THE ADVENTURER'S GUIDE TO SIGNS, SIGILS, AND SENTIENT PLANTS

The Adventurer's Guide to Signs, Sigils, and Sentient Plants

Megan Brown

ISBN and Copyright

This book was written and edited by humans.

Contents

To my family, especially my son, who still think I can do
anything – M.B.

1. The Guiding Light

Oracle entered the town with dust clinging to her boots and the hem of her cloak. Her familiar, Aquarius, had long ago curled up in her cloak pocket, leaving her to trudge on without company. Her feet ached. Her shoulders sagged under the weight of her pack. The town was empty and dark, save for a lone flickering light up the street. In her own light she could see worn cobbles and shabby buildings. Where was she?

She had trekked through dense forest which turned sparse. It then disappeared altogether. The trees were replaced with black rocks and brown grass, decorated with the occasional spiky shrub. For all her adventures, Oracle had never seen a place so brown.

As she stood, taking in the street before her, the flicker of the lantern beckoned her forward. Oracle was curious and couldn't read the shop sign from here, but what shop would be open so late? She tucked her hair behind her gently pointed ears, lowered her hood, and decided to find out. She extinguished the fire in her hand – a mote of light she used instead of a lantern – and approached the light.

In perfect lettering the sign above the shop read: *The Guiding Light Tea Room.* The warm glow of the lantern and the tea room's interior was enough invitation for Oracle. A cup of tea after so many hours on foot would be a nice refresher. She tentatively pushed on the door, unsure if it would open. It swung easily and chimed with three bells. The bells sung a merry chord, tinkling brightly in the silence of the room. Oracle's mood was definitely not merry nor bright.

Partially hidden by a wood booth was a tall and handsome man. He was reading a book. A bright blue mug sat steaming in front of him, and Oracle noticed how strong he was. She would have mistaken him for an adventurer if it wasn't for his plain clothes. Regular clothes for regular folk. Oracle guessed this was the proprietor, indicated by the apron he wore. He smiled warmly at her and stood up from his seat.

"I'm sorry, I thought you were open," Oracle said. She turned to go from the shop.

"No, please. The Guiding Light Tea Room is always open. Especially for weary travelers," the man smiled even bigger, and Oracle thought she might have seen filed down lower teeth. She wondered what a half-orc was doing in a town serving tea. It piqued her curiosity, but she had better manners than to ask outright.

"Do I look that bad?" She asked softly. The man froze, a look of mild panic on his face.

"Oh! No. No I didn't mean to imply you looked a way. I'm sorry I – " the man said quickly, his hands up.

"I'm kidding," Oracle smiled a little, "Sorry."

The man looked relieved and walked behind the counter. Oracle watched him move. He was graceful for being such a tall man. He was young, maybe her age or a little older. His arms and chest were easily visible through his shirt and Oracle wondered if he was maybe a retired adventurer, like she now was. Nobody that strong brewed tea for a living. He had short black hair that shined in the candlelight. It looked soft. He had dark brown eyes and while he probably didn't have to duck to enter or exit the door, he might have been close.

Large glass canisters lined a shelf behind the counter filled with all sorts of dried herbs and leaves in curious greens, browns, reds, and purples. There were several lit candles inside the room, and the wooden furniture had a well-loved look about it. The rugs were worn with foot traffic, and the tables were close together. The whole tea-room was warm, and Oracle sighed as she took it all in.

"I'm sorry to bother you so late. You don't actually have to serve me," Oracle said, still holding the door partially open.

"Tell you what, Traveler. You let go of my door there and pick a seat and I will brew you a tea like you've never had. After that you can give me an honest review of what you think, and we'll call it even for interrupting my evening tea. Deal?" He was perched with his hands spread wide on the counter. Oracle couldn't see a reason not to partake in the offer.

"Ok. Thank you." She let the door swing shut behind her.

"Let's see," the man said, studying her closely. Oracle looked right back at him, assessing him as well. She noticed how relaxed he was, and that he had a scar on his chin.

"You have obviously been traveling. I can tell by the deep layers of dust on your boots, and the fact that you're wearing what can only be described as 'adventurer clothes.' Since we're not really located near anything, it must have been far. Where are you from?" The man asked and turned to reach down the canisters of ingredients.

"New Clave," Oracle said, still standing in front of the door.

"Ah. City girl. Have you come all the way from the city?" He asked and motioned for Oracle to sit. She only moved a little further into the room.

"No. I have just come from the river town of Mendide," she said, peering at the glass canisters of ingredients from the center of the room. One contained a silvery green substance that shimmered under the candlelight giving Oracle the impression of glittering jewel dust.

"Business?"

"Not exactly," she refocused on the man. "My team had a contract there. I had to report back. Now I'm here. Where is here by the way? There wasn't a sign I saw when I entered."

"I think I know what to make you," the man said, ignoring her question. He weighed and scooped ingredients, mixing them just so, and put them into a strainer. He began to boil water over coals in a special fireplace stove behind the counter, and when the water boiled, he removed it and steeped the mixture. Steam rose in swirling circles above the container of tea. Oracle watched it in silence. The longer she stood, the heavier she began to feel. She turned and set her bag down, pulled out a chair, and plopped into it. Her feet hurt, and it had been a long time since she could say that.

Oracle watched as the man poured the concoction into a mug. In the candlelight it looked golden and sparkled like powdered diamond; a rare ingredient Oracle had used in a ritual spell once. She had never seen a drink that mesmerizing. The man walked around the counter with it and reverently set it down in front of her.

"It's extremely hot now, so wait a moment before you take a sip. I don't want you to get burned. You won't be able to taste it then." He smiled again at her.

Oracle was sure that his smile was genuine. He didn't sit with her. Instead, he sat back down at the table he was at when she entered. He sipped his own tea and surreptitiously studied her. Oracle pretended not to notice, but he wasn't very good at hiding his gaze.

She cupped the mug in her hands and let the warmth seep into her palms and fingers. The steam curled up from the mug and she leaned in a bit to smell the tea. It smelled lightly sweet and tickled her face. Cautiously, not knowing what to expect of the flavor, Oracle took a sip. It was earthy with a hint of honey and something else. It soothed a piece of Oracle.

A few more sips and she began to feel very relaxed. Her mood improved some and she felt better than she had in days. Somehow lighter. She took another sip of tea and let it slide into her belly, warming it. She hadn't realized she had been cold and the sensation was welcome.

"I feel...funny," Oracle said. She turned in her chair to look more directly at the man.

"Funny how?" The man sat up straighter in his chair, looking concerned.

"Not bad funny. You didn't poison me, right?"

"Not intentionally."

"That isn't reassuring." Oracle said and stared into the golden liquid. The weight lifted from her clearing mind. All she had room for was to appreciate the feeling. The man crossed over the room and sat on a chair across from her.

"Well, as long as you aren't allergic to any of the ingredients you should be fine. What are you feeling?" He leaned in toward her.

"I feel...floaty. Light. Almost carefree?" She watched the man, who was looking back at her.

"Your body or your head?"

"A bit of both. It's not unpleasant though. I kind of like it. How long will it last?" She asked dreamily.

"Not too long. It's meant to provide a little relief for the weary traveler. The effect is more intense the wearier the traveler is..."

Oracle closed her eyes and focused on the sensation. It was the best and most carefree she had felt in weeks. She finished the mug and looked at the man who eagerly looked back at her.

"This has to be magic," she said aloud, closing her eyes again.

"Some say so. I say it's simple alchemy. Maybe the simplest! Leaves and hot water," he laughed and Oracle smiled. It felt good to smile. After a few more moments she opened her eyes again. The stranger looked at her intently and Oracle suddenly felt hyperaware of herself. She shifted in her seat and didn't hold his gaze. She looked at the bottom of the empty mug.

"Atmir," he said.

"The tea?" Oracle said, looking back at him.

"No. My name. *I'm* Atmir," He grinned and held out his hand for her to shake. She took it and smiled back. His hand swallowed hers and he gave a firm handshake. Oracle marveled at how big his hand was compared to hers. He could crush hers easily if he wanted. She was silently thankful the man was a gentle giant. Or appeared to be right now.

"Oracle."

"Oracle? That's quite the name. Seer?" He released her hand and she put it back on the mug before her.

"Mage. Fire specialty. My mom thought I would be doing something different when she named me," Oracle stated plainly.

"Mine too. Atmir means 'silent flame.' My family is big on adventuring and glory seeking. I'm happy to 'mix leaves and hot water' as they like to call it. They support it, but they don't quite understand it." Atmir sat back in his chair, crossed his arms, and looked intently again at Oracle. She could feel her face flush. She hoped it wasn't noticeable, and thought she could always blame the tea. She searched intently for something to say.

"How did you know which tea to make me?" She asked.

"Well, there were a few clues. No offense, but the bags under your eyes; the very late arrival here at my doorstep; the dust and dirt on your cloak; and you said your team had a contract, but *you* had to report back. You had a falling out with your team?" He asked gently.

"Something like that, yeah," Oracle said softly, looking into her empty mug again. The floating feeling faded and she came back to reality. The weight that had lifted settled again on her body and mind and deep into her bones.

"If you don't mind me asking, where are you going?" Atmir put his elbows on the table and rested his chin on his hands, leaning slightly toward Oracle.

"I'm not sure yet. I am not going to adventure in the foreseeable future. Not like I had been anyway. But I'm not sure what I want to do. I've been traveling and thinking about it. I think I want to rekindle a childhood skill I had."

"Oh? What's that?"

"Plants. I want to grow and sell plants." Oracle looked at Atmir earnestly. He tried to keep his face from falling, but he couldn't.

"What's wrong with plants?" Oracle demanded.

"Nothing! Nothing is wrong with plants except... they don't grow here."

"What? Bad climate?" Oracle brushed a loose strand of hair from her face.

"No. They just don't grow here. That's why it's so dusty and barren around; we can't get anything to grow anywhere around here. We import almost everything, with a few exceptions. I travel to gather certain tea ingredients where things begin to grow again, for example. But nothing grows *here*." He pointed down at the table to indicate the town they were in.

"Where is 'here'? You never gave me the name of this place." Oracle was checking her pockets to do something besides look at the man directly. Her familiar was still sound asleep in one of them. Oracle thought she heard snoring.

He smiled coyly, "Noticed that? Guess I'm not as smooth as I think. The town's name is Greenspring, but there's nothing green or spring-like about this town. We are great at farming dusty sand and haggling prices, but plant farming? Forget it. Even houseplants can't survive here. It would take something miraculous for anyone to grow a plant here. So, I'm sorry to say, this is probably not your final stop."

"Oh," Oracle said. "I don't know where my final stop is, but I think I'll know when I see it."

They sat in silence for a few minutes. Oracle looked around the tea shop and Atmir looked patiently at Oracle.

"Does anyone know why nothing grows here?" Something pulled at Oracle.

"Not that I'm aware of. For as long as I have lived here it's been this way, and the long-term residents can't remember a time when something green grew here. Or something grew at all. I've asked." Atmir sat back in his chair, studying Oracle again.

They sat in silence. Oracle noted that it didn't feel awkward to sit quietly with Atmir. She didn't feel pressured to fill the void with noise. She reflected on his words and listened to the quiet crackling of the fire in the stove. She felt the mystery pull at her, and her adventuring mind prodded her to action. She forcefully ignored it.

"I should pay you and be on my way," Oracle said abruptly and pushed her chair back from the table.

"Hey, we made a deal. I need your honest opinion on the tea," Atmir said. He gestured at the mug. He grinned and leaned forward in his chair with his elbows on the table.

Oracle considered him for a moment and then replied, "I really liked it. It's lightly sweet but very...I'm not sure the word. Not bitter...earthen? Like clay, I guess? But lighter. And *the effects*. That will be your main selling point. It does taste good, but the effect is amazing. I've traveled all over and I've never had tea like this. It was magic."

"I am truly glad you enjoyed it. I hope it helped you some," he smiled genuinely at her, his eyes wide and sparkling in the candlelight. Oracle was distracted by the deep brown of them.

"I should be going," Oracle stood up and bent down to grab her bag, but Atmir put his hand on her hand. She froze.

"It's late and you're tired. You can't camp another night, I can see it. Let me put you up for the night?" Oracle picked up her bag, and broke Atmir's gentle grip on her hand.

"I am not going to be a part of a two person one bed trope, thank you," She said and slung the bag over her shoulder.

"Oh! No!" Atmir stood, blushing, and waving his hands. "Down-hereattheteashop! A spare room. I have a room for travelers!"

He marched behind the counter and pulled back a curtain. The room was dark and Oracle couldn't see inside. Atmir looked at her confused face, looked into the room, and realized his mistake. He snatched the nearest candle and held it into the room for her to see before she could get over there to light her mote of fire.

Oracle could see a small room with a bed and side table. There was nothing more, but what else did a weary traveler need at night except a bed? She approached the counter to get a better look. There was a small picture frame on the side table with a watercolored painting of a beautiful green plant. The tug of adventure pulled at her again. Maybe it was something else pulling. She walked around the counter to investigate the room and examine it more closely than she could from afar.

"I sleep upstairs. My home is upstairs," Atmir explained. "This room isn't often used, but as long as you don't mind the noise I make when I start business for the day, you can stay here. Free of charge."

Oracle looked at him suspiciously.

"Why?"

"Why what?" A bewildered Atmir asked.

"Why free? What's going to happen to me in the dead of night in this town?" Oracle demanded, ready for the unexpected.

"Nothing! Nothing will happen to you, I swear!" Atmir took a step back from her, still holding the curtain open. "I-I have family, like I said. They are adventuring types, and I know that sometimes a soft bed is few and far between. In my experience, adventuring parties are generally out to help people. I can't house a whole party, obviously, but I can do my part to help a person or two who travel through. I am no adventurer, but this is how I can help in my small way. So, no charge. No obligation either. I won't make you wash mugs or anything, and you can leave when you like. Assuming you can find your way through this curtain I'm holding - I bet a smart woman like you would have no problem with that."

Oracle stood there weighing her options as she looked at the tall man opposite her. A bed, any bed, would be better than sleeping on the ground another night. This didn't feel like a trap, but maybe it was a well-executed one, and that's why she'd never heard of this town. Travelers go in but not out. Still, she was exhausted. He did say she could leave whenever, and the curtain, to her senses, didn't appear magical. She shifted her weight and the floor creaked.

"Against my better judgment," Oracle growled and Atmir's face turned hopeful, "I will accept your offer for *one* night."

Oracle marched past Atmir into the little room. She sat on the bed and Atmir squeezed into the room to set the candle on the table. He immediately turned and walked out. Before he could close the curtain, Oracle spoke.

"Atmir?"

"Yes?" He turned around, thinking she needed something.

"I'm an experienced adventurer and a fire mage," she paused to let that sink in. "Don't try anything or you *will* regret it."

"Understood," came the reply.

After the clinking of mugs and soft puff of candles extinguishing, Oracle heard the creak of a door open and close and then the tea shop was silent. She was so tired she fell asleep almost before laying down.

2. Magic Teas

Oracle awoke to her familiar dancing on her pillow. The small dragon-like creature was stepping his stubby feet on her hair, gently tugging her awake. It didn't hurt, but it wasn't the most pleasant wake-up she'd ever had.

"Aquarius, what are you doing?" Oracle groaned in the way of someone still half-asleep.

"I'm waking you up! If you sleep any longer I might starve."

"Would you get off my hair please?" Oracle croaked. The little dragon creature marched off her hair and around to her face. He stood on her chest and peered at her with his ochre eyes.

"Oracle. What is going on? Where are we?" He demanded, tilting his head.

"We're in a tea shop. Now let me sleep."

"A tea shop! In what town? Also, I'm *still* hungry. Hungrier than the last time I said anything, which was just now," He peered at Oracle's closed eyes, willing them to look at him. "A happy dragon is less likely to breathe fire over their hoarded gold."

"You don't breathe fire." Oracle said exasperated. She covered her head with the pillow, though careful not to knock the little creature off of her.

"Water. Whatever. A hungry dragon is not a happy dragon."

"You're not even a real dragon," Oracle groaned, removed the pillow, and opened her eyes to look at Aquarius, who was inches from her face staring her dead in the eye.

11

"That's hurtful." He pretended to pout after he was sure she could see him.

"Sorry. I'll see what I can do about some food," she said, exhaling the words. Aquarius hopped down from her chest and smiled.

Oracle sat up and swung her cloak around her shoulders. Aquarius climbed into her front pocket on her cloak and sank out of sight. She pulled a comb from her bag and addressed the tangles from the night. She wondered why she cared about her hair, but thought it would be indecent to roam about with it a tangled mess. She put the comb back, tied her hair up, and noticed her reflection in a bowl of water where a towel sat next to it on the nightstand. She silently cursed being unaware and asleep when that delivery had been made. She washed and dried her hands, silently grateful the delivery *had* been made.

She peered out from the curtain into the tea shop. She saw Atmir's back. He must be taking an order from a customer, she surmised as she could hear light talking and glimpsed a man's bald head. She could see the lantern beyond him in the window, still lit. Oracle looked out the window. The sky was inky black, but lightening up toward the east. It was still early. She thought, a little sourly, that she could still be sleeping if it wasn't for her hungry familiar. The older man at the counter left to sit down and Atmir turned around. He caught her eye through the curtain, and it startled her. Oracle whipped the curtain open as if she was just exiting.

"Good morning! Sleep well?" He asked brightly. He was holding a kettle.

"I did," she said a little tersely. She relaxed a little and added, "Thank you."

"I'm glad. Hey, would you help me with this for a sec? My coals have cooled too much, and I need to heat this water. Would you mind...?"

Oracle stared at him a moment and then realized what he was asking. She walked out of the room and cast a small fire spell. Flames flickered forth from her hand and she placed them under the container of water. Atmir watched for a moment, handed her the kettle, and then went to fix the fire.

"Is that a mage?" The older man called from his seat. "Atmir you should know better! Nothing good comes from magic. I don't want mage tea."

"Harrad, it's fine. The *tea* is mildly magic. You know this," Atmir called right back. "And she's only heating the water for me while I get the fire going again. You're earlier than usual today."

Oracle didn't look at the old man. She just focused on heating the water. She couldn't help notice Atmir working just beside her. His white shirt sleeves were rolled up exposing muscled forearms, and he wore a dark blue apron. His hair still looked soft, and his skin con-trasted nicely with his white shirt – an olive tone. He deftly moved to position some wood in the specialty stove. Before he could light the fire Oracle reached in. The wood ignited and Atmir smiled broadly, impressed. He put his hands on his hips and admired her for a mo-ment. Oracle quickly turned away and focused on heating the kettle.

"Oracle," came a little voice from her pocket. "The food. I'm hun-gry!"

"What was that?" Atmir asked.

"Oh. Uh, my familiar is hungry. You don't have anything he could snack on, do you?"

Atmir looked at her a beat and then went out one of the doors at the back of the shop. He came back with a fluffy roll and handed it to her. She stuffed it in her pocket and Atmir heard a small squeal of de-light.

"Is that enough? I'm sorry it's yesterday's. The baker won't be in for a while yet."

"It's plenty. Thank you," Oracle replied. The kettle of water was boiling now. "What should I do with this?"

"Oh! Here!" Atmir took the container and put in a strainer. He set it down on an intricate black trivet and then he set a timer. It clicked quietly behind the counter. "Thank you. Harrad is always my first customer of the day and it feels like he arrives earlier than he used to. He likes the Topaz Root blend and gets it almost every morning."

"And what does that do?"

Oracle had a suspicion that all of the teas did something magical here.

"It eases joint pain," Atmir replied, picking up a notepad and taking down some canisters.

"What else does it do?" Oracle asked, walking up beside him at the counter.

"Why do you think it does anything else?" He asked playfully.

"Call it intuition."

"Ah. Well, good intuition, then. It also makes you levitate and curls your hair for about 10 minutes."

"It does what?" She moved back half a step.

"The joint relief lasts longer than ten minutes. The side effects are curly hair and levitation."

"Curly hair and levitation. Are you sure you're not casting some silent spells on these teas?" Oracle asked, incredulously.

"I can assure you I know no spells. I only know teas," Atmir said with a chuckle as he worked. He added, "I wouldn't be opposed to learning a spell or two if there was someone willing to teach me, though."

Oracle didn't reply. Instead, she heard the timer clicking stop. She turned and looked for a mug. She found them below the counter in neat rows; all kinds and all colors of mug under here. She picked out a crooked yellow mug and gently poured the tea into it. A faintly blue liquid steamed into the mug. Atmir contemplated while he observed her.

"What? Did I do it wrong?" Oracle said, a little snappish.

"No. Not at all," Atmir replied, "I just was thinking you had a handle on tea already and maybe you'd like to help a little bit. You know, since you don't have anywhere to be or a schedule to keep at the moment. I could use the help if - if you want."

Instead of answering, Oracle brought the tea to Harrad, a grizzled old man with a long grey beard and a few hairs clinging to a mostly bald head. He eyed her suspiciously as she put the tea in front of him.

"I didn't poison it, you old coot." She said as she set the tea down.

Harrad gave a *HARRUMPH* and took the tea anyway. Oracle returned behind the counter to see what Atmir was doing. She quietly peered at Harrad and noticed he had already begun to levitate in his seat. He was humming gently as he read a book and Oracle couldn't look away. Harrad paid her no mind and sipped his tea while he read, unbothered.

"He doesn't have enough hair to see it curling," Atmir whispered. Oracle smiled but tried not to.

"What are you working on?" She peered at his notes.

"I'm just taking some inventory. Market will be a little skinny. The usual guy I purchase supplies from won't be at the market and the other vendor doesn't sell everything I need so I can't always buy what I need there. I'm low on only a few things, so I'm not too worried, even if the courier will be a little late with some of my other ingredients." Atmir studied his list of ingredients and their quantities. On hand or to order, Oracle wasn't sure.

"Doesn't that stress you out?"

"Not really. It gets here when it gets here. I'm not going to die because a shipment was late."

Oracle's life of adventure had always been high stakes. When something went wrong it was usually catastrophic. Sometimes when things went right it was catastrophic. She briefly thought of her team and their last adventure. Her heart ached and shame crawled across her skin.

"Oracle?"

"It's nothing. I'm fine." She said quickly and turned to check on the fire in the stove. It was burning without trouble, but she still pretended it needed tending. She could feel Atmir's eyes on her before he turned back to his list. The doorbells chimed.

"Good morning Beatran, Gorman. What can I prepare for you today?" Atmir stood up straight and smiled for the customers. Oracle stayed crouched down and pretended to tend the fire some more. The fire illuminated her face and arms as she re-arranged some wood inside the stove.

A deep woman's voice replied, "Atmir, darling, I would like my usual. Has the baker been?"

"Not yet, Beatran."

"Pity." She gave a flourish with her hand.

"And you Gorman? What would you like?"

"I'll just take what Beatran is having to make it easy on you today, Atmir." The man said and knocked twice on the counter.

Oracle stayed crouched by the fire as Atmir leaned over her to reach canisters down from the shelves. She held still. She was very aware of how close he was to her and felt a warmth in her cheeks that didn't emanate from the stove. She cursed them silently. He moved and turned to look at the newcomers, then Oracle stood up.

"Oh, who's your friend, Atmir?" The lady named Beatran asked. She wore an elaborate hat with feathers and jewels – presumed to be fake because of the sheer number of them – and what looked to be a fake bird on the side. She had ostentatious rings and necklaces laid over a bright red, modest dress and jacket. Oracle gauged her to be a human, roughly in her sixties. The man she was standing with looked to be about the same. His wiry figure was draped in a suit of navy and gray. They were opposites in Oracle's mind.

"This is Oracle." Atmir turned to her and gestured with a hand holding a container of deep purple particles Oracle guessed were crushed leaves.

"A new hire! That will be a great help to Atmir. Pleasure to meet you darling! Our poor Atmir is run ragged by all of us demanding customers," Beatran winked and smiled widely at Oracle with a nod. She and her companion then turned and chose a table by the window to sit down.

"I'm actually –" Oracle started to say but went quiet when Atmir handed her a measuring spoon.

"She's just visiting from out of town, Beatran," Atmir called over to her, "She's helping today, and I hope maybe tomorrow, too." It was a sort of question-statement directed to Oracle. Atmir looked hopefully at her.

"Yes, I'm visiting. Not sure how long I'll stay," Oracle spoke up looking pointedly at Atmir, who withered appropriately under Oracle's gaze. He slid two containers of ingredients, water, and a kettle to Oracle. The thought popped into Oracle's head that maybe she could stay, but it exited almost as fast as it had entered.

"Two scoops of each in a big strainer. Steep with the timer on the two setting in the size two container after you take the kettle off the heat." He instructed, not looking her in the eye while he tended to his list. She stared at him a moment, her lips pressed together. When he didn't look up at her, she scooped the brittle leaves into a large strainer and put the water into the kettle and placed it on the stove to boil. Aquarius popped his head out of Oracle's pocket to look around, and she gently pushed him back down.

When it was ready, she poured the hot water into the size two container as instructed with the strainer and leaves positioned inside. She set the timer and heard it clicking, barely, over the sound of Beatran and Gorman loudly gossiping. She put the two containers back on the shelf and the doorbells chimed again.

A middle aged man walked into the tea shop. His belly was draped with a flour-dusted apron, and Oracle guessed he was the baker. He also wore a little hat that appeared to be dusted with flour, as well as carried several bags in each of his thick hands. Harrad was at the counter paying for his tea and mumbling something about mage water, to which Atmir rolled his eyes and said goodbye to him. He grinned at the newcomer.

"Hello Rory. I'm glad you're here. Beatran was already lamenting about arriving before you," Atmir said to the rotund man.

"Morning Atmir, Miss Beatran will be pleased to know her usual is in the mix as well. I'll collect payment tomorrow, but I need to get going. I have to deliver these to the inn." Rory held up one hand with a large bag in it and a few smaller bags.

"Thank you, Rory! You know how I love your sweet buns with my tea!" Beatran gushed loudly at him and batted her eyes from across the room. Rory tilted his head and gave a flat look to Atmir, not bothering to acknowledge Beatran, or Oracle. Then he placed one bag on the counter in front of Atmir, turned, and left without another word. Beatran cackled loudly behind him.

"I'll tell you all about it later," Atmir said when Oracle looked to him for an explanation. "The mayor – Beatran – likes to give Rory a hard time. Can you heat three more size 1 kettles please. The water barrel is right there, kind of hidden." Atmir pointed to the large barrel near the back door partially obscured by a curtain, and Oracle carted over three containers to fill. She put them on the stove to start heating up and the door chimed again. Three more people entered the tea shop. Oracle was amazed that Atmir knew how many containers and of what size to heat. Then she thought it must be a small town and surely these people were regulars.

The customers all talked amiably with Atmir as he took down some containers, instructed Oracle on measuring, and put away the baked goods in a case on the counter and the excess in the storage room. He took a small savory-looking pastry and pulled Oracle by her front pocket close to him. She leaned back, a container of water in one hand and a measuring spoon in the other, spread her arms wide and suppressed a squirm. Atmir stuffed the pastry in her pocket and let her go.

"O-other one." She stammered.

"What?" He asked.

"My familiar is in my other pocket."

Atmir smiled and hooked a finger on her pocket again, reached in and retrieved the pastry, then stuffed it in the other pocket. Oracle stared at him with wide eyes and hoped he didn't see her ears redden. Aquarius on the other hand, could be heard muffled by the pocket, cheering.

"We're never leaving this place, Oracle!" He cried out. Atmir was shocked for a moment and looked at Oracle, whose arms were still spread wide.

"I didn't know it could talk! It just sounded like squeals earlier." Atmir's eyes were wide.

"His name is Aquarius. You can meet later." She said hurriedly.

After a moment of staring at each other, they both heard timers click off and resumed what they were doing. The interaction was not lost on Beatran who leaned in conspiratorially to Gorman and whispered something Oracle and Atmir couldn't hear. A few more patrons arrived and Oracle and Atmir had fallen into a quiet rhythm, the dance of well-timed production. The clank of mugs, the chime of the door, and low voices made a sort of music to Oracle.

The sun had risen fully, and the day was sunny and bright. It served to accentuate the sand and dust outside. Oracle thought absently about what Atmir had said about plants not growing here. What could be the cause? She waltzed to and from the stove, the counter, and the ingredients while pondering why a town couldn't grow anything. With a name like Greenspring, plants surely must have grown here at one point.

Atmir had gone out of the back door to refill the water barrel. He was doing some housekeeping in the back room while the customers who entered had slowed. Oracle watched his muscles flex beneath his shirt as he lifted the barrel to carry it out. She admonished herself and turned back to the fire. She was putting wood into the fire when she heard a voice.

"Oracle, was it?" It was Beatran, at the counter.

"Yes." Oracle stood up and turned to face her.

"Welcome to our little town. A word of advice though? Don't go around using magic here. It always ends poorly. For some reason, magic users tend to disappear here. Take the Alchemist for example. He had a good business, I've heard, but you know what happened to him?"

Oracle shook her head.

"Nobody does, dear. That's the thing. He packed up one day and abandoned his workshop. It's been so long that not a soul knows why or where he went. This used to be a vibrant place, or so that's the rumor we've all heard. What's left here are old codgers who can't bear to leave, people who are too afraid to go, and people hiding from something. This is a quiet place. Dusty and brown, yes, but quiet. We all want to keep it that way."

"I don't intend on causing any harm," Oracle said, putting her hands on the counter.

"Generally, people don't, dear. We don't want to see anyone hurt. Least of all our dear Atmir. He's a genuine find and a treasure we hold dear."

"Oh, it's not like that!" Oracle exclaimed. Beatran patted her hand on the counter.

"Of course not, dear," she said with a sly smile. "If you're going to stay a bit you should go to the Alchemist's old building. It's empty and in no worse repair than anything else around here. If you want to discuss owning the building, just come see me and we can work something out. Greenspring is charming once you get to know the place. If you are looking for less permanent shelter we have an inn with a tavern, but between you and me," she leaned in and lowered her voice, " – it's not the most respectable place, if you gather my meaning."

Oracle nodded.

"Good girl. Will I see you tomorrow?"

"I'm – I'm not sure. I wasn't planning on staying even this long."

Oracle hadn't planned to stay at all, let alone overnight in the town. She didn't plan on staying much longer either.

"Oh. Well. You've been such a help today as far as I have seen and I think Atmir could use some assistance. He's run ragged between all the locals in for tea and biscuits. Have him show you the building. It's been ages since it's been occupied. Nobody here even remembers the Alchemist personally. We just have his dilapidated old sign as a reminder."

"I'll think about it," Oracle replied slowly. She knew she probably wouldn't think too long about it. She was *not* going to become an assistant in a tea shop. She did need a change of pace from adventuring though. She thought back to her mother and the peacefulness of the greenhouse she essentially grew up in. Maybe that was her change of pace? She didn't want to move back in with her mother though. The Alchemist's building sounded interesting. If she stayed, maybe that was the place?

"Good girl." Beatran patted her hand again and then removed it.

The rest of the day was filled with customers, of which Oracle couldn't quite remember all their names. She remembered that Harrad, the grizzled old man who levitated, was a bookbinder. Then there was a beast tamer who told her story after story about the beasts he had tamed. Oracle had politely listened while she worked. A hunter and his very large dog had come in and ordered tea. Atmir called it "Piercing Gaze Blend" but didn't tell Oracle what was in it. It was supposed to give the hunter more accurate sight for a little while. There were also a slew of women coming to ogle Atmir under the pretense of getting tea. She admitted to herself they had a point, then chided herself for having the thought.

More customers throughout the day entered. There was a pale man with pointed ears and a quirky woman with long, full, curly hair who seemed to make him nervous as she unabashedly flirted with him. A set of women that looked to be twins came in, but were not there to ogle Atmir. They sat quietly talking together. There was also another grizzled old man that was even more ancient than Harrad. He carried a walking stick. He told long-winded stories to anyone who would listen. Sometimes he seemed to tell them to no particular person, babbling on and on as if he had an audience. Most notably, there was a priest. Oracle wondered to which god and if there was a nearby temple or sanctuary. She'd ask Atmir later.

There were two distinctly busy times: the morning rush, and the late afternoon rush. Some patrons, including some of the ogling and giggling women she saw in the morning, also came in the afternoon. When it finally settled down in the early evening, she was exhausted. Who knew making tea could be so tiresome?

In her time at the shop Oracle saw miraculous tea side effects. From glowing fingertips – Atmir claimed the tea was great for reading at night in the dark and called it Reader's Delight– to steam pouring from the head for 30 minutes. There was a tea to relax the body, a tea to energize, a tea for mental clarity, and the Piercing Gaze Blend Atmir had served the hunter. It seemed like Atmir had tea for everything. Whatever Atmir was doing, he must have been doing it right. The Guiding Light was a very popular venue.

"Do you ever stop?" Oracle asked Atmir as she wiped the counter down and leaned up against it.

"I try to keep the doors open for those who need it. Tea is healing and everyone needs some of that." Atmir shuffled containers around as he looked for the right ingredients.

"When do you put the light out?"

"The lantern? Never. I have a bell to ring me if someone enters and I'm upstairs. The lantern is a guide. It brought you here, didn't it?" He stopped and looked at her with a crooked smile.

Oracle thought about this. She had felt a pull to the tea shop from the lantern, but had chalked it up to being tired and the shop being the only place that was open in the first town she had seen in a while. She wondered if the lantern was magical.

"It's not magical. Least as far as I can tell."

Oracle scowled at Atmir, and he laughed heartily. It was a stentorian, full sound. She liked it but didn't want to admit to herself she did.

"I didn't read your mind! I swear. Most people ask about it, that's all." Atmir held his hands up in defense.

"Uh huh. The 'not magic' tea guy, with the 'not magic' lantern, wants me to believe he 'can't read' minds." Oracle crossed her arms and looked at Atmir wryly.

"Hey, I only know what I know. I'm not magic. I'm ordinary. The tea has side effects, sure, but it's not from *me*," Atmir said and raised his hands palm out in surrender again.

Oracle eyed him, but didn't reply. She crouched and tended to the fire and Atmir finished wiping down the counter.

"Hey," Atmir stopped, and Oracle turned around. "Do you think I could meet your familiar now?"

"Well, that depends." Oracle stood back up.

"On what?" Aquarius and Atmir both said at the same time. Oracle rolled her eyes, but Atmir tried not to look too shocked again.

"If you'll, ahem," Oracle cleared her throat, "If you'll go with me to the Alchemist's."

"You want to go to the Alchemist's? Who told you about that?"

"Beatran."

"Well, I don't see why not. We can go now if you'd like? It will be quiet for the rest of the night, and I have a sign I can put out in case anyone comes while we're down there. It's not far, just a few buildings up the street."

"Uh, yeah. Yes. Let's go now. I'm curious is all."

"Not thinking about staying, are you? We don't need any trouble-makers sticking around," Atmir said grinning at her.

"Oh shut it. I do not look like a troublemaker. Weary traveler, maybe, but not a troublemaker."

"Ok then maybe weary traveler, let's walk down to the Alchemist's so I can meet your familiar and you can see what's to see there. Which isn't much if I recall. He's been gone long since before I arrived and I'm not sure if anyone living here ever met him because it was probably still green when he lived here. That's what the rumors say, anyway."

Atmir dropped the rag he was holding on to the counter and took his apron off. He hung it on a hook and then walked with Oracle to the door.

Atmir opened the door and held it for Oracle. The evening was warm, and the sun hadn't quite gone down all the way, streaming soft light into their surroundings. It was almost summer. Oracle missed the smell of spring. Here, it smelled like dirt and lightly of minerals. They walked quietly at first, and then Oracle reached in her pocket and took Aquarius out and let him rest on her palm. The scaly, blue, dragon-like creature had a wide mouth, stout body, and sat upright on her hand with bright yellow eyes and wide feet. He curled his tail around his body.

"Atmir, this is Aquarius. Aquarius, this is Atmir. He's been the one feeding you all day."

"If you continue to feed me, I might consider being *your* familiar," the little dragon chirped.

Atmir couldn't help but to stare at the blue creature. Oracle wasn't sure if he was dumbstruck by the cuteness or the talking.

"You're quite the little stunner, aren't you? What exactly are you? A dragon?"

"Aquarius is a closely related cousin to dragons, but not a dragon as such." Oracle stated plainly.

"Again, hurtful." Aquarius began to pout.

"Shush you. You're not a dragon no matter what," Oracle turned back to Atmir. "I don't know what their official names are, to be honest. I picked him up as an egg on a contract and I'm quite protective of who knows I have him."

"I do have dragon-like qualities though," Aquarius said, closing his eyes and jutting his chin into the air.

"I can see that," Atmir said, still in awe of the creature.

"Oh, it goes beyond looks. Watch this!" The little dragon got into a full four-legged stance and sprayed something out of his mouth before

Oracle could say "stop." The liquid shot out and hit Atmir. Or rather, Atmir walked into the path of it. He stopped, looking at his wet shirt.

"I'm so sorry!" Oracle said, "Aquarius!"

"Sorry," he said while he lowered his head and looked away.

"What – what is this?" Atmir asked.

"Water," Aquarius said proudly.

"Water? You can spray water?" Atmir looked at his shirt in disbelief.

"Hence the name," Oracle said with just a tinge of resignation in her voice.

"That is incredible!" Atmir looked up from his shirt at Aquarius standing on Oracle's hand. "What an amazing thing!"

"Don't encourage him," Oracle muttered and continued to walk.

"Seriously, that's really amazing. And useful. Especially for a fire mage, right? What a brilliant familiar!" Atmir only needed to take two big steps to be aligned with her again. They continued to walk.

Aquarius stood straight up with his chin in the air, basking in the praise. "I like this guy, Oracle."

"I'm sure you, do Aquarius."

"Have you had a familiar before?" Atmir asked.

"I haven't had one before this. Aquarius is my first. I did a ritual on his egg before he hatched to bind him to me, so he's been attached to me ever since."

"What does that mean?" Atmir reached out and stroked Aquarius on the head. Aquarius leaned into his hand.

"It means I can die and not be summoned back. I'm a living creature with free-will. Sort of. I do serve Oracle and there are some limitations I must abide by."

"Like?"

"He has to stay within a certain distance of me, unless I command him otherwise. He must obey direct commands. *Sit,*" Oracle emphasized, and Aquarius plopped down, looking sour. "I don't do that very much."

"I hate it when she does that," Aquarius said. Oracle released him.

"He doesn't like it, and to be truthful, I don't like it either. Aquarius is a friend. Probably my best friend." Aquarius stood a little straighter, and Oracle lifted him to sit on her shoulder. He obliged and sat perched there for the rest of the walk.

"We're here." Atmir said. They stopped in front of a decently-sized building with a large storefront window next to a door. There was a faded orange and black sign above the door with beautiful script lettering and delightful painted bottles. It hung squarely in place, with only the faded script to make it look old. It read "Alchemist's". The windows were so grimy you couldn't even see inside. "It should be unlocked."

Atmir tried the doorknob, and it twisted easily. The door swung in, and they were greeted by near darkness. Oracle lit her hand up so they could see around the place. It was dirty, but the bones were good. Nothing was broken or creaky. The wood was all solid, just covered in a layer of dust and a little bit of sand. It appeared to be a perfectly safe room.

"Why is it still called the 'Alchemist's'?" Oracle said as she entered.

"We don't get a lot of newcomers to town, and nobody ever moved into this building after he left, I guess. The sign out front is the only reason we know there was an Alchemist. Who knows? Maybe people think it's haunted?" Atmir replied while he followed her in.

There was a counter, a back room with a dusty curtain hung in the door frame, a main space, and a little apartment area upstairs. It was not a terrible place. The best part, in Oracle's opinion, was the skylight that let in the sky's sunset hues. It was huge. She thought it would be perfect for plants. In the daytime this whole space would be filled with natural light. The thought of staying popped into her head, and she had some difficulty shoving it back out. The call of plants tugged at her, burrowing roots around her heart.

"No clue why the Alchemist left, huh?" Oracle turned to look at Atmir, who was examining the back door, and leaned against a supporting beam in the center of the room.

"None. I've heard rumors, of course," He said as he turned around. "Nobody really knows, so they just make something up. His sign is the only record of an Alchemist actually being in Greenspring."

They looked around for a clue of some kind to who the Alchemist was, or how long ago they'd owned the shop, but were greeted only with cobwebs and darkness. Oracle lit her hand to see into the deeper crevices, but nothing of note appeared.

"I don't like this," Aquarius said into her ear. He was still riding on her shoulder.

"What? The dark?" She looked at him.

"No, this space. I don't like it. It's probably haunted. Or cursed. I don't want a curse, Oracle."

"It's a little spooky, but with some cleaning up, I think it will be a really nice space. That big window in front will allow a lot of light in. And the skylight is perfect," She turned to look out the window. It was still barely light outside.

"Too spooky. Too many cobwebs. It has terrible curb appeal."

"You're worried about curb appeal?" Atmir asked.

"Nevermind," Aquarius sighed.

"I think it's perfect."

"Perfect for what?" Atmir asked.

"No, no, no. This is *not* the place, Oracle." Aquarius said, pulling on her neck to emphasize his point.

"I think it is." She scooped Aquarius off her shoulder and held him in her hand.

"Place for what?" Atmir asked.

"For plants," Oracle said seriously while Aquarius breathed out the words in an exasperated sigh. She waited to see amusement on Atmir's face, but he didn't look amused.

"Are you sure that's a good idea? Nothing grows here. *Nothing*," he said. "I don't want you to be disappointed with our town and leave if your plans don't work out."

"I think this town has a secret, and maybe I'm not done adventuring yet. Maybe I'm just going to do it a little differently." Oracle said as she walked around the interior.

"By killing helpless plants?" Aquarius snarked.

"Nooooo," Oracle put him in her pocket now. He poked his head out of the top. "I think I can turn this space green. I have some experience with plants. And maybe once I do that, I do it *outside* the shop, too. And maybe I can turn this whole town green. Maybe Greenspring can return to being green. Who knows? But I'm willing to try. It sounds adventurous enough and I have enough coin to sustain myself here for a bit."

She turned to look at Atmir. He was looking at the floor, his brow furrowed in deep ridges. She stood in front of him and looked up into his face, craning her neck.

"What do you think?" She asked in a hopeful tone.

"I think you're crazy to try, but also," he paused, "if being a little crazy gets you to stick around for a while, who am I to argue?" He shrugged.

Oracle squinted at him with suspicion then took the space in again. It would need some work. A little elbow grease and time, but she had that and more. Atmir returned to the tea shop and came back with some cleaning supplies and a few candles.

"I can help tomorrow after the first rush, but this should get you started," he said. "I'll be back with some more."

"Aquarius and I will be fine. You've done enough already," Oracle was midway through swiping some cobwebs away. They were sticking to her hands and her sleeves.

"I'll be right back." And again, Atmir left.

Oracle watched him go, then shrugged at Aquarius, now on the floor, who again voiced his displeasure at the space. She began to clean with the supplies Atmir had brought her, starting with the room she intended for her bedroom. She and the broom did a dance as she swept and battled cobwebs and dust, the sounds of the broom scratching the floor the only music. Aquarius sneezed as motes of dust fluttered down from the rag and the windowsill Oracle dusted. The grime was so thick on the window Oracle scrubbed what must have been three layers off. It looked into the alley below. Oracle used a bubbly rag to wash the walls, while Aquarius rinsed them. Then she put the broom downstairs, and she mopped the water up from the floor. The room was looking better already.

Oracle wasn't sure why growing plants popped into her head. She wasn't even sure she would call Greenspring home. She just felt like she was done walking and needed something else. She knew enough about plants and magic that she was confident this could work. Oracle was about finished with the bedroom when she heard the front door open.

"Oracle?"

"Upstairs," she called. She heard some grunting and scraping and came out the door to find Atmir struggling with a bed frame on the stairs. She rushed to help him.

"Thanks," he grunted.

"Is this the bed from the tea shop?" She lifted one end of the bed and helped it pivot the stairs.

"I don't need this bed right now, but you do, and I'm happy to help. Now, where's it going?"

"Here," she led him into the bedroom, hefting one side of the bed.

"I'll bring the table and mattress too. Not much use for them without the bed," he said as they set the bed down.

"Atmir," Oracle looked at him as he stopped, halfway out the door. "Thank you."

"Don't thank me yet. I'm not paying you wages for today," he said with a grin and went down the stairs. Oracle rolled her eyes and smiled. She felt warm. She felt happy? She wasn't sure what she felt, but it warmed her, comforted her, and made her feel just a tiny bit bubbly. She went out of the bedroom and began cleaning downstairs with the help of the broom. Resigned, Aquarius began to help clean again with the water he produced. She might be up all night.

3. The Bookbinder's

The doorbells chimed merrily as Oracle entered the tea shop and the air was filled with the smells of tea and a little smoke. Atmir was busy mixing something together at the counter. Oracle knew this was his experiment time. When the shop was between rushes and he had finished cleaning and restocking, he usually tried new blends and new ingredients. As far as Oracle had seen, he hadn't made anything worth keeping around just yet, but the man was persistent. She liked that about Atmir. It spoke to a reliable and strong nature, that Atmir was someone she could rely on when things were tough to help get her through.

She pulled a tall chair up to the counter to watch what he was doing and leaned both elbows on the surface, resting her chin on her folded hands. She sighed. Atmir finished his last precise measurement and put the ingredient into the strainer with the others.

"Why the long face, Oracle? It's a beautiful day and you're in the finest tea shop for at least several miles."

"None of my plants have taken," Oracle said mournfully. "It's like the longer they try to grow the harder they die. And they aren't growing further than the seed splitting. I don't know what I'm doing wrong. They wither overnight in a wave of death. I wrote to my mother for advice, and now we wait until I hear back, I guess."

"Have you considered that you're not doing anything wrong?" Atmir put the strainer into the container of water he just removed from the stove. He didn't need to set a timer, but he did anyway. It click-clicked into rhythm as he turned his attention back to Oracle.

"What do you mean?" She asked.

"Nothing grows here, remember? I don't think you're the problem. Or what you're doing. I think maybe this is the wrong, I don't know, climate? Wrong something. Greenspring can't grow a single green thing. And that's not your fault." He reached out and put a reassuring hand on her arm.

"There has to be a reason nothing grows here. You can't just have dust festivals and sand harvest parties." Oracle said, frowning.

Atmir laughed and Oracle felt something stir merrily inside her. She told it to shut up.

"I think there used to be festivals. Or at least *a* festival. One festival. Not sure what it was about, and maybe it's just a rumor." Atmir took some containers from the shelves behind him and continued. "Something long forgotten about Greenspring that nobody remembers because nobody is old enough to have been there." Atmir leaned his elbows on the counter, stooping to do so, and rested his face on his hands, mirroring Oracle.

"Still. There must be a reason. What could possibly make this place not only barren, but barren with a vengeance? Something is determined to make this place brown." Oracle sat back in her chair and crossed her arms. The ticking stopped and Atmir turned to get the container. He poured a mug slowly and slid it across the counter, then returned to leaning on his elbows, face in hands.

"Don't burn yourself."

"You know I can't," Oracle replied, taking up the mug. She looked at the tea inside. It was a deep pink. She took a long quaff and set it back down again.

"Anything?" Atmir asked hopefully.

"I'm not sure."

"Did it taste good at least?"

"Yes. A little earthy and citrusy. With…. something like anise. Is there anise in there?" She picked up the mug to inspect the tea inside, as if looking at the tea would show her the flavors.

"Yes, there's anise in there. Very sharp," Atmir said, looking pleased. "Maybe that's the tea? Makes your palette more sensitive?"

"I don't think so."

They sat in silence for a moment. Atmir rested his face on his hands with his elbows on the counter again, looking at Oracle. She looked right back, arms crossed again.

"You know? I think something is happening. I feel different. Sort of happier, maybe. Perhaps the tea is a mood booster?" Oracle sat up and rested her hands on the counter.

"That isn't what I thought it would do, but maybe it is. Any side effects?"

"Not that I can tell," Oracle said, looking at her body, hands, and feet. "Do you see anything?"

Atmir stared at her with a little smile teasing his lips. He looked her up and down slowly, almost dreamily, before finally saying, "Nothing weirder than usual."

Oracle snapped forward and slapped his arm out from under his face. It bobbed a little before he caught himself. He stood upright and laughed. She tried to force her lips together, but they curled up at the edges.

"Well, that's enough teatime for me today," she said. She stood up and returned the chair to its rightful spot.

"Are you sure? I have another blend to try. It *might* make you weirder than usual. One can hope, anyway."

"Very funny. I am going back to the Alchemist's to get rid of my latest batch of murdered plants. I'll keep you apprised of their funerals."

"I have a better idea." Atmir came around the counter to stand in front of Oracle, blocking the exit.

"What's that? Roast me again over tea?"

"No. Go visit Harrad. He's got a whole library. He's a bookbinder and I think he inherited them. Some of them are quite old and might have something interesting. Also, stop calling it the Alchemist's. You bought it, it's your space now."

"I'm not open for business yet. I'll call it the Alchemist's until I find a name for it. And Harrad hates me, remember?" Oracle put a hand on her hip, narrowing her gaze at him.

"Hate is a strong word." Atmir mirrored Oracle.

"He literally said 'I hate that mage' the last time we were in the same space. He was not quiet about it."

"Ok, Harrad is a bit of a curmudgeon, but I assure you he doesn't actually hate you. He's just scared of magic. He's lived a long time and has plenty of bound up stories in that place of his that speak ill of it."

"And you want me to march over there and say 'Hi Harrad. I know you hate me, but can I root through your library? Promise not to besmirch it with my magic?'"

"Maybe phrase it differently?" Atmir offered a shrug.

"Ugh," Oracle rubbed her face. "I wish you could go over there and do the talking. He likes you."

"Everybody likes me."

"*Almost* everybody," Oracle said and put her hands on her hips.

"Don't act like you aren't among the adoring masses." Atmir's eyes sparkled and he posed for Oracle, looking off into the distance, chin raised and fists on hips like some kind of hero. Oracle again felt something stir in her. She willed it to stop fluttering.

"I have to go. There are books to besmirch with my magic." Oracle walked around Atmir and opened the door, the chime bells tinkling.

"See you later, adoring fan!" Atmir called as the door shut behind her. She could hear the smile without looking at it, and she could picture it without meaning to. She tried not to think about Atmir's smile on her walk, but the thing about trying *not* to think about something means you're going to think about it even harder. And so, Oracle spent the entire walk to the bookbinder's trying to get the various smiles of Atmir out of her brain. She was unsuccessful.

When she arrived at the bookbinder's shop, she stood outside for a long moment, steeling her nerves. She ran through several hypothetical situations in her head about what Harrad might say to her. Would he yell? Throw her out? Say something rude about mages to her? She decided she could live with all that, took a breath, and opened the door. The bell that rang was quite a bit deeper than the bells at the tea shop. It rang one clear *dong* and then stopped.

It turns out the bell was wholly unnecessary. Harrad sat at a desk covered in papers, glue, inkpots, and binding tools. His workstation took up most of the small entry they were in, and there was barely enough room for the door to swing open. Oracle wondered why Harrad had the bell at all. Harrad paused mid-stitch and looked up at her, scowling deeply at her.

"What d'you want mage?" He grumbled.

"Hello Harrad." Oracle let the door shut and took a step inside. She held her hands clasped in front of her body, doing her best to look prim and proper.

"What d'you want?" He looked back to his work and continued to stitch.

"I was hoping you could help me with something." Oracle crossed another two steps to his desk.

"Not about growing things, I hope. Nothing grows here. You're foolish to try it and even more foolish if you think your magic is gonna do anything. It's not welcome here." Harrad said as he continued to work. He didn't look up at her.

"I haven't really been able to grow anything, yet."

"*Yet*," Harrad snorted. Oracle watched him stitching.

"Well, I was going to ask if I could look through your library. Atmir says you have a lot of good volumes you have collected. He recommended I ask you for permission to read some of them." She was struggling to look polite because she was growing impatient, but she did her best to keep her hands from drifting to cross in front of her.

Harrad finally looked up at her and firmly replied, "There's no magic in those books."

"I'm not looking for magic." It was only a half-lie. Oracle would definitely be looking at anything magic if it turned up. Harrad stopped what he was doing and put down his tools in a huff. He scooted back, his chair screeching against the wood floor in protest.

"Fine," He pointed a finger at Oracle, "But nothing funny and you better be careful with my books. And you better not be magicking in my house."

"Understood and agreed. I promise to take care of your books. I appreciate your kindness and – "

"Shove it, mage. I'm doing this because Atmir is such an upstanding man. If anything happens, he'll make it right."

Oracle promptly shut her open mouth and followed Harrad into a back room. It was huge. The room was spacious and two stories tall, full of books. It smelled wonderful. Not like freshly bound books, which sometimes smelled of glue, but of well-loved volumes. It smelled like a *library,* of which Oracle had always been fond of visiting.

"Did you bind all of these?" Oracle asked in awe.

"Child, binding is an art. This is several lifetimes of artistry. No, I didn't bind them all." Harrad grumped at her. Oracle went to grab a book from a nearby shelf.

"No magic in here. Mind yourself," Harrad warned and went to exit the room. After he left, Oracle took a nearby book, opened it, and Harrad reappeared before she could read a single word.

"There's a small reading desk you can use. The chair isn't much, but comfortable enough," He set down an unlit candle on the desk and mumbled, "no magic" on the way out again.

Aquarius woke and hopped from Oracle's pocket. He skittered around the shelves.

"Oracle, this is like a whole library. Look at all these books!"

"I know. Isn't it great?" She whispered. Then realized she wasn't in a library and probably didn't need to whisper.

"I love the way it smells," Aquarius said, delightedly inhaling. He continued to climb up the shelves to the top. "Try not to besmirch it with your magic," he teased.

"Be careful, Aquarius. Mending broken limbs isn't in my repertoire." Oracle said, ignoring his remark.

"I know, I know. I'm just taking it all in. I'll help you look, just wait a minute."

The book Oracle had opened was titled *A Short History of Orc Names* and appeared to be just a list of names without context. She found 'Atmir' almost at the bottom of the second page and once again she was distracted when the image of his smiling face wafted into her mind's eye. She pushed it out and shut the book, trying to focus on her mission.

She gently put the book back in its place, then looked around. How was she going to find anything in here? She began on the shelf next to her, reading title after title, feeling the spines and taking some books in her hand to feel the texture of the covers or the weight of the book. Some books were small, some were large, and some were part of a series. There were books on every topic. Fiction, non-fiction, lists, maps – mostly outdated - and even a few technical manuals with charts and diagrams Oracle had no use for and didn't pay much attention to. She had made it through the first level of shelves and found nothing useful, replacing book after book. The books she did find that related to plants had basic information. Information she already knew from her mother. Sighing, she lit the candle and continued to the next level of shelves.

Aquarius picked a book and brought it clumsily down from a shelf in his mouth. As she read the cover she thought it would be useful. It was called *Greenspring: A Guide*. It detailed how the town looked before turning to the brown dust it was today. It sounded like Greenspring was lush with greenery at one point. The guide detailed many places in town, some of which still existed.

As Oracle continued to read, she wondered if maybe there was a clue or book that Harrad himself didn't even know would be helpful. Oracle made a mental note to try to get some information out of him if she could. Maybe over a cup of tea. Or maybe she could get Atmir to do it. An unbidden smile came to her face thinking of the way that conversation would go. She was delighted to think of the unflappable Atmir getting frustrated as he tried to pry information from an unwilling Harrad.

She closed *Greenspring: A Guide* and put it back on the shelf. The next book to catch her eye was a book on plants. It listed native plants to the area – none of which grew here anymore as far as she could tell. Disappointed, she leafed through it and then replaced it on the shelf. It gave her an idea of what *might* grow here if she could figure out how to grow anything. She finished looking through the second-row shelves, a little disheartened.

Partially through the third level's first shelf, Oracle hit paydirt: a book titled *Soil Amendments for Stubborn Plants.* Aquarius, at this point, had curled up on the reading desk to sleep. He had been helpful, but his endurance left something to be desired. Oracle had laid her cloak down for him, making a little pillow of scrunched fabric and covering him with an end for a blanket. Oracle read the book once and then kicked herself for not bringing anything to make notes with. She checked the little desk and was delighted to find pen, ink, and a bound notepad inside waiting for her to use them. She took them out without waking Aquarius and began writing details down.

Harrad was wrong about one thing. There *was* magic in the books. The *Soil* book included small growth spells, fertilization spells, watering spells, and a few others. Some of them she had seen before, helping her mother plant, others were new. She carefully wrote them all down. She cautiously put the book back in its place and looked at the remaining bookshelves. It was getting late, the candle's flame was nearly into the little bit of wax left the wick was so low, and she wasn't sure when she would have another chance to look at Harrad's books. Her eyes were drooping though, and her brain, which felt energized a moment ago, seemed to fizzle and then fog. The rest of the books would have to wait for another time.

She tidied the desk up and put away the pen and ink and notepad. Carefully she tucked her notes into her cloak, and gently scooped Aquarius into her pocket. He stirred but didn't wake. She took the candle, burned low by now, and walked out to the entry room. She expected to find Harrad at his workstation, but he was not there.

"Harrad?" She called hesitantly. There was no answer. She assumed he'd gone to bed and noted to thank him the next time they met. She would buy his next tea.

Before she left, she glanced at the books on his workstation. Of course there were some unfinished books, but there was a freshly finished book as well, its pages crisp and its cover bright and new. Harrad must have been working on that one when she arrived. Oracle then noticed there was a book squarely set on the desk, facing her. It only would have been more noticeable if it was propped up. She looked at the title: *A Gardener's Guide to Greenspring's Plants.* She blinked at it, wondering if it was possible Harrad set it out for her. She hesitated. Then she blew the candle out, set it on Harrad's workstation, and let herself into the night. She had the book tucked under her arm and a smile on her face. She would definitely be buying Harrad's next cup of tea.

4. Something Green

The sun hadn't risen yet when Aquarius paraded himself around the pillow on top of Oracle's hair. She groggily tried to roll over, but Aquarius protested at almost being pinned under her head. Oracle sat up.

"Aquarius, why must you wake me so early? The sun isn't even up yet."

"You're in charge of taking care of me, remember?"

"I suppose that's a valid reason."

"You suppose? It *is* a valid reason!" Aquarius huffed.

"Ok, I'm up. Let's get you some food, and then you can water the plants."

Oracle rose from the bed and got Aquarius a piece of dried meat and some dried berries. She found that the market that came to town every seventh day was bountiful with all kinds of useful and delicious items. She ate a small pastry from the tea shop. Atmir had been saving her the ones she liked when she came in – almost daily – for a cup of tea. Oracle liked the jam filled pastries. The flaky dough contrasted the sticky jam in a way that made Oracle's mouth happy and if her mouth was happy the rest of her was too.

She had fallen into a routine, and she wasn't upset with it. She would rise, feed her familiar, and tend to plants. Or rather, seeds in dirt. She was almost at peace with her decision to stay in Greenspring if it wasn't for the plants that refused to grow. Sometimes they would grow, but soon after they would die in a wave of heartbreak. Oracle's frustration was only second to her stubbornness.

After reading the book Harrad had left out for her, and compensating him with the appropriate number of teas, Oracle had carefully measured, cast spells, and planted various greenery in different pots and put them where they had the best light. Every day Aquarius ate his breakfast and then watered each plant to keep them moist. Oracle inspected each pot, and when she found them devoid of green, she'd march herself down to the tea shop for a consolation tea.

Today, Oracle woke, gave Aquarius his breakfast, and went down the stairs to look at the pots. She froze.

"Aquarius. Look," She whispered.

He paused with a mouthful of berry and looked up at her from the cloak pocket, then at the pots she was staring at. A small, barely visible green sprout was protruding from the dirt in one of the pots. Oracle rushed toward it to inspect it. She touched it gently, caressing the little lone leaf.

"Aquarius. It's *growing*. We did it! This one has lasted longer than all the others!" She couldn't take her eyes off the little shoot.

"Thanks to my impeccable watering schedule, I bet," Aquarius said after swallowing the berry. He looked curiously over to the pot, but didn't move to examine it further. He was eating, after all.

"I bet," Oracle said back. She picked up the pot and rotated it around, inspecting the green protrusion. She held it right up to her eyes. Oracle rotated it this way and that way, hardly believing what she saw. "It's still growing." Her voice was full of awe.

She lightly set the pot back down in its place and then proceeded to inspect each pot for any semblance of something growing in them. She was only mildly disappointed when she discovered the rest of them contained only dirt thus far.

"I'm going to the tea shop to tell Atmir! Water the plants when you're done."

"Bring me a pastry back!" He cried with a mouth full of food. Oracle hardly heard him as she rushed out the door and down the road to The Guiding Light. She burst through the doors and before the bells had finished their chime, she was already speaking.

"Atmir!" She cried excitedly. He turned from the stove, his eyes wide.

"What is it? What's happened?" He asked urgently.

"I did it! I have something green!" She nearly ran to the counter where Atmir stood, crossing the room in a flurry.

"That's amazing! What is it?" He set down his tea supplies. Oracle leaned forward on the counter, bouncing on her toes.

"A plant of course!"

"I knew that. Which kind of plant?" He asked and rested his hands on the countertop.

"Oh! An inside plant. One to keep in the window and enjoy its long tendrils of leaves coating your space in *green*. This is the first step! Greenspring can become green again!"

"How big is it?" Atmir whispered and leaned toward Oracle, his eyes wide.

Oracle shyly held up her finger and thumb in approximation.

"I see," Atmir said. "And how many leaves?"

Oracle held up a single finger.

"That's a start. Which is further than you've been able to go before. Incredible. Do you think it will survive?"

"I am going to do everything I can do to make sure it does! This is the longest anything has stayed green!" Oracle seemed to accentuate every other word with a bounce.

"This calls for a celebratory – "

"- tea?" Oracle cut him off.

"I was going to suggest an ale after the late afternoon rush, but if it's tea you want, I'll happily oblige." Atmir smiled at her and Oracle's stomach did a little flip. She scolded it.

"I could maybe do an ale. I haven't been to the inn yet, but Beatran had told me it's seedy."

"Seedy? It's not that bad. Beatran is a bit of a gossip, in case you hadn't noticed," Atmir looked at Oracle with raised eyebrows indicating she most certainly should have noticed. "She likes to exaggerate a bit. She's a great mayor, but don't tell her anything you don't want someone else to know. Anyway, how about just after the evening rush we can meet at the inn?"

"Yes, that will be perfect. I need to tend to my *plants*. Well, plant. There's just one growing right now." Oracle couldn't help the grin that spread across her face.

Atmir smiled again and stood up to his full height. "I'll see you then."

Oracle left the tea shop and walked into the sun. The wind pushed her hair around her face a little and she tied it back to contain it. She paused outside for a moment longer, shook her head as if she was dreaming, and then walked back up the street to the Alchemist's building. Did she just agree to a date? She couldn't help but to feel a little excited about the possibility.

When she entered the shop, she went upstairs and pulled her adventurer's pack from under the bed and set it on the bed. She carefully unloaded the contents one by one until she felt what she was looking for: a small sack. She pulled it out from her bag and undid the string on the sack and looked inside. A medium sized glowing seed was at the bottom, about the size of a gold coin.

Oracle turned the bag over and the seed slid out into her hand. She examined it. It was oval, mostly flat, and softly shining yellow. The seed itself was an off-white color and smooth like a pumpkin seed. Oracle spun the seed in her hand and flipped it over a few times. Making up her mind, she stood up and went back downstairs. If a plant could grow, this little seed could too. She couldn't explain it, but she felt a change somehow.

Aquarius was done watering the plants and taking a nap in the corner on a small hammock. He was almost invisible on the blue fabric. She prized how she loved Aquarius' presence, even if he wasn't doing anything in particular. His presence was steadfast and sure. She could rely on him.

Oracle pulled out a pot from under her bench and gathered her components: dirt, vermiculite, manure, and a little sand, to name a few. Soil magic was not complicated, but there was a subtle art to mixing the various parts together and she recalled how her mother had always told her that when mixing. Her mother had always instructed her to mix with her hands so she could really feel the soil components and know if the balance was right. She said you could feel it by touch and you'd know it was right. Striking a balance in the mixture was a starting point. Oracle would also have to cast the appropriate spells as well.

She scooped and mixed. She used her hands and felt the cool dirt between them. She concentrated on each element in the special mixture and tried to infuse her will into the soil. That was the first step. She transferred the mixture into the pot she had gotten earlier and gently patted the soil down. She stuck her finger in the center to make a hole and softly placed the glowing seed inside. She covered it loosely with dirt and then began the third part of the growing ritual. The spellcasting.

Harrad's book didn't have any spells in it. The book he'd left out had a lot of knowledge about different soil mixtures, growing plants, a little on types of plants, and basic care instructions. Most of those plants had been outdoor varieties, which was not going to be very useful right now. The book that Harrad must not have known he had, called *Soil Amendments for Stubborn Plants*, contained a variety of simple spells and rituals for helping plants grow. Oracle had known some of them already from her mother, but one spell in particular attracted Oracle the most. She had made sure to cast it on every plant she had tried to grow since then. It was an easy ritual with a simple, plain incantation.

Oracle brought the planted seed to a table in the backroom behind the counter and placed it within a ritual diagram made of chalk. The diagram was a simple circle made up of smaller circles shaded in to represent the phases of the moon. There were two full moons and two new moons to complete the circle diagram. In the center of the circle was a small mound of dirt she had mixed by hand, and this is where Oracle placed the pot. She stepped back and focused a hand on the diagram, ready to cast the spell.

"By phases of the moon,
by light does it grow,
protect this seed
that I have sown,
Let the energy of the earth
feed it green,
may it bloom and rise,
a sight to be seen."

The diagram glowed soft white for a few seconds and then faded. An invisible wind smudged the chalk, ruining the diagram as Oracle expected, and then she removed the pot and set it aside. She cleared and redrew the circle for the next time she planted, taking care with each section, feeling the chalk move across the wooden tabletop. Oracle took the pot out to the main room and looked around at the various pots and planters she'd put on the floor in the sunlight under the skylight. It was time a plant occupied the window. She set the pot down on the floor and went upstairs. She picked up the side table Atmir had brought her and carted it downstairs to the window to find the perfect spot.

After getting the placement *just right*, Oracle took the pot with the glowing seed hiding in it and placed it on the table. The late afternoon sun streamed through the window and it warmed her as she stood in the sunlight. Oracle took a breath and admired the dirt, imagining the plant that might arise from the glowing seed. Today would have been a year with her team.

The seed she had been given was part of a reward for a contract she and her team had completed. Most of her team hadn't cared about their seeds. They were very unique, individualized, valuable, and rare, the man had told them. The seed, he told them, would bond to the person who carried it and when planted there would be elements of that person in the plant it produced. He could not or would not say what those elements would be, or what plant would come out of the seed. It was a layered mystery, but Oracle hoped it was one that would be solved soon.

Oracle pondered what the seeds would have produced for her team. It made her sad. Though they hadn't known each other for very long, she had known from the start they were good people. A few hiccups in their time together had her feeling self-conscious about her abilities as a mage. A few failures had cemented the idea for her. Maybe focusing on fire had been a mistake. Maybe she should have gone into full-time greenhouse work like her mother did. Maybe she should have trained to be a seer like her mother had wanted.

No. She was a fire mage. A profession usually imagined as a violent boy who grew up to cause chaos and destruction as a man. Truthfully, Oracle did like the destruction part of fire, the potential for unreserved power, and just the way it *looked*, but she had never been reckless or even chaotic with her power. It had always been her favorite tool for most problems, but not the only tool she had. She could do other spells; they just weren't as fun.

Magic was her calling, and fire magic had brought her around the world in a way that other magic probably wouldn't have. The only traveling seers you encountered were either hiding from someone or a fraud and she had no idea why her mother wanted her to become one of those. She thought she might ask one day.

"Am *I* a fraud?" Oracle wondered aloud.

"A frog?" Aquarius asked, yawning. "I haven't seen a frog for ages. How has the plant fared so far? Not withered and crispy yet?"

Oracle snapped out of her reverie and strode back across the room to the sprouted plant. It basked in the sun from the skylight. Aquarius met her there.

"Looks the same," Oracle said, crouching down to examine it instead of picking it up.

"Do you have any growth spells to speed it up?" Aquarius got up on his rear legs and peered over the edge of the pot at the plant. He was only about 8 inches tall when standing like that.

"I do, but I don't want to use it. I want it to grow slow and steady," Oracle said, scooping Aquarius up into her hands. "But look at this."

She walked back over to the table in the window and placed Aquarius down on it. He stood upright again and peered over this plant pot.

"Ah. Amazing. A pot of dirt. Very similar to the several others over there. What am I looking at?"

"I planted it."

"The mystery seed?" Aquarius peered up at Oracle in disbelief. "You know it could be a seed that dooms us, right? It could hatch a monster."

"I don't think it will hatch a monster. The man who gave it to us was sincere and grateful for getting rid of that creature on his property. Remember? It destroyed most of his field and ate a helper."

"I remember. I also remember the creepy plants he had inside. Do you remember the one that grabbed me? I was almost eaten by a plant!"

"It didn't grab you. You just got tangled in its long strands."

"It *grabbed* me." Aquarius insisted, turning his attention back to Oracle.

"You're very dramatic, you know that?"

"*Grabbed.*"

"You must." Oracle breathed the words out and looked amused at Aquarius.

"If this seed grows some kind of sentient plant that tries to eat us, what are you going to do?" Aquarius asked and paced across the table.

"Burn it. Obviously."

Aquarius opened his mouth to reply, but shut it and rolled his eyes instead. "Burning things is how we ended up here," he muttered under his breath.

"I heard that," Oracle scolded, crossing her arms.

"It's true," Aquarius said quietly back.

"You don't have to say it aloud. I know why we're here," Oracle said, her tone morose and down. She held her hand out for Aquarius to climb onto.

"Sorry," he said as he walked aboard her outstretched palm.

"It's fine," Oracle replied, resigned. She walked back to the counter and placed Aquarius on it. She took out a piece of dried meat and placed it in front of him. He started gnawing at it, making happy little sounds while he did so. Oracle looked out at the mostly empty room, save for the pots, and imagined what it would be like when it was full of green. She pictured long leaves and deep foliage covering the whole space. She folded her arms on the counter and rested her head on them, so she was eye level with Aquarius. He was happily eating his little piece of meat.

"This place is going to be beautiful when we're done. This is just the start. Also, you'll need to water the new plant. I didn't do it."

"Did you do the spells on it?" Aquarius said between chews of meat.

"I only did the ritual one. This plant feels like it needs just a little help. A little protection for now. I don't think I should do the growth spell or the fertilization spell on it. I'm definitely not going to do the deep root spell on it. Not yet anyway."

"You don't think it's your spells doing all the hard work here? I mean, how many plants did you kill before we got that little sprout to survive?" Aquarius said between bites of meat. "This last batch of plants you put all the spells on and they're still struggling. You don't think it's a good idea to cast some on your precious mystery seed?"

"I can't explain it, but it doesn't feel like it needs it. Not yet anyway."

"You're weird," Aquarius said, then burped.

"Gross, Aquarius." Oracle recoiled. He just smiled back at her and then continued to eat his snack. Oracle raised her head up, took another look at Aquarius and sighed. He was happily shredding what was left of the piece of meat. She loved her little friend, even if she didn't always understand him.

"I'm going to get cleaned up and then Atmir is going to meet me at the inn for a celebration ale this evening."

"A date!" Aquarius squealed.

"It isn't a date. We're just meeting to celebrate the little green sprout," Oracle said, her voice rising slightly in pitch. She was trying to sound convincing.

"Are you going to tell him about the mystery seed?" Aquarius asked seriously.

"I might."

"Are you taking me with you?"

"I don't think I am."

"It *is* a date then!"

"Aquarius, stop. It is not a date. We're just going to check out the inn and have an ale and then Atmir will have to get back to the tea shop and I'll be back here. Not a date. Just a…I don't actually know what to call it, but it's not a date!" Oracle exclaimed, a little flustered.

"Uh huh. Daaaaaaaaate," Aquarius sang the last word at her and did a little prance on his stubby legs.

"Ok. I am going to do something productive now. Finish your food."

Oracle turned and went up the staircase, not looking back at Aquarius. Aquarius turned back to his piece of dried meat and contin-

ued to happily shred it to bits. When she got to the top of the staircase
and entered her room, she caught herself in the mirror. She almost
always wore her adventuring clothes. They were practical, comfortable, and she never bothered to think of something else to wear.
Tonight, she thought maybe she would wear normal clothes. She did
have some.

Oracle tried one outfit, then the next, then a third. She went back
to the first, then decided the third one would be the right one. It was a
plain green tunic, a brown leather vest, and simple brown pants. She
looked put-together without looking like she was dressing up. She
brushed her long brown hair and tied it carefully behind her head,
making sure the sides just slightly covered the tips of her ears. She examined herself in the mirror, looking for any detail out of place. Satisfied, she grabbed her cloak and left for the tavern.

Oracle smelled the inn before she arrived. It smelled of warm
bread and hearty stew, and her stomach grumbled and she realized
she'd forgotten to eat lunch. Oracle didn't have to open the big
wooden door on her way into the inn as a stream of people walked
out laughing and joking with each other. She held it for them. It was
heavy. She expected the inn to be crowded but found it was not over-
run with rowdy patrons. It was a little busy, but not the raucous party
she was led to believe it would be. She laughed at herself for picturing
the inn being full of shady characters, men and women of the night,
suave bards, and drunkards. After all, this was a small town, not the
city. She shook her head and took in the sight.

Music from the bard floated to her. Tellamund, the man playing
the guitar, had been into the tea shop looking for something to soothe
his throat some weeks ago. Oracle wondered if his throat was still
bothering him. She saw Harrad eating something soupy in the corner
as she walked further in. She waved but he pretended not to notice
her. In the low light she thought she saw the baker with someone, but
she wasn't quite sure. There were a few tables of folks she didn't know

and few she recognized by sight. She took them in as the barmaid bustled here and there.

She had been to their market stalls or chatted briefly with them at the tea shop or elsewhere in town, but she didn't really know any of them well. Most of the townspeople seemed wary of her, and she didn't press her presence upon them. Once they found out she was a mage, and news had traveled quickly, they seemed hesitant to engage with her. They weren't impolite, or downright grouchy like Harrad, but they definitely were not so friendly with her. She wanted to chalk it up as being the newcomer to town but wondered if it wasn't because she was a mage. It seemed, by all her accounts, that it was because she was a mage.

As she scanned the room she found Atmir sitting at a corner spot with a book. It was a tall table with four tall chairs, three of which waited for her arrival. Oracle looked at him for a long time before she walked over to the table, captivated by the big man. She admired his quiet nature. She approached the table and sat down. She found herself grinning back at Atmir, who had set his book down and was grinning at her. They shared a little secret that the town didn't know yet – something had grown. Atmir put his book down as the barmaid approached.

"Good evening, Atmir. Away from the shop? Must be something special to do that," She nodded at Oracle, who looked a little confused.

"We're celebrating tonight, Sunny. This is Oracle. Have you two met?"

"We have not," Oracle said cheerily, "I'm Oracle."

"Senaila Neesa, innkeeper extraordinaire. You can call me Sunny. Pleasure to meet you, Oracle. What can I get you two?"

Sunny was a beautiful elven woman with long golden hair tied back in a braid, impossibly bright blue eyes, and a tall, lithe frame. Oracle guessed Sunny to be in her early 40s, but that was hard to tell, and she wasn't going to ask.

Oracle could smell many more savory foods wafting out through the kitchen. She looked to Atmir and said, "I will take your recommendation. This is my first time here."

"Ok then, two ploughman's and two ales. Light?" Atmir asked, looking at Oracle.

"Yes, light."

"I have just the thing for you," Sunny said. She smiled broadly and walked off to her duties.

"With something green surviving now, more things will follow," Oracle said.

"Have you thought about a store name yet? With all the green you'll grow, you can't call your plant shop 'The Alchemist's.' It'll be very misleading." Atmir put his book away in a satchel slung on the back of the chair he was perched upon.

"I've thought a little bit about it," Oracle said, leaning back in her seat.

"Come up with anything good?" Atmir turned around and leaned an arm on the table.

"Well, my family name is Moss, so I wanted to incorporate that. I was thinking maybe Moss' Plants, or Moss and Green," Oracle said unsure. She looked away from Atmir at other patrons in the inn.

"What about Blooms and Moss?" Atmir asked and leaned forward in his chair.

"Blooms and Moss…" Oracle felt the words in her mouth as she said them, "Blooms and Moss."

"I think it's nice."

"I think I like it. Blooms and Moss sounds nice to say and it's memorable. Hopefully," she said. She sat forward in her chair and leaned her own arm on the table, mirroring Atmir.

"Well, if you continue to get things to grow, I'm sure it will be very memorable."

They fell into a short silence before Oracle asked, "What's a ploughman's?"

"You don't like surprises?" Atmir asked with a half-smile and cocked head.

"Just curious," she replied, putting her hands up in defense.

"I think you'll like it. It's like adventurer fare, but much, much better. It's more like a snack, so I ordered two. I don't know how hungry you are, but I am hungry and will definitely eat what you don't," Atmir stated.

"What do you know of adventurer fare?" Oracle teased.

"I know a little! I know adventuring is hard work, risky, and sometimes it pays well. I know it isn't the life for me."

"How did you come to tea?"

"I've always made tea. My parents, aunts, uncles, grandparents, all had slightly different paths in life, but most of them were adventurers at some point. I grew up with stories of their exploits. It was exciting when I was a kid, but I gravitated toward brewing teas with my aunt. She was the druid sort, but instead of living in the woods she lived a few houses down. I think she did the whole woods thing when she was young, but by the time I came around she was accustomed to permanent shelter."

Oracle laughed, which made Atmir smile enthusiastically at her. Sunny returned with two flagons of ale and said she'd be right back with the ploughman's platters.

"So, your aunt taught you to brew teas?" Oracle said and took a sip of the ale. It was crisp, bitter, and tasted like lemon, hops, and something grain related. She was pleasantly surprised.

"My aunt and my father. My aunt was good at identifying plants, harvesting them, and growing some of them. She did simple brews, mostly for their magic effects. My father, however, could take ingredients and make something that *tasted* like magic. My aunt could make nettle tea, but my father could make it palatable. He said he learned from an old witch. I have no idea if he meant his mother or an actual old witch. I never met his side of the family," Atmir explained and took a sip of his ale.

"An old witch? Sounds like he got off easy if all she did was teach him to brew teas," Oracle said with a smile.

"He never elaborated, so maybe he didn't get off easy? I have no idea."

"Are your parents still around?" Oracle asked.

"No." Atmir stated matter-of-factly. "Yours?"

"My mom is, as far as I know. My father left when I was very young. I don't have any recollection of him, but if everything was normal in his life, I imagine he's still alive somewhere. My mom tells me he was a 'where the wind takes me' type of man; he is my elf side, and their relationship didn't last very long. Sorry to hear about your parents, though. That has to be tough."

"It gets a little better with time. It's actually my uncle who mostly raised me after my parents. His death was really tough."

"I'm sorry, Atmir."

Atmir heaved a breath out and Sunny arrived with two platters she set before them. There was a chunk of bread, a selection of cured meats, some cheeses, nuts, cured olives, and a little cup of yellow stuff that Oracle assumed to be some kind of mustard. She didn't tell Atmir she didn't like mustard or olives. They happily dug into the plate after they thanked Sunny. The salty meat was very satisfying and Oracle layered it with bread and cheese trying not to be voracious in her eating.

"Anyway," Atmir started again, "I'm here now, brewing teas, keeping the lantern lit."

He ate casually, as if he wasn't too hungry, despite his proclamation earlier. Oracle had a mouth full of food and had to wait to chew and swallow before speaking again.

"How did you end up in Greenspring?" she asked.

"Well, that uncle that died had left my cousin Eli his house. The house I essentially grew up in."

"That had to be a blow."

"It was. Eli's a good man though. He is dedicated to one of the lesser gods and was going to turn the house into a small place of healing. He had the thing torn down before my uncle was cold, which didn't really sit right with my other cousins," Atmir said and took a big bite of bread and cheese.

"What about you?" Oracle asked.

"It chafed. It hurt. It felt unfair." Atmir said and wiped his hands on his napkin to reach for his flagon and take a drink.

"And what happened? You just left?"

"Not at first. I had to help clean out the house before Eli tore it down."

"Ouch," Oracle winced in commiseration.

"It was painful, yes. I did get to keep a lot of my uncle's things, and I found a letter. It was unsigned, but obviously from my uncle. It was folded up in a volume of poetry and the folds were worn, so he had obviously opened it and closed it a lot. In it, he told me what a joy and pleasure I had always been to him, and how he admired what I did – which at the time was mostly play peacekeeper for my cousins and brew teas. He said he pictured his house as a place of comfort and knew his garden would be a legacy he could trust in my hands. In it, he said he was leaving everything to me."

"What? Your cousin stole it?" Oracle was shocked.

"No, no. Eli wouldn't do that. What happened was there was another letter," Atmir took a long swig of ale.

"Another letter? This is sounding scandalous." Oracle took another bite of food.

"Yes. And in this letter my uncle had expounded on Eli's good traits, etcetera. It was similar to the letter I found, but addressed to him. The difference being Eli's letter had my uncle's signature and the barrister stopped looking after finding it among my uncle's papers."

"No! You didn't fight it?"

"I didn't have a whole lot to work with, and I didn't want to fight with my family. I'd had enough fighting by then. I just wanted my uncle to rest in peace and keep what was left of my family – which is now just my cousins – intact. Eli hasn't come around since I left, but my other cousins do."

"So how long have you been here? Five years?"

"About five years now, yes."

"You've seemed to make a lot of friends over those five years. I never had a lot of friends back home." Oracle looked at her plate.

"Most of the people in town are customers, not friends. I'd like to think you're different though. I consider you a friend. It wasn't easy to come to this town. I had to make some difficult choices to fit in."

"Such as?"

"You may have not noticed, but my teeth for one," He bared his lower teeth for her. She could definitely see the filed down tusks now.

"Half-orc, then? I was pretty sure I saw your teeth the first time we met."

"Yep, half-orc. My mom was an orc and my dad was a human. I had to lean into my human half to blend in here and make it a little easier. Orcs do not have a great reputation in most towns."

"I understand about leaning into your human half. I'm half elf, as anyone can guess by the ears. In the city it's not so bad, but in many places humans consider me 'other' and elves consider me 'lesser.' I try to keep the points hidden."

"I like your ears."

"Thanks," Oracle said shyly and reddened.

"I felt a lot like you. Orcs considered me 'lesser' because I was not as big. I had to make up for it by being extra tenacious and extra ferocious. That's not me at heart, but I was good at it," Atmir said, a little uncomfortably. He fidgeted when he explained. "Humans tend to look at me as 'other' also. Now, I can pass for a very large human, unless someone looks too closely. I am fortunate not to have the green-tinted skin that would give me away."

"Where were you before?"

"In the village. My human dad and I lived in the orc village where my mom was from. My cousins are all mostly there as well. They have their own adventures to be getting on with, so they aren't always at home. It's not too far from here, actually. Maybe one day you'll meet one when they stop in. Every few months or so one of them pops in for tea, to tease me a bit about my profession, and then they disappear for several more months. They take it in rotation it seems like. They are never here at the same time. But maybe that's because they know I only have 1 spare bed."

"Speaking of which, they're going to be in for a surprise if I don't get that one back to you, huh?"

"They'll survive. They're not adventure-shy and from what I know, a bed is few and far between for your type."

"My type?"

"Aren't you an adventurer?"

"Well, I was. I mean, I am, but I don't have a type. Or, I mean, I am not a type," Oracle said, a little flustered. Atmir sat there, amused.

"Don't worry about the bed, you can keep it as long as you like."

They fell into silence and ate their food. Sunny came around and replaced their flagons with fresh ones full of ale. Oracle noted again that the ale was very good, and wondered where it came from. The inn surely didn't brew it, there was no room here, and importing everything seemed a large task.

"So, what about you? How did you end up here in Greenspring?" Atmir asked after a draw of ale.

"I was on a contract that went wrong. I'm in self-exile."

"That seems a little dramatic?"

"I was being a little dramatic, but truthfully I *am* in self-exile. The contract did go wrong. My party – my friends – were taken from me, and I feel like it's my fault. So, after completing my duties to report on the contract, I walked away. Literally. I had no idea how long I had been walking when I came across the lantern in your shop."

"I see," Atmir said gently. "Do you might if I ask what happened?"

Oracle was lost in thought for a moment, then replied. "I guess I can tell you. Do you know what an arcane conduit is?"

"I don't."

"Ok, well, picture a spider web with a spider in the center. And the whole thing is underground. Under a town or city to be exact. The web is the conduit which magic flows through. It's generally used to power machinery, magic lanterns, and some arcane objects. The spider at the center is an arcane condenser. It accumulates and channels the magic through the conduit. We were sent to examine an arcane condenser under a small town. There was a local wizard, a very old one, who wanted it investigated because it was interfering with something he was doing. He said he was too old for the job. He was ancient, so I think that part was true."

"So, he didn't set you up for failure."

"No, I don't think he did. He was very consoling when I reported back. Or tried to be, I guess. There wasn't anything anybody was going to do for me at that point," Oracle stared off absently watching people eat. She took a long drink of her ale, still staring off into the middle distance.

"Your friends and you went underground for this arcane conduit then?"

Oracle regained herself and said, "Yes. We were to find the arcane accumulator and inspect it. That's the piece in the center. It shouldn't have been working, but weird pulses of magic kept coming from this old, abandoned town and it was ruining whatever the wizard had going on. We got to the city. It was in ruins. Not hardly a building standing any more. Not sure what happened to it, but it happened a long time ago. We eventually found our way to a magic regulating station and entered a passage that led us underground."

"Was it scary?" Atmir was leaning in toward Oracle, his forearms resting on the table and his hands clasped.

"Not too bad really. It wasn't our first adventure together and far from our first adventures at all. We figured out how to light up the path by channeling magic into a grid that charged some lanterns. It was a huge underground tunnel. Massive. I have no idea why it needed to be so tall, but it was cavernous," she said, holding her hands wide. Oracle paused to take another sip of ale. Atmir watched her quietly.

"We wandered down the tunnel until there was a collapse in it. The lights didn't work here, and the cavernous opening was now going to be a squeeze for most of us. We crammed ourselves into this passage, making our way further and further into the conduit tunnels. We weren't entirely sure which way to go."

"The wizard didn't have anything for you to help?"

"He did. He had an old – we're talking disintegrate in your hands old – map. It showed roughly where we were, but before any changes had been made. It's my understanding that the conduit can change with what the town needs above it. We had an idea of where we were, but we weren't certain. We just kept traveling deeper, guided by the map as best as we could muster. Eventually it opened back up again. This goes on for a while."

"Like hours? Days? How long?" Atmir asked.

"Several hours at least. Being underground in the dark is weird and kind of messes with your body. Time feels different because there's no sun and moon."

"So, you're just going hours deep into a spiderweb."

Oracle let out a laugh, "Yes! That's pretty much the essence of the thing."

"And did you find the accumulator?"

"We did," Oracle said and shifted in her seat. "It was dead as far as we could tell. I did some tests. My friend Margo did some tests – she's brilliant at technical magic. Or she was. She was really good at technical magic. And we determined that the accumulator was dead. There wasn't any magic pulsing coming from it." Oracle sat back in her chair.

"The old wizard did set you up then?" Atmir asked, surprised.

"We thought about it at first. Wondering why he sent us down there and if he had some kind of plans to our detriment. We determined there was something else making magic pulses erupt and generally we believed the old wizard just wanted them to stop. We just weren't sure if the pulses were coming from there or up top in the town somewhere." Oracle paused for a drink of ale while Sunny came by and took their platters away.

"That sounds like a good way to get lost in an endless maze of tunnels. No thank you," said Atmir, drinking his own ale.

"We set up camp because we were all tired. We had no idea what time of day it was, but we knew it was time for a rest. We set up some devices to sense the magic pulse and alert us. We left Peter to stand first watch and we all sort of just dozed off when the arcane pulse hit. Looking back, we should have continued to rest because we were all so tired, but we decided to pursue the mystery instead." Oracle leaned against the table now, and rested her arms on top of it. Atmir shifted to mirror her position.

"We trekked over a lot of rubble from collapsed tunnels heading toward what we thought was the source. We guessed it was some natural array making an accumulator that filled up and then let out a burst when it was too full. We weren't really prepared for what was down there. We entered another cavernous space and you could just hear the emptiness of the space in there. I had entered last and I didn't – I didn't," Oracle took a breath and looked at her lap. Atmir put his hand on hers.

"You don't have to tell me," he said softly.

Oracle looked at him. "It's fine. It's fine. I haven't really re-lived the moment out loud." She took another breath and continued. She didn't pull away from Atmir's hand letting the warmth seep into her hand. "I went last through the crevice. I could feel how big the space was and the lights we had only lit up a fraction of the floor. What we didn't expect and what we were not prepared for, was an arcanely charged wyrm."

"I'm sorry, I don't know what that is. I know what a worm is, like for gardening."

Oracle smiled, the tears welled in her eyes, and she wiped them away with the back of one hand.

"No, a wyrm. Like a wingless dragon. Arcane wyrms are huge burrowing beasts that use magic pulses as a type of detection system when they are hunting. The beast had taken up residence under the abandoned town and it couldn't get to us from where we had been, but it knew we were there. We walked right into it."

"How did you get out? I mean, I know not everyone did. What happened?" Atmir didn't take his eyes off Oracle.

"It attacked of course, and we attacked back. The wyrm had lashed its tail at us and collapsed our escape. We had to find a new way out, or at least away from the beast. The wyrm didn't have a lot of maneuvering room, and it took a moment for it to turn around and plan its next attack. They're not extremely smart, but they are extremely aggressive. It managed to attack Tevin, and, well," Oracle stared off again before continuing, "it killed him."

Atmir squeezed her hand reassuringly and waited for her to continue. She paused a long time before she did.

"There was another section of collapsed tunnel, but it looked like a safe bet to get through. We charged inside as fast as we could get and the wyrm couldn't follow us. When the space opened up again, we took a moment to try to heal Tevin. It was no use. He was gone. None of us knew what to do next, but Hellene carried Tevin and we moved forward. We were just trying to navigate back to where we entered or to another place where we could exit to the city above."

Oracle turned back to look at Atmir, her face marked by a tear streak.

"We turned down a tunnel we thought would lead us back around, listening to our surroundings, moving quietly and cautiously. It wasn't enough. I think we were in a wyrm tunnel and not a conduit tunnel. The wyrm came up behind us. We started to run, and the tunnel came to a dead end. There was a small opening we could squeeze through and I stopped before going in and cast a spell, hoping to buy us some time. The spell hit the worm, catching it on fire. I remember the awful sound it made," Oracle made a face. "The pressure from the blast threw us all backward and the wrym couldn't stop it's forward momentum. It slammed into the tunnel wall collapsing the entrance. I landed in the crevice beyond the collapse. Just me. And Aquarius."

"There's no possibility your team could have survived?"

"I checked," Oracle said so softly Atmir had to read her lips.

"I'm so sorry Oracle. That's a tragedy."

"It's...well...it's not fine. But I can't change it." She replied, still barely above a whisper.

Atmir got up, went around the table, and gave Oracle a long hug. She wiped the tears from her eyes and said in a half laugh, half cry, "We are supposed to be celebrating!"

Atmir didn't let her go for a long time and when he released her he said, "We don't have to celebrate. We can just be sad if you want."

"No. No way. We need to celebrate damn it," Oracle called Sunny over and ordered more ale. "I *grew* something and that's why we are here. So, let's celebrate and forget all the old pains we have. At least for now."

Atmir raised his eyebrows and smiled. He returned to his seat. "Ok. Let's celebrate then. To you, Oracle, and your little green things."

She wiped tears from her eyes and looked directly at Atmir. With a sniff, Oracle replied, "To green things."

5. Foraging

The day was cool yet. It would be sunny and warm later, during which Aquarius would find a sunspot to soak in the heat and laze the afternoon away. Atmir and Oracle were headed to where they could forage tea ingredients. The plants Oracle had grown suffered another wave of death. Her magic seed's sprout seemed to survive, but Oracle wasn't sure it would last much longer. Atmir suggested they go for a hike and forage to ease her mind and Oracle reluctantly agreed. They hiked through the sandy trails until it turned to dirt. They passed columns of black rock, and low spiky bushes until the path eventually started to grow trees. After a while longer they were in a forest, deep with green and wildlife.

Aquarius was in Oracle's pocket, his head poking out of the top. He looked around as they walked, making comments here and there about the scenery. Atmir led the way, as he knew it best. They both carried packs. Oracle carried her adventurer's pack, and Atmir carried a satchel meant for storing their finds. They also both carried water. The days had grown longer, hotter, despite the misleading coolness of morning and evening. Summer was on the cusp of arrival.

"How long before we're there?" Aquarius asked.

"Not too long, little buddy," Atmir replied back. Oracle didn't say anything, just marched behind Atmir. Something was bothering her, but she couldn't place her finger on it.

"Good, because I'm hungry."

"You already ate. I fed you a roll half an hour ago," Atmir said.

"I'm growing! A paltry roll isn't going to satisfy me for long."

Atmir rolled his eyes and shook his head, though Aquarius couldn't see it.

"Doing alright back there?" Atmir called over this shoulder to Oracle.

"Yeah," Oracle said. "Just marching along behind you. We're not too far off now that the trees have gotten thick, right?"

"No, we're getting close. I'm glad you remembered."

"I recognized this part of the trail is all."

"That's remembering," Atmir said. Oracle could hear the smile and she smiled too.

Soon they reached a small clearing of tall grass with a slope on one side. Tall evergreens reached to the sky, which was a bright blue now. This was Oracle's third or fourth time foraging with Atmir. She liked the hikes, and she particularly liked the quiet time with Atmir. She didn't want to admit that part, especially out loud. She reached down and removed Aquarius from her pocket. She set him gently down and he scurried off to find a sunny spot to sunbathe.

"Don't wander too far, Aquarius," she called after him. She heard a little sound of assent and watched him go until she couldn't see him anymore. She looked at Atmir and set her pack down.

"What are we seeking today?" she asked.

"Loroot and maybe Idlesprout. Idlesprout might not be out yet, but since the weather has been warming up so much, I think we're close."

"What do you use those for? Which teas?" Oracle asked as she stretched her arms and rolled her shoulders.

"Loroot goes in quite a few. It's readily available almost year-round. Idlesprout is for three or four brews. I find that it smooths out some of the more potent concoctions. When a tea's ingredients get to be a little harsh, I add the dried Idlesprout, and it tames it. Makes it more palatable. A trick my dad taught me." Oracle listened intently to Atmir. She liked seeing him talk about his ingredients. She wasn't the only one with a passion for plants, it just happened that Atmir's plants grew outside instead of inside.

"You said your aunt taught you about the plants, right?" she asked.

"Yes, that was my aunt." Atmir was not looking at Oracle now. He was focused on the ground, scanning back and forth. Oracle watched him, unsure of what he was searching for or if she should do something.

Instead, Oracle asked, "Was she your uncle's wife?"

"No, his sister. Ah!" He reached down and pushed some tall grass out of the way. "See this?"

Oracle walked over and looked at what he was holding. In his grasp, not yet pulled from the ground, was a long, pale green, flat stalk. It was barely taller than the grass around it, and the top flared slightly wider than the base.

"I do. What is it?" She peered closer at the stalk.

"This is just the blade, you have to gently pull." Atmir did so as he was talking. Oracle was surprised that the blade continued to come out of the ground until it ended in a long brown root. She was also a little distracted at Atmir's flexing arms. They gently tensed as the muscles flexed in his forearms and Oracle couldn't look away. There was something about his sleeves being rolled up she liked. "And you get the Loroot. Pull too hard, and it'll snap off in your hand and the root will be wasted. Digging them out is a pain. It's best to be strong, but gentle."

Atmir stood up and showed off the blade and root. Oracle admired him for a moment, but didn't let it show on her face. She was trying her best to look like a conscientious student, but she kept thinking about Atmir being both strong and gentle, too.

"You think you can find more? They are a challenge in the grass, but that's their favorite place to grow. You have to be a little lucky." He began to strip the root from the blade and placed it in his satchel when he was done.

"I'll do my best," Oracle replied not unhappily.

So they began, scanning the meadow, walking in a grid pattern. Atmir took one side and Oracle took the other. They'd meet in the middle somewhere. Atmir stumbled across Aquarius, sunning himself. He was outstretched on a bed of fallen needles, eyes closed, breathing gently. Atmir thought he was asleep until he spoke.

"If you paint me, you can stare at me whenever you like."

"Very funny. How's this sunspot?" Atmir asked, still looking at Aquarius.

"It's nice, but I don't think it'll last too long. I'll have to move again soon."

"That's a shame," Atmir said, and continued to scan nearby. Then he stopped. "Aquarius?"

"Yes?" The little creature opened one eye to look at him.

"Can I ask you a question?"

"Sure." Aquarius opened both eyes, stretched, and sat up. A few needles stuck to his body, and he swept them away.

"Do you like being a familiar?"

Aquarius looked thoughtful and didn't respond right away. He then said simply, "I do."

"What do you like about it? You don't think it would be better to be free?" Atmir walked back closer to Aquarius.

"I have freedom enough. Oracle takes care of me, and I her. When she said I was her best friend, she didn't say she was mine. But she is. Being a familiar is a responsibility, of course, but I take it seriously. As I grow I'll be able to do more for her. Neither of us know how big I'll get, but I'm determined to be the best familiar there is. It's a bond more than a bind. Oracle is a friend, but she is also family. My family. And I don't need freedom from that."

It was Atmir's turn to look thoughtful. Aquarius waited patiently.

"Thanks," Atmir said, and then continued on his way. Aquarius watched him for a while, then went to seek out another sunspot.

When Oracle and Atmir met in the middle, they compared what they had found. Oracle, as it turned out, was exceptional at finding

Loroot. She had found almost double what Atmir had and she felt a little proud of herself for doing so. Next, Atmir taught her about Idlesprout.

"It grows at the base of trees. It's challenging to find it sometimes, and like I said, it might not be ready yet. You'll recognize it when you see it. It's a reddish-brown plant that looks like it's newly sprouted."

"Why is it called Idlesprout? Is it lazy?" Oracle asked him with raised eyebrows.

"It's named for Hickam Idle, the man that discovered it."

"Oh." She said, disappointed.

They walked side by side into the woods, checking the base of every tree for a little reddish-brown plant. The smell of the trees and of the forest floor was a scent Oracle missed. She inhaled deeply several times, trying to commit the smell to memory. She liked the bouncy feel of the forest floor, too.

"Oracle?"

"Atmir?"

"Do you mind if I ask about your life in the city?"

"No. But turnabout is fair play."

"I'll remember that," he said, with an easy chuckle. Oracle suppressed a smile. "What was your life like, before adventuring?"

"I grew up in the city, like I said. My dad wasn't around and my mom makes her living growing plants in a giant greenhouse that I pretty much grew up in. Mostly medicinal plants, but a few for fun. I was newly seventeen when I started my apprenticeship to be a mage. I didn't tell her at first."

"Was she mad?" Atmir asked, sweeping his eyes across the tree trunks.

"I wouldn't say mad. Upset, yes. She knew I'd always dreamed of adventuring because that's all the books I'd ever read. I talked about it nonstop. She knew I'd find a way, but she wasn't too pleased about the fire aspect. Especially when I accidentally lit a few reference books on fire once."

"Didn't burn the place down though."

"Didn't burn it down, no," Oracle laughed.

"And what about after you learned to be a mage?"

"Oh, I spent most of those with my mentor, Attican Braun, until I started out adventuring with a team," Oracle replied as she bent down to examine the base of a tree. Atmir stopped and watched her. They resumed walking when Oracle's search turned fruitless. Atmir's hand brushed against Oracle and Oracle realized how close together they were. He smelled like citrus. She thought it would be nice to stroll holding hands, and then she forbade herself from thinking that again. The forbidden thought was persistent, distracting, and drummed in her head.

"And what did you learn from him?" Atmir asked.

"Almost everything I know about fire magic, and magic in general. He was fantastic. He believed in me," Oracle said, and then fell silent. After a few steps, she added quietly, "Even when I didn't believe in myself."

"It's nice to have that kind of support."

"It is," she agreed.

"Do you miss the city life?"

"Not really. I saw a lot of places when I was a full-time adventurer, but I always thought I'd retire to a smaller town. I love the bustle of the city, but I figured I'd be tired someday and want to slow down."

"And now that you've slowed down, how do you feel about it?" Atmir asked tentatively.

"Honestly, I'm not sure. I miss adventuring, but also, I don't miss it? I like Greenspring. I like..." she trailed off. She couldn't have possibly said "you" at the end of that sentence. "I like the people. There's *some* adventure to be had locally. It's been satisfying so far, and I don't feel the pull of adventure trying to take me to far off places anymore. That's not to say I never will again, but right now, I feel the pull of...the pull of..."

"Home?" Atmir offered.

"I guess so, yeah." They walked on in silence, listening to birds call to one another, and checking trees off and on for any signs of the Idlesprout. They eventually decided they'd wandered far enough and turned around to check the trees' other sides as they walked back. Oracle let Atmir's hand brush her as they walked, wondering how they might hold hands.

"What happened to your parents? Oracle asked.

"They died on a contract together when I was eight. I don't have all the details because nobody in their right mind gives that to an eight-year-old, but I do know they were together, it was supposedly quick, and there's some wizard out there responsible for it," Atmir said, his voice low and monotone.

"Did you ever think of going after the wizard?"

"I used to. When I was a kid, I thought that's what I'd grow up to do, take the wizard who killed my parents down. As I got older, I learned that revenge really wasn't for me. I told you I had to be more tenacious and ferocious than the rest of the kids and my cousins, and that served me. For a while."

"Yes, I remember."

"I might have been sugarcoating it."

"How so?"

"Orcs don't get their reputation for nothing. While my family cared for me, there were certain...expectations. I was expected, for example, to take care of my own problems. Which, of course, led to mistakes on my part. Kids make mistakes, right? I have a hard time shaking the ones I made."

Oracle walked quietly next to Atmir, letting him talk. When she didn't say anything, he continued.

"When I said, the other night, that I was done fighting, I didn't mean arguments."

Atmir held his breath but didn't dare look over at Oracle. She asked, "Are you running? Hiding?"

He exhaled. "No."

"What are you doing in Greenspring then?"

"I *have* always enjoyed making tea. I have always been good at it, too. But it wasn't my whole life. It is now. If I could give up the orc in me entirely, I would forfeit it no questions asked. But that's not how life works, and I still love my family. I am *ashamed* of the things I have done, and I know I can't make them right. So, I have committed my-self to a simple life of teas because I know I want a different life than the one I had before. I don't know if it's atonement. I do know that it's better. That I'm better, now. Tea saved me. It was an escape with a fresh start and it's one little way I can honor my uncle. He believed in me, too."

They re-entered the meadow and Oracle sat down. Atmir followed suit and sat next to her instead of across from her. He sat close enough to touch if either of them leaned in the slightest bit.

"Why Greenspring?" Oracle asked. She couldn't stop herself from hoping maybe Atmir would lean in a little.

"Like you, I just sort of stumbled across the place, but it was before I moved. I didn't take much when I left. A few things of my uncle's, a few things of my own. It's about a three day walk to my village. When I first arrived, I figured it was as good a place as I'd find. I didn't want to be too far away, but I knew I needed a fresh start. I moved to Green-spring about two weeks later, filed my teeth, and took up residence in what is now the tea shop. I was still mourning my uncle, and he's part of the reason I left."

"Why is that?" Oracle began to fidget with the grass between her legs. She pulled it out, twisted it, tied it in knots.

"He believed in the side of me that liked to make the teas. He was a gentler man. At least by orc standards. When he died, something changed in me. My life sort of lost its meaning in a way. I felt lost. When I lost the house, I felt lost even more. I decided to leave then. Leave it all behind and start fresh doing what my uncle would have wanted me to do – take my talents to do something good with them." Atmir picked up his own blade of grass.

"And how do you feel now? Time surely has eased some pain."

"It has. I still feel a little bit lost, but I find I'm gaining new footing every day. I'm always worried I'm going to revert to the person I was. That something will bring out that side, because I know it's still in there," Atmir said and then paused. "But, I like my life now. I like who I am now. I want to brew tea for people and keep the lantern on. I want to provide a soft place for an errant traveler to land for a night. I just want to do better than I had before. I'm going forward, not backward. I can't change my past, but I can build a future I'm proud of."

Atmir dropped the blade of grass he'd been playing with. Oracle was looking at him, but offered no reassurance in her expression. He looked vulnerable just now, but Oracle was considering his words carefully.

"I think you've done better," she started quietly. "You're doing better, I mean. We can't live in the past, we can only take its lessons, take its beatings, take its memories, and move on with it guiding us to the future."

Oracle had a small epiphany then, about her own life, as the words came out of her mouth. Atmir's shoulders relaxed and he breathed out heavily. Oracle watched him lay back in the grass. He soon started laughing his deep rumbling laugh. She wasn't sure what he was laughing at, but she still liked the sound.

"I'm an idiot," he said, still laughing. "We're supposed to be foraging."

When they were done foraging, they headed back out of the forest, their feet sinking in the sandy trails. Rocky black protrusions marked their approach to Greenspring. It was there that Oracle saw something unusual. Carved into the back of one such rocky protrusion, or the front from her perspective, was a strange marking. It was a faintly glowing symbol Oracle didn't recognize. She stopped walking to look at it up close.

"What is it?" Atmir asked.

"I'm not sure," Oracle said, cautiously approaching it. She gently put a finger on the marking. It made no motions, no sounds, and it didn't stop glowing.

"It's some kind of sigil. I don't know what kind though."

"So, no idea what it does?" Atmir asked but didn't approach.

Aquarius popped his head out of Oracle's pocket and said, "We should probably leave it alone, Oracle. Who knows what it does? It could be dangerous."

Oracle let her finger fall away in a gentle swipe and the faint glowing stopped. The sigil had a smudge mark where Oracle's finger had been. "That's curious."

"What is?" Aquarius asked.

"I think it's supposed to be glowing, but I must have accidentally turned it off. I'm just going to sketch it out in my notebook and then we can keep going."

Oracle took out her notebook and sketched the sigil in it.

"We should visit Lady Lady's sometime," Atmir said while Oracle put her notebook away. "She has a lot of insight to things like this."

"That could be a good idea. She's at the market, right?"

"Yes."

They continued into town, idly chatting together, but Oracle was having a hard time keeping up conversation with Atmir. He'd eventually given up trying to engage with Oracle in any meaningful way and kept it to casual chatter about their surroundings, the walk, town, tea. Oracle was a little distracted by the sigil they'd seen, but tried not to let on. She wondered what it could possibly do and why it was on the outside of town. It tugged at her brain. When Atmir walked her to her front door, she found a neat white envelope with a green seal on it. Her mother had written her back.

6. Leaves and More

Oracle had painted the shop door a muted green since the rest of the wall was red brick and she thought it would stand out nicely. The preparations were made. Her sign was up. There was just one last thing to do. Oracle and Aquarius stared at the door of the shop from across the room.

"It's a big day, Aquarius."

"It is a big day, Oracle."

"Are you ready?"

"Shouldn't I be asking you that?"

"Maybe. Am I ready?"

"Maybe."

"I think I'm ready. I think so."

"Ok, so do the thing you are waiting to do. I'm getting bored staring at the door."

"Ok, here goes."

Oracle went to the front door of the Alchemist's building, which now had doorbells of its own and a beautiful newly lettered sign reading "Blooms and Moss" in a handsome script. She flipped the hanging sign in the door's window, from "closed" to "open." Oracle exhaled a lungful of air and stood looking out the door's window to the empty street. It was morning, the sun was up, but nobody was immediately outside in her view.

"That was anticlimactic," Aquarius said. He was perched on her shoulder.

"Yeah. It sort of was, wasn't it? Oh well, it's a slow day out there. Doesn't mean it's a slow day in here." She lifted Aquarius and set him down on the side table nearest her. "Get to watering these ones while I grab my watering can. I'll help you water and then we have some propagation to do."

Aquarius did just that. He used his special "breath weapon" to water the nearest plant. If the pot was low he just poked his head over the top to water, but if it was tall he'd stretch up and then poke his head over the top. The first thing he watered was a gangly thing with lots of small round leaves. It was a yellow-green color with very long draping tendrils that spilled over the side of the table and almost touched the floor. This was easy enough to water because the pot was round and low. The next plant he watered was an upright sort. It had green leaves streaked with pink and white and it curved into the window seeking the sunlight. It had to be rotated ever so often because it would lean heavily into the window to get to the sunlight. He could water this one by getting on his hind legs and poking his head over the top. Aquarius purposefully skipped the magic seed plant.

The magic seed plant was now a small, thick vine with little soft protrusions on it. Oracle had gotten into the habit of talking to it, and to everyone's surprise, the plant seemed to *like* it when she did. It had a certain body language. Droopy when it was underwatered, or overwatered. It had a little twist to it when it was sad and twisted the other way when it was upset for some other reason. And whenever Oracle talked to it, it stood up and sort of trembled, almost indistinguishable to the naked eye.

Oracle said it was vibrating with happiness, but Aquarius thought the whole thing would grow up to eat them and so avoided it as much as possible. The little vine wasn't long enough to reach out past its pot yet, so Aquarius didn't need to take an alternate route around it. He simply scooted past at the base of the pot and watered the next plant from the opposite side where he was both out of reach and could see the vine plant in case it did something weird. It was currently just a

little droopy at the tip, and Aquarius hated that he knew how the plant
"felt."

Oracle walked back with her watering can and fed the little monster with a water and fertilizer mix she made. It seemed to relax. Then
she began to talk to it a little bit and sure enough, it stood up and vi-
brated. Oracle was just narrating what she was doing – watering other
plants – but the mystery seed vine plant somehow knew she was talking to it.

"Do you suppose we should name it?" Oracle asked.

"Yes, so we know who to beg for our lives from lest there be any
confusion when that time comes." Aquarius moved to the next plant
and watered it – another plant with long skinny ropes of bulbous
leaves.

"You're worried about nothing. It's friendly. I think," Oracle paused
her watering to consider the small vine.

"Friendly to you, maybe," Aquarius then muttered, "For now anyway."

He continued to make his rounds, watering each plant. Oracle watered the ones he didn't. She grew to like this part of the day. The tinkling of tricking water, watching the dirt absorb it, and moving her
body through her space among all the green made Oracle feel at peace.

Over a few short weeks, and after a few growth spells, the plants
in Oracle's care had flourished. The front room, once devoid of any
green, was almost a jungle. There were plants in the window, on tables, on little stands, and on the floor. There were plants hanging
from the ceiling, on the front counter, and in little displays. The room
was a green paradise, and it smelled wonderfully fresh inside. The un-
spoken words were that no wave of decay had ruined them yet. Oracle
didn't want to jinx it.

At the seventh day market, Oracle had gotten some small trinkets
and accessories to decorate the space. Nothing too magical from the
market. There were some plant lights that looked like they were dancing in the dark and a few spare watering cans for sale she had or-

dered from the courier. Shears for trimming plants were on the wall with some work gloves to wear when dealing with some of the more prickly varieties of plant. There were bags of fertilizer and plant food that Oracle had mixed and bagged herself. Aquarius hated them, but Oracle had found some little figurines to decorate some of the pots. Oracle suspected he didn't like them because she had found several that resembled him but were not entirely flattering.

Oracle bent over to adjust a plant out of direct sunlight when she heard the doorbells chime. She stood up quickly, her heart skipping a beat. Her very first customer. She quickly turned around and found Atmir standing there. He admired the plants around him while Oracle stared. She caught herself soon enough.

"Hi!" She said, too enthusiastically.

"Hi," Atmir replied. He smiled broadly at Oracle and she could feel something melt within her. When she didn't say anything he continued. "This is nice. I'm sorry I haven't been up to see it in its full daytime glory. Am I the first one in?"

"Yes. Why aren't you in the morning rush?"

"I put the sign up so I could come down and see. This is amazing," Atmir said as he gazed from plant to plant.

"Thank you," Oracle replied, looking at a plant instead of at Atmir.

"Are these little Aquarius figures?" He asked, picking up a decoration.

"They are not! They don't look anything like me!" Aquarius squeaked from his hammock.

Atmir raised his eyebrows at Oracle in question, and Oracle smiled and gave him a small nod. Atmir set the figurine down.

"Are they hard to take care of? Now that they're grown?" Atmir was looking at a big plant with large, shapely leaves.

"Some of them are a little finicky, but most of them are hearty with the right care. Most of them need little care besides some food, water, and a bit of natural light. You know, like people," Oracle explained as she picked up a small bushy plant. "Take this little guy. He needs water only every few days and will happily live away from a window as long as he gets a little light for most of the day."

"Like on my counter?"

"Yeah, he'd live there just fine as long as you remember to water him. You have to feed him too, but luckily plants aren't big eaters. A little of my special food mix would do the trick to keep him happy."

"Do I have to trim it?" Atmir approached Oracle and looked down at the plant she was holding.

"Only if you want to. I like him as is though. It's cute in an odd way. What?"

Atmir looked at Oracle for a long time with a small smile on his face.

"I'll take it."

"You will?"

"Yeah. I'd like to be your first customer. I'll take the little odd plant and he - it – it can live on my counter if you say it's a good spot for it. The tea shop could use a little more cozy and I think some of these plants might do the trick. Plus, the more the locals come in and see what you've done via the plants at the tea shop, the more likely they'll come in to buy something of their own. It's really miraculous what you've done here, you know?"

"I hope it lasts. I am worried this is some kind of fluke and I don't actually know what I'm doing and none of this is going to work for very long," Oracle said, and held the plant for Atmir to take.

"Give yourself more credit, Oracle. You've kept more plants alive than anybody in memory has been able to," Atmir put a hand on her shoulder, causing Oracle's heart to beat a little faster. "It's going to be great."

Atmir took the plant out of Oracle's hands and said, "You've made this space your own. It suits you."

"Thanks, Atmir."

"Listen I have to get back to –"

"Oh! Right! Yes! I'll ring you up later, just take the plant and go back! We'll meet up later."

"Promise?" Atmir smiled again.

"Yes, now go back to work so you can afford that plant!" Oracle could feel her face and ears warming.

Atmir's smile dropped to a feigned affront, but he turned and left anyway. Oracle watched him walk past the window and down the street cradling the plant as he went. It was then that she noticed a face staring *in* the window at her. It was Harrad. He scowled for a long time at her, and she tried to wave him in, but instead of entering he continued down the street back to the tea shop Oracle assumed. Oracle shrugged and went to her workbench. She put on her gloves to handle some prickly plants, but before she could start her project the doorbells chimed again.

Oracle called out, "Welcome!"

She took off her gloves and turned around to see… nobody?

"Hello? Welcome to my plant shop. Can I help you?" Oracle looked around but didn't see anyone. Then she noticed a plant with a hat. Or rather the hat was behind the plants. She walked over to it and peered over the top. There was a child there feeling one of the plant leaves that was actually soft and fuzzy.

"Hello there," she said boldly. It startled the child, and they jumped back.

"Sorry! I didn't mean to scare you!" Oracle walked around the plants to address the child.

"You didn't! You didn't scare me," the child said defensively.

"Oh. Some of the plants are pokey and some of them aren't nice to touch. Maybe ask the next time, ok?"

The child nodded and looked around at the plants that were taller than them.

"I'm going to do some work at my workbench," Oracle turned to walk away but didn't get more than a step when the child spoke.

"I've never seen plants in Greenspring before," the child said softly. "Nothing grows here. I've seen plants in other places, but not here. Do they only grow in your shop?"

"No, they should grow in other places too." Oracle approached the child again.

"How do you do it? Are they all magic plants?"

"No, they aren't magic at all. I have a special blend of soil and plant food I use for them."

"Oh. I was kind of hoping they would be magic."

Oracle smiled at the child, and the child smiled back.

"My name is Evan."

"Nice to meet you Evan. My name is Oracle."

Evan reached out and shook Oracle's hand, then continued to look around the shop in awe. Oracle watched him take in the plants. She took a certain joy as she watched his face wonder at them all. She might not be great with children, but she didn't mind them. Maybe she would learn to like them if they all looked at her plants this way.

"Evan? Did you come just to look today, or would you like to buy a plant?" Oracle watched Evan shift uncomfortably and wondered if maybe her abrupt tone was off. She would need to work on that. Maybe Atmir would help.

"Actually," Evan started a little timidly, "I was hoping you would have something with flowers. I think my mom would like something with flowers because she always talks about flowers that my dad brought her one time. He is away for a long time sometimes, but when he comes back he always brings us gifts. She says she liked the flowers best, but it's been a long time since my dad brought flowers home. I was hoping she could have flowers all the time."

"Well, that's very sweet of you. I don't have anything that's flowering," Oracle said, and Evan's face fell. "But I do have some plants that *will* flower with a little bit of time and care."

The little boy's face lit up, and he eagerly asked, "Can you save it for me? I need to go home to get money, but I don't want anyone to get it before me!"

"Of course I can. Let's take a look at them."

"Yes, please."

Oracle walked back around the tall plants to a cart near the skylight. There were several plants that looked like fingers erupting from the pot. They had thick stalks and thin spikes. They grew in groups of four or five. Aquarius pushed a few forward so Evan could get a better look.

"These ones will have a single flower on each tip. All different colors – pink, yellow, purple, red. These other flowers," Oracle turned to another nearby cart and indicated another plant, "they will show up throughout the plants. I like these ones because they grow like a little tree. These flowers will all be the same color on one plant. I have dark pink and light pink. And lastly, I have these. They are pretty small, but the stalk will grow taller and unfurl into a large, single bloom. It'll go from green at the base, to brown, to a deep red on top."

Evan contemplated his choices. He went back around to each plant she had shown him carefully inspecting them.

"Which one will bloom first?"

"The one that looks like a little tree is very nearly ready to bloom. You can see the little buds. Look."

Evan came back to that plant and looked at the buds Oracle pointed out to him.

"Are they hard to take care of? What happens if it dies?"

"They like being in the sun, so placing them in or near a window that gets a lot of light would be perfect. I will send you with a little bag of plant food and a measuring cup for water. It likes to have moist soil. In about a week, the buds will open to flowers."

"What if it dies?" Evan looked worried.

Oracle bent down to his level and said, "If you do everything I say and it still dies before the flowers bloom, I'll replace it for you."

"Really?" His eyes lit up.

"Yes."

"Ok! I'll take it! Well, I'll have you save it. I have to go get money," Evan said.

Oracle walked to the front counter and wrote "RESERVED" on a little paper she affixed to a stake. She placed the stake in the pot and said to Evan, "There. Now it's reserved for you. Just make sure to come back before the week is up or it will bloom before you get it home. The flowers don't last forever once it's started to bloom, and you won't want to miss out."

"Ok, Miss Oracle. I'll be back with money!"

Evan rushed out, the bells chimed, and the door struck the frame. Oracle watched the boy run down the street, framed by her growing plants and pleased with the interaction.

"Don't start singing or anything," Aquarius chirped at her.

"Is it such torture? To be here growing beautiful plants and making people happy?" Oracle looked out the window, the sun beamed on her face, warming it.

"I suppose it's ok. It would be better if we had more of the baker's biscuits though."

"I'll get you some more if you promise to improve your attitude." Oracle gave Aquarius a look.

"Done!" Aquarius exclaimed.

Oracle tended plants, mixed soil, and made fertilizer bags. She was hesitant to admit it, but she liked the way she felt here. She thought she'd always be an adventurer and considered her mother to be a bit mad for loving growing plants so much. She was starting to think her mother might have been wiser than she had credited her. Her mother had written her to give her great advice for sustaining the plants, but now Oracle thought it prudent to maybe ask about maintaining a plants shop and the business thereof. She'd write another letter soon.

Before she could clean up, she heard another chime of the door-bells. She turned around to see Beatran at the front of the shop. She wiped her hands on her apron and quickly walked over.

"Welcome, Beatran!" She said with a proud air.

"Oh darling," Beatran said brightly, "this is simply amazing! How did you do it?"

"The plants will grow, but sometimes something kills them. I'm not sure what, so that's been my main challenge."

"That's strange business."

"I am beginning to suspect something is afoot."

"Like what?" Beatran eyed her over small spectacles.

"I don't know." Oracle rubbed her chin.

"Are you saying there is a danger here in Greenspring? That's a se-rious matter." Beatran's tone was very serious and lower than normal.

"No! No. I don't know. I just think that things should grow here because I've proven they can grow here. And it's concerning that the waves of death keep happening. It's definitely a wave of something that comes through and kills the plants. There's not really another ex-planation, is there?" Oracle looked at Beatran expectantly but knew Beatran wouldn't know the answer or else everyone would have also known the answer.

"I don't know, darling." Beatran began to walk through the shop, looking at the beautiful plants, touching one here and there. "I never thought I'd see greenery here. You've done something amazing."

Oracle followed close behind. When Beatran had made it all the way through and back again, she faced Oracle.

"Darling, you've done a wonder, but now I'm concerned you're right about something being truly wrong here."

"I'm sure it's nothing too severe. An annoyance maybe."

"Darling, we can't grow crops here. That's more than an annoy-ance. We're fortunate to have the mine and the glassworks to export. Our little town thrives only because we have so many exports. It bal-

ances out what we need to import to survive. We're not exactly self-
sufficient though. Not without crops."

"That's true."

"Maybe you'll be figuring out what is the matter for us?"

Oracle set her face and looked directly at Beatran, tilting her chin
ever so slightly downward and putting her hands on her hips.

"Good girl," Beatran said, patted Oracle's arm, and asked which
plant would suit her best. Oracle helped Beatran while she wondered
if it wasn't time for a little adventure. Maybe one would present itself
soon.

7. Hostile Takeover

"Oracle!" Aquarius shouted in her ear instead of his usual dance routine. She sat bolt upright and readied a spell. Her hair covered half her face.

"What?!"

"There's shouting outside. I don't know what's happened, but it sounds angry."

Oracle dissipated the spell and hopped out of bed. She swept her hair out of her face and eyes and tied it back. She listened hard. She could hear sporadic angry yelling but couldn't quite decipher what was being said. She went cautiously down the stairs. She was greeted by a jungle.

"Oh no, what's all this?" She asked. She swallowed a rise of panic. She peeled thickets of leaves and stalks away to make it down the stairs. The shop was covered in bushy green. She knew which plant this was. She also knew it was only supposed to grow to be medium to large. Not to take over her shop. She heard more angry yelling that was muffled by the greenery.

It took effort, but she made it to the front door. The window of the door was broken and the bushy green plant had busted its way outside. Oracle tried the door. It was stuck. She pried and pushed and pulled to get back the way she came. She diverged to the back door and found it was not blocked entirely. She clawed her way through and opened it. She walked through the alley to the front of the building. The green had spread outside the shop, clinging to the brick. It spilled onto the sidewalk piercing its way into the cobblestone, growing up from there. There was a man, red in the face, angrily yelling and shaking a fist standing at the edge of the green opposite Oracle.

"You! You there! Is this your doing?" He yelled at her.

"It's my plant but I didn't –"

"Get rid of it! Why did this even happen?" The man didn't wait for her to finish.

"I don't know why it happened. I will get rid of it as soon as I – "

"Get rid of it now! This is why Greenspring doesn't need magic! Nothing ever good comes from it. Some folk say it's fine, but look at this! What if this plant was poisonous?" He demanded. He was visibly angry and gesturing at Oracle as he yelled.

"I'll get rid of it! Just calm down! It's just a minor inconvenience. And I don't grow poisonous plants!" Oracle shouted back at him, annoyed.

"Don't tell me to calm down!" The man almost spat the words at her. He reached down and started to tear at the bush. It looked like he had been at it for a while, his face was red and sweaty.

"Who are you?" Oracle asked.

"A concerned citizen right now!" The man replied as he tore at the bush, releasing clumps of green behind him.

Oracle thought for a moment. She wasn't sure what happened with the plant and she wasn't quite sure how to get rid of it. She didn't want to burn it, but that was her first instinct. Instead, she tried a shrinking spell she knew. It wasn't very powerful, but it was useful sometimes. It had no effect. The man swore and grunted while he pulled.

Oracle tried a wither spell, that did a little bit, but not enough to control, contain, or eradicate the plant. She tried a slashing spell that worked somewhat, but she knew it was not very precise and didn't want to risk hurting the yelling man, or anyone else that might show up.

Oracle went back inside through the alley door. She traversed the bushy overgrowth until she got to her shears. She then forced her

way behind the counter and grabbed another pair of shears. She told
Aquarius to stay put on the stairs or upstairs, wherever he was then.
She returned outside to the front of the building.

"Here," Oracle said, tossing the shears near the man. "Those will be
more useful."

The man begrudgingly took up the shears. He looked like he
wanted to retort, but he started cutting the plant instead. He quickly
became even redder and sweatier than he was before. Oracle too began to sweat as she cut the plant. The green strands that forced their
way through the window left shards of glass mixed in with the plant.
Oracle was careful not to cut her hands as she worked. She broke bigger strands and sheared the smaller ones.

As they worked, more townsfolk arrived. Some gasped and murmured, some gawked silently, and a few said a derogatory phrase or
two that made Oracle's ears heat up. Oracle and the man said nothing.
After making little to no progress, the man dropped his shears.

"I've had enough of this. This isn't my problem, it's her problem.
See this?" He raised his voice to address the crowd, "This is what happens when you trust in magic. Weird things happen. *Uncontrollable*
things. Is this what you want for Greenspring? Magic taking over our
town? Unreliable and uncontrollable!"

Oracle could feel her face redden now as she listened to the man
rant. She chose to work a little faster at clearing the greenery. She
could burn the plant after she got the road free of it, and then she
could worry about what to do inside. The man outside was a stranger
to her, but she thought she recognized him from somewhere. She
couldn't place him. She wondered why he was so infuriated at the
plant and at her. It couldn't have been magic alone that perturbed him.
And plants never made anyone angry unless they were weeds.

Oracle steadily cut away at the plant. The man finished his tirade
and walked off, grumbling to himself. The small crowd of people that
gathered to watch mostly left, with a few exceptions. One person

came up and grabbed the shears the man had dropped and began helping Oracle.

"Don't worry about him, he's got his own issues to deal with and I think this was just the straw that broke the camel's back, if you know what I mean?" This was a young man, dressed cleanly in simple robes. Oracle recognized him as the priest that visited the tea shop sometimes.

"Thanks for your help," Oracle said, not looking at the man.

"You're welcome. I'm Feldan. You've heard of me?" He said as he snipped and pulled at the plant.

"You're the traveling priest, right?" Oracle's forearms were beginning to get tight.

"I am."

"I didn't think plant maintenance fell under priestly duties," Oracle commented and looked over at him while she worked.

"It doesn't necessarily," Feldan said. He smiled at her. "But helping others does. I serve the god of charitable works, friends, and healing."

"Haspian." Oracle stated.

"Yes, Haspian." Feldan replied.

The two worked in silence for a while with just the snipping of the shears to be heard. Oracle still couldn't open the front door. She began to gather up what they had cut to burn it, but realized the plant was attached to the sidewalk cobbles. She took up the shears again, but Feldan hadn't stopped. The pile of loose plant was growing. Oracle hoped the rest of the plant had stopped growing. Atmir came up the street just then. He greeted Feldan and looked around at the green intruder.

"What happened, Oracle?" he asked, bending to pull up some of the plant still rooted to the ground.

"I don't know. I woke up to this plant taking over," she said.

"A hostile takeover," Feldan offered. Atmir chuckled, but Oracle was feeling sour.

"Can I help you?" Atmir asked.

"That would honestly be great. Can you take the loose plant matter somewhere so I can burn it?" Oracle responded.

"Yeah, I can haul it away."

The three of them worked in silence. Sometimes someone would pass by, and the reactions varied from a whispered "magic is awful" and "the mage can't be trusted with her own plants" to "Wow that's amazing!" and "Something is growing outside..." Oracle pretended she couldn't hear any of them and diligently worked on freeing the place from the plant's grip. Eventually, Atmir had to return to his shop. Feldan stayed and, after explaining what happened, some of Oracle's friends – regulars from the shop - arrived and chipped in to help when they arrived.

Oracle began to see the front of her shop again. Her poor sign was still entangled, but the door was clear. The window was broken and the shop was still filled with overgrown plant, but it was a start. Oracle and Feldan forced the door open together with some effort. The plant's dense resistance was no match for teamwork. Oracle threaded her way through the tendrils and leaves and made it to the plant's pot. They had the idea to cut it there. Oracle set to work with the shears. She snipped and cut until the plant was free of its roots.

The work took all day and into the evening. Her friends had hauled away what had been cut, and Oracle would ask where it went later. When Oracle's regulars had to leave, Atmir had reappeared to help again. She had paused several times to tend to Aquarius and make sure he was fed and fine. He was less than impressed with the day and made it known to Oracle. Oracle returned to the work.

It was late into the evening when they had finished. Only Feldan and Atmir remained to see the final bush remnants removed. When Oracle could finally see around the shop again, she saw some of the other plants in the building had withered to husks as if they hadn't been watered in weeks. Her vine plant was fine, thankfully. Oracle inspected each one and then sat on the floor, cross legged, and sighed.

She felt her throat tighten and her eyes water, but she shoved the tears down.

"Do you need more help, Oracle?" Feldan asked.

"You've really done enough, Feldan. I am grateful you helped me. I will find a way to repay your kindness, unless you want coin. In that case, name your price," She replied, exhausted.

"I don't need coin or repayment. If anything, I would like you to pay the kindness I have shown to someone else who needs help. It would be the best repayment you could offer. Haspian wouldn't want it any other way," He smiled at her.

"Are you sure? Can't I even buy you a tea from down the street?" She stood up and walked over to where Feldan stood.

"I'm sure. I will visit The Guiding Light another time." He said sincerely.

"Well, I will buy your tea and you'll have no say in it. That's a kindness I will pay immediately," Oracle said.

"Thank you," Feldan said with a small bow of his head. "If there's nothing else I can help you with, I am going to go now."

Oracle walked the few steps to the door to open it for him. "Thank you again, Feldan. I appreciated your help more than I can describe."

"It was my pleasure to do so. Farewell Oracle, Atmir," Feldan said and walked outside.

Oracle closed the door, looking at the window without glass. She took a deep breath in and then forced out a big sigh from her mouth. She turned around and walked back to a spot on the floor and sat down again. Atmir sat next to her. It was late.

"Would you like some tea?" Atmir asked gently.

"No."

"Would you like something to eat?"

"No."

"Would you like a hug?" Atmir asked softly.

"Maybe."

Atmir scooted next to her and put his arm around her shoulders. She leaned into the big man and took a long breath of him. He smelled good, like cinnamon and orange peel.

"Is that better?" Atmir asked, without releasing her.

"Yeah," Oracle said just above a whisper.

"What do you think caused the plant to grow like that? And what about these other ones? Did they just get strangled?"

"I don't know. I don't know," Oracle said. She sat upright, but Atmir didn't let go of her. "It was obviously magic that did this. I don't think it was mine though. I have the same routine for all the plants."

"Do you suppose that there's something magical keeping Greenspring from growing anything? Could that magic be affecting your plants?" Atmir asked. He let go of her and looked at her face. Oracle rubbed her temples and her eyes.

"It's possible. Maybe that sigil has something to do with it," Oracle said and ran her hands down her face. "Ugh. I am tired. I'm tired of the intermittent people saying 'magic is bad' and the whispers. I'm tired of feeling like I should be out taking contracts and helping people instead of growing plants. I'm tired of thinking about that stupid sigil. I'm tired of feeling tired."

"I'm sorry."

"I'm tired of you being so nice," she said, only half grumpy.

"I'm not tired of it," Atmir said, smiling down at her warmly. "What are you going to do?"

"I still want to figure out what's wrong with Greenspring," Oracle said slowly.

"What do you think is wrong with it?"

"You know, the not growing things? I want to figure out what's causing it," she said plaintively and looked up at Atmir.

"You don't want to keep growing plants?"

"I can do both. If I do some adventuring on the side, maybe that will keep me content with growing plants. Plus, it will help Greenspring if I can solve that mystery. Maybe I can change a few more peoples' minds about magic along the way. I can't sit here feeling sorry for myself and watch my plants meet their demise for unknown reasons. I have to do something and I think that's the right thing to do."

"If you say so." Atmir looked around the shop. Aquarius investigated the room. He'd come downstairs when it was mostly clear of plant matter.

"What? You don't think so?"

"If anyone could have fixed this problem, you don't think it would have already happened?"

"Are you saying I can't do it?" Oracle was getting testy.

"No. Not at all. I'm just wondering if you go up against the impossible and then feel like a failure if you can't beat the impossible. I know you have a tenacious spirit. I would hate for it to be broken."

"It sounds like you think I can't find the problem and fix it." She was angry now.

"I'm not. I promise," Atmir raised his hands in surrender. "What do you think is wrong?"

"Well, I think that sigil has something to do with it. That's obvious enough." Oracle settled down.

"If not the sigil, what else could be wrong?" Atmir put his arm back around Oracle's shoulders.

"I don't know. I'm sure I should start with the sigil. It has to be connected to something. Either Greenspring or something else. I need to start somewhere and that's the only lead I have." Oracle leaned into the big man, his body warm and comforting.

"That's a good idea. If that's your lead, you should follow it."

"You want to help?" Oracle asked after a pause, still leaning into Atmir.

"How would I help?" Atmir looked down at her with his eyebrows raised, dubious of his role.

"Be my moral support."

"Ah. I can do that. When do I start?"

"I think you already have." Oracle smiled up at him.

8. Adventure Returns

The plant shop had steady hours and steady customers. The shop had become a gathering hub of sorts. Less quirky patrons came in and left, not lingering for longer than it took to browse the shop and buy what they needed or wanted. The shop's regulars often didn't buy things but came for the conversation. It was a gathering of strange folk, but Oracle had learned to like the company and Aquarius had learned to especially like Tullus, an old man who had wandered in to wonder at the plants one day. He always brought a treat once he learned of Aquarius' existence. Aquarius was often found stationed in Tullus' lap.

The group of regulars took to wandering the shop, conversing, sometimes running errands for Oracle, or helping with the plants. They usually didn't stay all day, but they did often stay for most of her opening hours. Sometimes they would bring tea from The Guiding Light. Oracle had set up a small table under the skylight, and the group would sit and drink their tea amongst the plants. Each one was unique and Oracle enjoyed their company for different reasons.

Tullus was a retired commander from somewhere in the North. He was ancient and grizzled, but had a soft heart and a very deep voice. He didn't talk about his time in the military much, but that was ok. Once Tullus started on a topic, it was hard to get him to stop talking. Oracle liked that he was kind to Aquarius.

Adam was a scribe but was recovering from an injury to his hand. He was tall and pale with black hair and a morose look about him. Oracle had recognized him from the tea shop. Adam was trying to learn to use his nondominant hand, but he was not having much luck with it. Before the plant shop, Adam would spend long hours writing at home until the daylight waned. Then he would take a break until it was dark enough to light candles and work some more. He genuinely enjoyed his work, but was essentially a shut in. He didn't mind. Oracle got the sense that the awkward man liked Indy, but wasn't sure what to do about it. She had seen him cast glances her way, and anytime something funny was said, Adam would look to Indy first to see her reaction.

Indy, the woman that hung on to Adam at the tea shop the day Oracle had worked there, was relentless in flirting with him. This made Adam stutter, turn red, go silent, or all three. She would touch him often. On the arm, the shoulder, his neck if she could get away with it. Poor Adam had no idea what to do with Indy, and so he continued to suffer her advances while not knowing how to return them. Oracle thought she might give him a clue one of the days when she could get a private moment with him.

Jenna and Edalyn were not as regular as the others. Edalyn sometimes brought her son Evan, who had purchased the flowering plant, with her. The sisters worked part time in the evenings, one of them at the inn and the other at a small tavern across the town. They were both married to sailors who were gone more often than not. They found the company in the plant shop more agreeable than the company they met at work, so they were in most mornings as well to fill their social buckets. Atmir had a whole new rush of morning folk who wanted their tea to go so they could sit in the glory of the green plants and discuss.

Oracle and Aquarius had a routine that they kept to most days. They would rise early, care for plants, take customers, prepare more plants for growing or sale, and keep up on inventory and supplies, and if there was time, tea at the Guiding Light. Seventh days were for the market, gathering tea ingredients with Atmir, or writing out her order for the courier and then having tea at the tea shop. Oracle still had to take care of the plants on seventh days, but it was a much easier day without the worry of customers.

She often made time for tea. Aquarius, for his part, would have liked her to fall in love with the baker instead. He voiced this often. Oracle denied anything but friendship with Atmir, but Aquarius, and indeed the rest of the world, was not blind. Nobody could figure out what they were dancing around but thought it best not to mention it.

Atmir's little plant was thriving in his shop. Oracle had shown him how to re-pot it twice already. She suspected that once was enough but didn't protest when he told her he thought it needed to be done again. The locals that enjoyed their tea now also enjoyed a plant or two at their houses or places of business. After Oracle's shop opened, it was not long before people flocked to see the green wonders. It was a short time after that they began to purchase the little miracles.

Oracle gifted a hearty and easy to care for plant to Harrad. She had hand delivered it, but she had reports that it had died. She figured he didn't take care of it and probably would say something about "mage plants" if asked. It didn't bother her. In fact, she felt very much on top of the world. She wasn't sure when she would tackle growing plants in the ground here but for now, she rode this wave.

This particular morning Oracle was having tea with Atmir after the morning rush at the tea shop. They discussed the market convivially, and Oracle was letting the warmth of the tea, the room, and Atmir seep into her bones. The door chimed and Atmir stood up to help whoever entered.

"Beatran! How are you?" Atmir beamed at the woman.

"Fine, fine, darling. How are you?"

"I'm great! What can I get for you today?" Atmir stood behind the counter and spread his hands wide on the countertop leaning forward slightly, ready to make whatever she wished. Beatran put a paper on the counter in front of Atmir.

"I was hoping you'd do me the favor of brewing a tea from this old recipe," Beatran's said. Atmir took up the paper and read the ingredients. He took canisters down from his shelves. He got a pen and paper and wrote a note or two.

"Beatran, I am afraid there's two ingredients on this list I don't have, and I don't think I can get."

"Nonsense, darling. These are all common, aren't they?" Beatran peered at the upside-down paper and pulled her shawl a little tighter. She couldn't tilt her head, or her flamboyant hat would fall off her head. Oracle kind of wished it would.

"I can't get Ruby Leaf or Drizzlebramble without going quite far. The courier won't be able to source them. I can't leave the tea shop for that long to go to where they grow. I'm sorry Beatran, I can't brew this for you."

"Oh dear," Beatran's face fell, and Oracle felt a pang of guilt. She stood up and walked over.

"What's this she's looking for?" Oracle asked gently.

"This old tea recipe needs Ruby Leaf and Drizzlebramble. I have everything else, but those two things grow beyond where I can comfortably forage. It's already a long trip to forage grounds. I just can't leave the shop that long. I'm sorry Beatran," Atmir said again.

"What if I go?" Oracle asked.

"Would you, darling?" Beatran's face lifted again, hope returning to her voice. "This recipe is important in many ways to me. If you could get the ingredients, I will be in your debt young lady."

"Are you sure Oracle? You have your own shop to care for," Atmir said quietly.

"I can go on a simple errand and not be gone for more than a couple days. Aquarius can tend the plants – except Noodle. You'll have to water Noodle."

"Noodle scares me."

"Noodles aren't scary, dear. They are delicious. I don't know about adding water to them besides to cook though," Beatran interjected before either of them could say anything.

"You'll be fine. I'll be gone one day, two days max," Oracle said encouragingly. "So, you'll just have to water it once if I am gone for two days. And it shouldn't take that long, right? We daytrip the other ingredients regularly. How much farther can Ruby Leaf and Drizzlebramble be?"

"A little farther than you're anticipating, I can tell," Atmir said gravely. He crossed his arms and looked at her.

"Well, I'm an experienced adventurer and I think I can handle a few days in the wild picking leaves. Seriously. How much further is it to get these?"

"Probably, another half day to the area where you *might* find them. And I say might because animals love Ruby Leaf and Drizzlebramble. Drizzlebramble is in season right now and Ruby Leaf is just coming out of season. It's going to be a challenge to find them both."

"I can do it."

"Listen to the lady, Atmir," Beatran said, "She sounds like she knows what she's talking about."

Atmir looked at Oracle. He wasn't skeptical. It was something else. After a moment longer than Oracle would have liked, he finally said, "Ok. I'll draw you a map and write down exactly what you're looking for."

Oracle and Beatran almost leapt with joy. They shared a grin as a resigned Atmir got started with paper and pen. He took several minutes to draw and label the crude map.

"I can leave tomorrow morning," Oracle told Beatran.

"That would be lovely, darling," Beatran replied.

Atmir paused and narrowed his eyes at them, as if they were plotting directly against him right in front of his face. He continued to write directions and information down for Oracle. Oracle offered to brew Beatran a cup of different tea, and she enthusiastically accepted.

Oracle chatted with her as she reached for canisters, measured out the leaves and herbs, and heated water on the stove. She moved with a quiet confidence she'd earned after spending so much time there, both drinking and helping to make teas. Atmir wrote notes and Oracle and Beatran visited over their teas. He paused to look at them, at home in the shop, and smiled to himself. He finished his notes as Oracle finished her tea.

"Don't get up," he said as he came around the counter. He handed Oracle the paper he had written on and handed Beatran the recipe back. "I wrote down a copy of the recipe, so you can have this one back. Oracle, are you sure you want to do this? I mean, do you trust me to look after the plants and Aquarius –"

"Of course I trust you. And Aquarius is surprisingly resourceful for his size. He should be fine. Adam, Indy, or Jenna could help too. It's just one day. And *yes*, I do want to do this. I need to get out and stretch my muscles a little bit. I've been cooped in the shop for too long and it'll do me some good to get out and about. A little adventure is the perfect place to start." Oracle finished, grinning.

"That's what I'm afraid of," Atmir said, mostly to himself as the women resumed chatting.

-

As the sun was rising Oracle adjusted her pack and moved off in the usual direction she and Atmir would take to gather the regular ingredients. It took half a day to get to where anything besides some scrub brush grew, and it wasn't long after that where trees sprung from the ground instead of just rocks and dust and sand. It was a beautiful transition Oracle had come to appreciate. It wasn't sudden unless you weren't paying attention to your surroundings. The giant black rocks that jutted out near Greenspring didn't jut out so much where the grass started to grow back. Then even less when the first trees sprung up. Then disappeared almost entirely by the time the trees grew thick. Different rocks could be found here, but also plants, trees, bushes, a wealth of animals, and even a stream.

Up the stream was her goal. The Drizzlebramble grew in a known marsh several hours hike up the stream. The Ruby Leaf was known to grow at the edge of meadows. There was one such meadow nearby that Oracle hoped would have the Ruby Leaf. Atmir had given her directions to a second meadow if the first didn't have what she needed. It felt good to be out and about in the sunshine. Even if the quest she was on didn't involve complex mysteries, forces of good and evil, or monstrous beasts, she felt content to be on an adventure at all.

Going with Atmir when he foraged was nice, but it didn't feel like they were doing anything out of the ordinary. They consulted Atmir's notebook for any important details and went to the same six or seven places for the same eight or ten ingredients he needed to cure or dry to brew. It was nice. Oracle might even call it relaxing. But tending to plants was relaxing and Oracle wanted a little more spice to her life sometimes. Going on a fetch quest was the perfect balance of relative safety and the unknown. It would be easy, too. No need for magic spells. Probably.

When Oracle reached the part of the walk where the trees began to thicken, she stopped for a break. The sun was about halfway to midday. She made good time. She looked at the map and notes Atmir had made for her. She'd travel up the stream until she saw the Drizzlebramble – Atmir had sketched its likeness for her – and harvest any of the little shoots growing out of the marsh banks. Drizzlebramble had a woody appearance but was hollow. It was grey and the shoots grew to about 2 feet tall. Much taller than that and the woody structure of the shoot became hard and the Drizzlebramble wouldn't offer any beneficial properties. The shoots had little bramble tops marked by a swooping down leaf; the drizzle on the bramble. The leaves were soft, but the bramble tops were spiky though pliable.

Atmir estimated he needed about 10. Oracle planned to bag up at least 15 for him. Though she did consider that, if she got him fewer, the sooner she could have another adventure. She expelled the thought almost as soon as it entered her brain. Doing a good job with her task was important. When she felt sufficiently rested, she continued to the stream.

The stream varied in width and made a soft *whoosh* sound as the water ran over the rocks and around fallen branches. Oracle watched a leaf float down in the current, swirling around and bumping the edges. She entered the stream. The water soaked her boots and chilled her feet, but the stones weren't very slippery. Her boots sloshed against the current and she splashed a little more than strictly necessary for walking. Eventually the water grew too deep to walk in and Oracle made her way along the bank. Soon the bank flattened out. Oracle had arrived at a gummy marsh.

"Ok, Drizzlebramble. Where do you grow?" Oracle said to the marsh.

Fortunately, there was no reply to her inquiry. She found Drizzlebramble almost immediately and harvested 20 pieces of it rather quickly by slicing through their stalks with her knife. It was a bit of a pain to position them in her bag. The spiky bramble tops would tangle while the long stalks wouldn't bunch together nicely. Oracle considered she might have wanted to start with the Ruby Leaf.

The sun was past midday now, but Oracle knew she'd have plenty of time before it was dark, and what was a little darkness to someone who could conjure lights? She set off back the way she'd come and then turned left to head away from the stream. There was a meadow not far from here according to Atmir's map. Of course it was sketched without a cartographer's knowledge, but it was accurate enough. She wondered when Atmir had been there to know where the meadow and marsh were.

The woods were a pleasant affair as well. There were birds chirping and squirrels in the trees. She had seen several rabbits. It was peaceful. Even when the sun dipped too low to be seen in the sky, and the forest grew dark, it was serene. The birds stopped chirping and the only sound Oracle heard was the crunching of her own boots on dead leaves and twigs. Parts of the forest were too thick to walk through. The rest of it was a scramble. She felt good, until she heard a strange scratching noise.

Oracle froze. She tilted her head and listened hard. A definite, almost rhythmic, scratching noise was coming from nearby. She ran through a list of animals it could be. Surely an animal would have heard her or smelled her and fled? She strained her ears searching for another clue to what it might be. She then remembered she was a fire mage, and whatever it was should be afraid of *her*. She crept closer to the noise. It was just behind a fallen log and a few bushes. She'd be able to peer through the bushes if she climbed over the log.

She carefully straddled the log, then brought her feet down towards the bushes. She pressed into them. The bushes rustled quietly, but the scratching persisted. Oracle used her hands to pry a hole in the foliage and what she saw sent a small shock through her body. A broom was sweeping the leaves into a pile. By itself. The scratching was the broom bristles on the leaves. They fluttered this way and that way with every swing of the broom.

Oracle peered around looking for its master. Surely someone must have enchanted the broom for this task, and whoever it was must be nearby. She listened as the light faded and the scratch-scratch of the broom continued. Finally, she decided to confront the broom, and possibly whoever was attached to it. Nobody in their right mind would be aimlessly sweeping a forest floor, and they must need help if they were, Oracle judged.

Slowly, Oracle peeled back more of the foliage from the bush she was hiding in. She moved with care and exited the bush with only a few twigs and leaves in her hair. She looked like the crazy broom owner, had anyone else been around to see. But the broom only paused a brief moment and went back to sweeping the leaves. It wasn't sweeping them into a pile like a rake, it was sweeping them off the spot.

"Hello, broom. Where is your master?" Oracle asked cheerfully. She hoped not to scare it.

The broom paused again, but resumed its sweeping. Oracle walked a little closer.

"Broom, where is your master?" She insisted this time.

The broom paid no heed this time and continued to sweep.

"Ok," Oracle said deliberately. She tried to think of what else she could ask it, or if she should touch it.

"Broom, are you lost?"

The broom abruptly stopped mid-sweep and made a little bow. Oracle became excited at the gesture. The broom didn't start sweeping again.

"Do you need help?"

Again a little bow. A nod.

"Ok. Yes, you need help. Do you need to get home?" Oracle asked quickly in her excitement.

The broom swept a little side to side.

"That's a no? No, you don't need to get home, but you are lost and you need help. I can't ask you where you want to go because you don't have a mouth. Ok, think, Oracle. Where would a broom want to go…A town maybe? Are you trying to get to town?"

A sweep from side to side.

"No, not town. Hmmm. Do you want to go to a person?"

A little nod.

"A specific person? Are you looking for someone?"

A sweep.

"You want to go to a person, but not a specific person," Oracle said slowly.

A little nod again.

"You want to go to a person. You aren't looking for someone you know. You want to go to…"

A big, undeniable nod.

"You want to go to…"

The broom encouraged Oracle more with several quick nods.

"You want to go with...me?" Oracle asked, unsure.

The broom spun in a circle, kicking up leaves as it did.

"You don't know me. Why do you want to go with me? Wait, why am I asking you questions you can't answer? I can't take you with me. I have to find Ruby Leaf and get back to my home. Why are you – nevermind. Do you want me to take you to town?"

A nod.

"Ok. I guess you can follow me? Can you follow me?"

A nod.

"Is there someone nearby?"

A sweep.

"Is there some*thing* nearby?"

A nod.

"Something dangerous?"

A sweep.

"If you turn out to betray me, Broom, I will use you for kindling," Oracle said and lit up her palm with a mote of fire.

Several sweeps.

"I guess...follow me."

Oracle set back off, this time around the bushes, back to her original path and the correct direction. She wasn't sure how well the broom could follow, but it appeared to keep up without trouble. It was soon apparent the broom was correct. Not too far from where the broom was Oracle heard chittering. Assuming this was the something the broom indicated was nearby, Oracle relaxed. A small creature no doubt. She listened hard and kept walking. The chittering grew louder.

Oracle rounded a tree and a surprised squirrel bolted up the trunk. She turned around to look at it, but it scampered off into the canopy. Oracle turned back around to continue walking when she heard a scratch-scratch. She faced the broom.

"What?" She stared at the broom. The broom was motionless behind her, next to the tree. After waiting for a moment she moved to continue on, but the broom made another sweep across the ground. Oracle looked at it.

"What? What are you sweeping about?" She demanded and put her hands on her hips.

Again, the broom stood motionless. Again, Oracle turned to leave. The broom made another pass on the ground and Oracle wheeled around, ready to lay into it. But the broom was sweeping at the tree trunk where the squirrel had been. She peered closely and the broom stopped sweeping. It moved to the side and Oracle saw a hole.

"It's, like, a nut trap or something. Just a place squirrels keep food. Why are you telling me about this?" Oracle looked at the broom. "I am talking to a semi-sentient broom that can't talk back to me. This is…not how I pictured my return to adventuring."

Oracle marched over to the base of the tree. It was getting really dark now so she cast a small spell for light that made her palm shine. The broom twittered away.

"Relax, it's not fire. It's just light. Now what's over here?"

She shone her palm like a torch into the hole and used her other hand to pull away some dirt. She dug a couple handfuls of dirt out from the hole until she hit something solid. It felt just like a tree root, but had a sharp corner to it.

"What in the world…" Oracle moved her palm to try to get a better look, but she couldn't see much. "This is going to set me behind schedule."

She set to work digging out the hard object. After laying on her stomach and getting covered in dirt, Oracle dug out a box. A small wooden box with a simple design of two different woods. She tried to open it, but it wouldn't release. It was hard to open with one hand, so she tried two. It still wouldn't open.

"Ok, I don't really have time for this, can I just take it to go with us?" She asked the broom.

A little nod.

"Alright, let's take it to go," She said. Oracle dusted off the dirt from the box and put it in her pack. Then she dusted her hands and clothes, which made the light from her palm flash. It wasn't total darkness yet, but she could already see stars in the sky. She continued on course until the trees thinned and opened to a beautiful meadow. She consulted Atmir's sketch and determined the Ruby Leaf would be here, but Atmir told her it needed to be harvested during daylight or it would be ruined.

Oracle looked around. There were millions of stars above her and a slight breeze that swayed the tree limbs and made some creak. The moonlight lit the meadow up, but the forest beyond was pitch black deeper past the first row of trees. She turned to the broom.

"Have you been in the forest for long?"

A nod.

"Have you been to this meadow?"

A nod.

"Is the meadow safe to stay in overnight?"

A nod.

"Are you lying to me?"

A sweep.

"Ok, if something happens to me, you know what happens to you, Broom."

A nod.

"Do you need sleep?"

A sweep.

"Ok. I guess, alert me if something isn't right. Sweep me or something? I don't know. I'm trusting you, Broom."

A bunch of nods.

Oracle picked a spot in the meadow just at the tree line. She opened her pack and removed her bedroll and laid it out on the tall grass. She took out some food Atmir had packed in a red and white tea towel. She smiled as she looked at what he had sent her. A little brewing kit and a special blend of tea in a sachet. There was a note: "Real adventurer fare for a real adventure. The tea should help you sleep. Don't be gone too long. – Atmir." Besides the tea Oracle discovered he also sent an apple, a small wedge of cheese, some dried fruit, and some nuts. She set to heating the water with a spell and snacked on the food. She hummed to herself, and the broom swept nearby.

When the tea was ready she put the food away, stringing her pack into a tree. She climbed into her bedroll and sipped on the tea. It tasted like vanilla and fig and made her feel warm and sleepy. It felt a little like her body was humming, but in a soothing way. When she finished the tea, she packed up the set and set it aside. She waited a little bit for some slightly magical effect to take hold. The breeze caressed her exposed face and she slipped off to sleep with the gentle rustle of the broom's sweeping and the creaking of high up branches. She rested deeply, not hearing the swish-swish of the broom throughout the night.

The next morning she awoke to the same rustles. The broom apparently swept all night as evident by the tall grass that was now bent over. She felt refreshed and didn't delay getting her pack and putting away her bedroll and the tea set. She'd have to ask Atmir about the blend later. Today she needed to get the Ruby Leaf and start back to Greenspring. She could make it home today.

"Home?" She said out loud. "I guess it is for now."

The broom swept the meadow while she packed up. She looked for Ruby Leaf near her camp and was almost immediately rewarded. Ruby Leaf was, as the name implied, a red leaf. It grew low to the ground, but stood out against the tall green meadow grass. She gathered about fifty or sixty leaves and put them in her pack. Oracle felt satisfied and looked to the broom.

"Now what do I do with you?" She asked. "Come on, Broom. Time to go."

Of course, the broom had no reply but simply trailed behind her and swept as she walked. Oracle wondered where the broom had come from and what she was going to do with it when she got back. Perhaps put up signs. Someone must be looking for their semi-sentient broom. It's not exactly an everyday object to own.

As she trekked through the woods, Oracle also thought about her plants, her new home, and her new friends. She also thought about her old friends. When she reached the stream again, she decided to put her bare feet in the water for a bit, and have part of the snack Atmir had sent along with her. The water was very cold, but it felt good on her feet. The sun was shining and the forest was peaceful. This is what adventuring could offer.

When her toes started to go numb, Oracle resumed her journey out of the woods. When she reached the transition section of the trees, where they thinned and the black rocks started to appear again, she noticed something strange. A little ways off, and partially obscured by a large granite rock, was a circle of iridescent little mushrooms. They glimmered in the sunlight changing from blue to green to purple or from yellow to orange to red. She approached.

"I wonder how I missed these on the way up," Oracle said out loud. Then she asked the broom, "Do you know what these are?"

A little nod.

"They're Glimmer Mushrooms, aren't they? I've heard about them, but have never seen any before. How many do you suppose I can take before the fairies get angry with me? There's quite a lot here." Oracle surveyed the patch. There were a good number of mushrooms.

"Maybe just five of each color. That's hardly any for a patch this size. I'll get a variety of sizes to experiment with. Atmir might like to try some in a tea. Actually, I would like to try some in a tea."

Oracle harvested the mushrooms by carefully cutting them at their base. She gathered five of each color, ranging from a small size that fit in her palm easily, to ones with heads about the size of her fist.

"That's enough," she said, then a little louder to the people watching she couldn't see, "Thank you."

She walked on, feeling really good about her trip. The broom continued to follow, pausing to sweep here and there.

"You're going to have nine hells of a job when we get back. The whole town is covered in dirt and dust and sand. You're never going to stop."

It was then that Oracle stopped. Ahead of her, on the back of a rock – or the front from where she was now – was another strange sigil carved into the stone. It had a faint pulsing glow, like it was dying. Or breathing. Oracle studied it for a minute, then she walked up to it. She traced the sigil with her finger and found it was slightly warm to the touch. The light that pulsed from the sigil was a soft pink. Perplexed, Oracle tried a spell on it.

She intended only to figure out what the sigil did, but her spell did nothing. Oracle opened her pack and took out a notebook. She drew the sigil as best she could and took some notes about it on the next page from the first sigil she had seen. She marked them on a rough map. She swiped her finger across the sigil, but nothing happened, unlike the sigil she had touched when foraging with Atmir. Broom swept behind her, reminding Oracle that she was not alone and was due back tonight.

"This place keeps offering surprises," she said to herself. She packed her notebook away and made a mental note to tell Atmir about the sigil.

The sky was just getting dark when Oracle arrived back in town. She thought it best to check in with Atmir before retiring so she could drop off the supplies. Honestly, she was looking forward to sitting in a chair and drinking a hot tea with him. She remembered she would have to thank him for the set he had packed and the special blend he had given her.

The lantern was shining through the window when she approached The Guiding Light. She paused outside in the settling darkness and watched inside. Atmir was reading a book, standing behind the counter. There wasn't anyone else inside. She watched him absentmindedly run a hand through his hair, sip his tea, and lean an elbow on the counter while he read. She looked at his expression to see if she could tell if he was enjoying the book, but he just looked focused. When the broom started to sweep again, she realized she was being creepy. She shook her head at herself and walked into the shop, smiling as Atmir looked up at her.

9. Seventh Day Market

Nobody had even pretended to claim Broom. At first, Oracle was sort of desperate to find its owner, but eventually she grew accustomed to its presence. Its rhythmic sweeping became the soothing soundtrack to her day, and Broom was surprisingly adept at tidying a whole room. In the mornings, when the dust was caught in the early sunlight, Oracle started to open the door for Broom which would sweep out the dust and dirt collected during the night. Then, Broom would continue to sweep what had already been swept. Occasionally, Oracle thought Broom would bump into pots to spill a little dirt for something to do. She couldn't be sure.

The wary townsfolk had mostly avoided Broom and turned to scurry away whenever it was outside. Some brave souls entered the plant shop and ignored Broom as best as they could manage. Broom was harmless and Oracle would often laugh at how terrified some people were of it. Broom became a constant companion in the shop and even Aquarius liked its company. Oracle began to appreciate the help Broom offered and felt more fondly of it each day.

Today, Broom was busy sweeping while Oracle and Aquarius finished watering the plants. Oracle was going to the market today. It had been a few weeks since she had gone, but she needed to get more provisions for Aquarius and the hunters had the best dried meat at the market. They were otherwise hard to account for since they were always off in the woods. She made a note to ask one of them about the sigil she had seen and if they'd ever seen them before.

Atmir hadn't known anything about the sigil. He suggested Harrad's books again, but after two days in his library, Oracle couldn't find anything very useful. The best she could find was a book with some basic information that said things she already knew, like sigils are carved for a variety of reasons, and they could be for protection, curses, traps, or alarms for example. Sigils could be connected, or singular. They could be on a variety of surfaces. Sometimes they glowed, but not always. Overall, it was too generic to help Oracle figure out what the sigil did.

She did find some interesting folklore about Greenspring in his library. There was a god a thousand years ago that planted some kind of seed for a village that had helped him achieve a victory against another, less benevolent god. The seed grew into a mighty plant and the god had told the villagers it must always be fed and it would be content to offer minor blessings in return. She borrowed the book from Harrad to study it more when she had time. The information was perplexing, but interesting, and Oracle wanted to know if the book mentioned sigils or if the village was actually Greenspring before it turned into a town.

Oracle watered Noodle, the plant that sprouted from the special glowing seed she had. Noodle was now several very long vines worth of plant. The base of the plant was over by the window with some others. The long vines crept over the door frame, along the wall, on the ceiling, down a beam, down a post and generally looked like it would keep going. It had little poky points all over the vines. They weren't sharp, and the vines themselves were soft and fleshy-feeling. It tended to be a little cheeky as well.

For whatever reason, probably because Aquarius was afraid of it, Noodle the vine plant would use a tendril and follow Aquarius whenever he watered the other plants in the window. If Oracle hadn't known better, she almost thought the plant was laughing every time Aquarius saw the vine following him, shouted, and scurried off as fast as his little not-dragon legs would carry him.

Oracle noted that the vine plant would react to her moods. Its body language would change depending on how she was feeling. She logged the vine plant's different actions and her various moods. She discovered there was definitely a connection. What that meant, and how she could use it, escaped her for the time being.

She was happy today, and Noodle the vine plant reflected that by being a little extra perky itself. She finished giving it water and then did the rest of the plants Aquarius didn't get. She put away the watering can and put on her cloak.

"Do you want to come today Aquarius?"

"To market? I don't think so." He said as he lazed in his hammock.

"All you do is stay here in the shop anymore."

"Someone has to alert the authorities when your pet plant takes over the place. I'm the last line of defense."

Oracle snorted.

"You go on, Oracle. Bring me back some dried apricots though."

"Anything else for his majesty?"

"That will do, peasant. Now, be gone!" Aquarius settled deeper into his little hammock and closed his eyes.

Oracle left for the market, which was held across the town in the town square. She peered into The Guiding Light as she passed it. It was empty and the sign was up, meaning Atmir was also at market today. She tried to keep herself from hoping to run into him, but failed. She admonished herself for liking the man so much. *They were friends.* Nothing more.

Oracle entered the crowded market and passed by the food vendors. Each week, with a few exceptions, the vendors rotated their sections. This week, the food vendors were on the side closest to Oracle's shop, thus the side she entered from. In other weeks, it had been the trinket-sellers, the books, scrolls, and bookbinder booths, and once it had been the fruit, vegetables, and for some reason, a pet vendor.

Oracle paused at the next intersection. She could go right to what looked like general provisions and spices, or ahead to the hunters and vegetables. One way went her actual mission, and the other way likely led to Atmir. She didn't have to really think about it, and turned right toward the spices.

There were two spice vendors. One that did herbs and spices and one that just did spices. One wasn't a local; instead traveling around a few different towns and making it to the seventh day market in Greenspring every few weeks. Atmir, Oracle knew, could find a lot of what he needed daily from these two. Sometimes he had to order in from the courier who traveled between town and the city, and sometimes he had to forage for things. Oracle liked it best when he foraged, because it was an excuse to go with him on what essentially was a nature hike. She had spent several seventh days in his company, wandering inside the woods or just before them, chatting, looking for the plants he needed, or just enjoying the sounds nature made. It was another reason she hadn't left Greenspring for the city.

Oracle had decided that when she left Greenspring, she would return to her home city and regroup by studying with her old mentor. He would have some wisdom for her, and enough tasks to bury herself in she wouldn't be able to think of anything else. Not of her fallen companions, failed jobs, old rivals, or even of Greenspring. It was freedom through absolute scholarly focus. She just wasn't quite ready for that again.

Atmir had been making an order with one of the two spice vendors when Oracle spotted him. She smiled as she walked up to him and bumped her shoulder to about his elbow. He was too tall to go shoulder to shoulder.

"Hello stranger," she said.

Atmir brightened when he saw her and wrapped one arm around her shoulders, giving her a quick squeeze. The aroma of all the different spices and herbs made Oracle's head light.

"Good morning. How is the greenery today?" Atmir asked, his arm still around her.

"Very well, thank you. How are *you?*" Oracle asked, and she felt the big man's laugh more than she heard it.

"Sorry. How are *you*, Oracle?" Atmir asked and looked down at her with a big grin.

"The plants and I and Aquarius are all doing well today. And how are you?" Oracle exaggerated the words, making her teasing tone more flamboyant. "Making a large order I see." Oracle could see several bags of spices on the table in front of them and Atmir's list in his hand, with little checkmarks next to what he'd already gotten.

"Yes, Gordon told me he won't be able to make his usual round next week, so I have to go double the time without seeing him." Atmir let go of Oracle.

"Mr. Atmir is sad to not be seeing my beautiful face," Gordon, who objectively did not have a beautiful face, interjected. "And who wouldn't be sad? Look at me!"

Gordon pretended to preen and posed for laughs. Atmir and Oracle obliged.

"But seriously, Miss Oracle. I cannot make it back for several weeks longer than my usual schedule. You'll either have to buy from my competitor, or stock up now," Gordon said. He leaned forward and stage-whispered, "I recommend myself. Never know what you're actually getting with the other guy."

Oracle laughed again while Atmir chuckled.

"I will keep that in mind. I am fully stocked with what I need at the moment. It's just me, so I don't run through things quite so fast as Atmir here. But, now that you say it, I should buy some salt."

"I have flavors today, if you're interested?" Gordon said, and pointed out his salt containers. "Smoked, wine, ale, sweet and salty...I can go on?"

"No, thank you. Just the regular salty variety will suit me fine."

"As you wish," was the reply, and Gordon bagged a pouch of salt for Oracle. She paid him and then scooped up her pouch and some of Atmir's bags. Atmir finished his order, and Gordon promised he would have the rest of Atmir's order delivered to the shop by the end of the day. Atmir and Oracle left, side by side, and walked up the market avenue.

"What else are you at market for, Atmir?" Oracle asked, watching the people at different tents browse and make purchases. Their casual pace was a slight impediment to others who were shopping for their week.

"I was thinking of making a stew, so I need to visit Lestle or Imantep for some fresh meat."

"That's perfect. I need to see them as well for dried meat. Which do you prefer?"

"Fresh meat of course. The dried stuff is too hard to chew. Makes me feel like some kind of animal."

"No, I meant between Lestle or Imantep."

"Oh," Atmir said, embarrassed. "I like them both, but I think Lestle has better fresh meat and Imantep has better dried meat. I think they both kind of do the same thing, so I don't know why one is better than the other."

"Little nuances I suppose. The same way tea can be brewed," Oracle said and shifted the weight she was carrying.

"You're right. The same way spells can be cast," Atmir replied. He turned to show his pack to Oracle, who got the hint and placed the bags inside it for him to carry. Freeing both her hands, she put the salt pouch on her belt and then they continued their meandering stroll through the market.

They walked in silence, neither one suggesting they go the direct path to the hunters. Oracle watched as a stall vendor showed off a trinket to a gathering crowd of children, who squealed in delight as the necklace burst into smoke and disappeared. There were always a lot of junk sellers. People who sold almost worthless items. Somehow they made a decent living and were posted up each week selling the same things that you could buy at any market in any town: fake potions you weren't supposed to drink; necklaces that burst into smoke, or burst into birds, or just birds' feathers; small figurines that didn't move; little balls that hovered just above wherever they were placed; dancing lights that didn't dance or light up enough. Just about everything they sold would break fairly soon. Maybe that was the secret to their success. If it broke it would need to be replaced.

"Have you been to Lady Lady's yet?" Atmir asked, looking down at her as they surveyed the market.

"I've been by, but it looks like the other vendors that sell junk from fancier tents than these guys." Oracle motioned to the stall vendor giving the demonstration.

"You've got it all wrong. Lady Lady's is legitimate magic. That's why she's not quite as popular as the other vendors. Greenspring isn't a fan of magic, beyond those little toys people buy."

"Why is that?"

"To be honest, I don't know. I don't have a problem with magic," Atmir said, then a short time later added, "Or magical people."

"You know, anyone can learn magic. It's not like it's a well-guarded secret. It takes some patience and study, but everyone can do it," Oracle stopped and looked at Atmir, "And your tea. Your teas are magic. Nobody has a problem with them."

"I think they're in denial," Atmir shrugged it off and went to start walking again, but Oracle stopped him with a hand on his arm.

"Maybe, but they can't deny the teas are magic. They are overtly magical."

"Speaking of overt magic. Are you ready to learn anything more about the sigils you found? We can go to Lady Lady's now?"

A woman walked by with a warm, sugary bread, and Oracle paused to smell the scent closing her eyes. It was cozy and caloric, the wafting smell of butter, sugar, and cinnamon.

"Should we get one of those, or are you going to be ok?" Atmir asked.

"I'll be ok, but I still might want one of those," Oracle opened her eyes. "And yes, I'm ready to learn more about those sigils. Not about sigils in general, but specifically the ones I documented. And the one I might have turned off."

They began to walk again.

"Do you think there could be more?" Atmir asked.

"I don't know."

"Maybe it's a pattern or grid?" Atmir suggested.

"I don't know." Oracle dragged a hand down her face.

"Or could it be a trail marker of some kind?"

"I don't know!" Oracle said, throwing her head back, exasperated.

"Sorry. You're the only magic expert I know."

"I didn't mean to respond like that."

"You're frustrated. I understand," Atmir said softly, not looking at her. Oracle didn't look at him either, but instead the ground ahead of her. His arm brushed against hers as they walked.

"Yeah. Sorry. I've gone over and over it and I'm not getting anywhere." The frustration gnawed at Oracle's brain. The image of the sigil burned in her mind. The way it felt, the way it glowed or stopped glowing, the way it was positioned on the rock all lead to dead ends for her. She chewed the inside of her cheek as she thought about it.

"Maybe you need a break. Look at it with fresh eyes after resting them. Let's go in." Atmir held open a tent curtain to Lady Lady's Magic Emporium and More. Oracle hadn't noticed they were approaching the large purple tent. She'd only been watching to avoid people in front of her, and was a little shocked she hadn't let a giant purple tent register in her brain.

10. Lady Lady's

Atmir held open the purple tent flap for Oracle to enter Lady Lady's. It was giant. It stretched about four tents long and went back too deep to see. From the inside it was spacious, but also dark. There were several rooms divided by curtains of sparkling beads. The entrance was a small hallway, and the beads made a slight clatter as they touched when Oracle and Atmir passed through them. The next room was dimly lit with floating orbs of colorful light. There was furniture in this room, like a sitting room in a fancy house. It felt festive, but also too quiet. It felt like your joy was to be contained.

"I wish it was a little brighter in here," Atmir said, and the soft glowing lights grew a little brighter. "You've got to be joking," Atmir said quietly.

"Oh. Look." Oracle pointed to the tea table in the center of the room.

"What does it say? Honestly, I never come in here, but I have been before. It's just been awhile. I don't remember it well," Atmir said.

"It looks like it's about Lady Lady herself," Oracle said, looking over a plaque.

They looked at the plaque, embedded in the table under a pane of glass. It detailed that Lady Lady had been born to a poor woman who named her Lady in an effort to sound noble. Lady grew up and married a lord and hence became Lady Lady Noblewoman – they never give her surname. After her husband died, Lady had begun to deal in magical artifacts, trading her considerable wealth for magical wealth and hiring adventurers to obtain magical items for her. She now travels with her emporium to various locations to barter, sell, and bargain for magical items of all kinds. It's her way of adventure. Lady Lady still hires adventurers from time to time for magical artifacts and is always looking for the next great item to add to her collection.

"She sounds like an interesting…ah…lady," Atmir said when he finished reading.

"She does. A little mysterious, too."

Nobody was sitting in the furniture or anywhere else in the room, and so Oracle and Atmir continued to the next room. It was a small room with shelves on all sides. Each shelf had potions on it that were illuminated by the soft colored lights in the room. The effect made each potion glint in the light and the whole room was a prism of colors reflected back at them.

"These are…real," Oracle said in awe as she picked one up and examined the tag affixed to it.

"I told you Lady Lady's was the real deal," Atmir said, behind her.

Oracle looked at more of the potions, reverently picking them up, reading the labels, and setting them down again. Healing potions, potions to cure and cause sickness, potions for hair growth and hair removal, a potion to make your feet grow, and one to make you smell nice. There were a few others that caught her eye: A potion of temporary forgetfulness, a potion of temporary blindness, and the one she read twice to believe: a potion of plant healing.

"Atmir, look at this," She held the round bottle out for him to read the label. Atmir took it from Oracle and read the label.

"That has potential in Greenspring. I wonder why nobody has tried it before."

"Probably because nobody comes in here you said? And if they do, they're too afraid of using whatever they find." Oracle couldn't take her eyes off of it.

"Fair points. Are you going to use it?" Atmir handed the potion back to her.

Oracle considered for a moment, turning the potion in her hands and watching the metallic deep green liquid swirl inside. Atmir stood just next to her, also still looking at the potion.

"I think I should buy it as a 'just in case' item. I don't know that I need to use it right now, but if there's a problem with one of the plants and my usual methods don't work, this could be useful." Oracle cupped the bottle in both hands, wondering about the contents. Could this really work?

"Do you think the plants will ever grow without magic interference?" Atmir interrupted her thoughts.

"Interference?" Oracle looked up at him, a little stab in her heart.

"I mean, do you think anyone will be able to grow plants in Greenspring again? Outside? Not just a skilled, talented, knowledgeable and very pretty mage." He added with a grin.

Oracle let the little stab fade, and her body replaced it with a warm bubbling.

"Well, if anyone could grow plants here then there would be no use for said mage," she said mock gravely. "And that mage would have to leave town to find a different adventure."

"We wouldn't want that." Atmir said, inching a little closer to Oracle.

"Who is 'we?' Does 'we' have plans for this mage?" Oracle asked, and Atmir inched even closer to her. She pretended not to notice how close he was getting and tried to focus on the potion in her hands.

"We would like it very much if the mage had plans to stay, I think," Atmir said softly. He was facing her now, almost touching, and looking down into the top of her head. Oracle looked up at him, into his deep brown eyes, and he looked back at her into her brown eyes, unblinking. The colorful lights danced off their bodies and faces, the potions a kaleidoscope of color surrounding them, and Oracle could feel a certain heat begin to rise inside her body.

"HELLO!" a man's voice rang out as the beads clattered, and the spell was broken. Atmir stepped back. Oracle hurriedly put the potion back on a shelf, then picked it back up remembering she wanted to buy it. The man who had flitted in was very skinny, with light brown skin and a human appearance. He had a very long nose and very short black hair. He wore white robes with light brown accents and soft shoes, also white.

"My name is Kangorrac. You may call me Kang," The man said with cheer and a bow. "I am so pleased to have you here at Lady Lady's Magic Emporium and More! I see you've found our potions selection. There are certain custom potions that can be made by request, but you'll have to see the catalog in the back for those. If I can help you find anything, please don't hesitate to ask. That's what I'm here for."

"Thank y-" Oracle started to say, but the man continued right along.

"We have a small collection of enchanted armor and weapons, an even smaller selection of magical books and books on magic, and a special section of enchanted jewelry for adventurers and admirers alike. Haha," Kang laughed a short merry burst and kept going, "We're here for the discerning lords and ladies who know what they want. If you have a special request, Lady Lady will try to accommodate you. If you're just here to browse, please feel free to do so, but know that the premises are monitored with anti-theft magic and you will *not* be pleased with the results if you try to steal. Not that you darlings are thinking about that."

"Ok –" Oracle tried to say again, but again Kang kept right on going with his spiel.

"When you're ready to make your purchases, you can meet me or another associate and we'll take care of you. Lady Lady's has a card oracle here today if such things interest you. She charges a reasonable rate and can be met in the room off of the jewelry room. Do you have any questions for me?"

Kang looked expectantly at Oracle and Atmir, who were both a little taken aback by the man's energy.

"Uh, yes, I have a question," Oracle said slowly, waiting to be cut off again.

"Yes, honey. Ask away."

"The magic books you have. Where might I find those?"

"Go through this room and you'll enter a small hallway with three entrances. The one to the right goes to the jewelry, the center goes to the armor, and the left goes to the library."

"Thank you. I think, that's - Wait, is Lady Lady here?"

"Why yes of course she's here."

"I thought it might just be a namesake."

"No darling. Lady Lady is always with the Emporium," Kang said, smiling broadly at her, as if she was a silly child.

"And who do I ask if I have questions about a product?"

"Me or any of our other associates in the tent. You'll know us by our attire," Kang indicated at his robes, his smile not faltering.

"I think that's everything I wanted to know. Atmir?" Oracle asked, looking at Atmir.

"I think you answered all of my questions. Thank you, Kang." Atmir replied.

"You're so welcome," Kang said and flitted out the way he came in, the beads giving a soft clatter as he left.

"He was…interesting." Atmir said, staring at the beads in the doorway.

"He would be right at home in the city. I wonder how he got this job? Traveling town to town selling magical items?"

"What do you think about the card oracle they have?" Atmir looked at Oracle as she stepped to his side. "You want to get your future told?"

"I do not." Oracle replied.

"Scared of what it will say?" Atmir looked at her with a teasing smile and bumped into her side gently.

"Oracles are either faking it or on the run from someone they told the truth to. I neither want a fake reading, nor to expose myself to whatever trouble a real oracle is in. That's why she's traveling and not a permanent part of this place. Trust me, you don't want to be involved in whatever mess she's gotten into. I've met enough of them to know this is almost universally true." Oracle stated with exasperation.

"Does this apply to you?"

"I'm not *an oracle.* It's just my name because that's what my mother wanted me to do. Why? I'll never know." Oracle was getting frustrated with the big man, and Atmir took the clue.

"Well, I hope you're not faking it," Atmir muttered.

"What?"

"Nothing. I didn't say anything," Atmir said a little too quickly, "What do you want to look at next? The books?"

"Yes. There might be something there on the sigil." Oracle said, looking around for the exit to the next rooms.

They traversed into the hallway, then turned left and entered the room containing all the books. It was lit with regular floating candles, and a little brighter than the other rooms and dark hallway they had been in. Oracle was in awe again. There were all sizes and volumes of books, and some she recognized. There was also a case of scrolls. Oracle knew that scrolls were one-time use items that would cast whatever spell they contained by channeling the user's own magic. The more powerful the user, the more powerful the spell.

She carefully browsed through the scrolls as Atmir looked at the books. The parchment the scrolls had been created with was dry on her fingers and she worried that some would crumble. She carefully unfurled one – a fire spell – and then another – a wind spell – and compared them. They were inked beautifully, but by obviously two different wizards. She was careful not to read the incantations aloud or the spells would be cast and the parchment dissolved. They were beautiful. Oracle had only used a scroll once before, in training.

"Are all of these books magic themselves, or are some of them references?" Atmir asked.

"Some of them are references, yes," Oracle said over her shoulder, still looking at the scrolls. "I saw some I know that are books with spells inside of them. A few I also recognized as being magic themselves. Don't touch any of the ones that are glowing. They are under a magical lock and will shock you."

"Good to know," Atmir said, putting his hand down as he was about to touch a book. "I think maybe I'll just browse the titles. Anything I should be looking for besides the word 'sigil?'"

Oracle rolled the scrolls up and put them back, left the scroll case, and went to Atmir across the room. She glanced over the tall bookcase, and briefly noted the books it contained.

"Ok, these are safe for you to handle. Except the glowing ones. Still don't touch those. You can read the titles on the spine. Look for anything with sigil, of course. Maybe something about magical marks, or possibly wards or even curses. It's frustrating because there is such a wide variety of uses for sigils. They aren't common, but they can be used for so many things."

"I think I'll just stick to calling out the titles and you can touch the books," Atmir said.

"Ok," Oracle smiled, "You just tell me if you see anything interesting."

And so Atmir and Oracle began combing the bookshelves looking for a book regarding sigils. Atmir called out titles he thought might be useful, and Oracle opened a few to look inside, but nothing came to fruition. Oracle and Atmir noted that neither Kang nor any other associate of the Emporium had bothered them to check in or otherwise. They kept searching.

They moved on to the third and fourth bookshelves. Atmir called out "Arcanist's Guide to Symbols and Runes?" which Oracle looked at and determined wasn't a fit. Then he called out "Rosewater's Guide to Curses: Rituals and Sigils Edition" and Oracle almost kissed him in joy.

"That has to have something to lead me in the right direction!" Oracle said with excitement. "Even if the sigil I saw wasn't a curse, this might put me on to a clue that will help. Maybe I can get my old mentor to send me a book. I don't know why I didn't think of that sooner. He probably knows which book I'd need."

"You can do that later in addition to getting this book. We're getting this book right?"

"Absolutely. Let's finish scanning the shelves for anything else useful."

Oracle ended up with the Rosewater book, a book on magical plants, and a book on identifying edible and medicinal plants in the wild. It was geared toward the whole region they were in, so not everything would be useful, but some of it would be.

"You know what? Maybe we should see if we can talk to Lady Lady. About Broom. See if she's seen anything like it, or maybe knows who is missing one? And about sigils maybe," Oracle said. She and Atmir were leaning in close together reading the last few books' titles on the last shelf.

"I see you've found several books from our selection. Very nice!" The chipper voice of Kang rang out, startling Oracle and Atmir, who both jumped as the curtain clattered and Kang swept in. "Apologies! I didn't mean to startle you. What else can I help you with?"

Oracle and Atmir shared a look. Then Oracle said slowly, "We were just wondering if it was possible to gain an audience with Lady Lady. I have a magical artifact I have questions about and I was curious to know if maybe she could shed some light on its nature, or perhaps its owner."

"I see," Kang said, smiling in a way that wasn't quite natural, but not quite forced either. "Are you available now?"

"I think we are, yes." Oracle looked at Atmir, who nodded.

"Great!" Kang whipped out a small book and opened to a page. "What are your names and can I just state your nature of business as a question of an artifact? Will that be sufficient?"

"Atmir and Oracle," Oracle replied, "I think that will be sufficient explanation. We won't bring the artifact. It can be a little unwieldy when packaged. And I don't think I'd like to bring it right through town during market. It's a little unwieldy when it's not packaged, too. Plus, I'd have to go home to get it."

True, the broom was stellar at sweeping the shop, but Oracle found when it got outside it tended to wander off sweeping the next pile of dirt and the next unless she gave it the "follow" command. She didn't have to wonder how it had gotten so far into the woods at all. She still wondered about its sentience, and ability to understand her and communicate back. When Oracle had tried to bind the broom up at night, it had fought vigorously and knocked several plants over, spilling them and their dirt all over the floor. Broom didn't seem to mind this after breaking free and swept up the dirt as usual, but Oracle was displeased. She decided to let it roam free and just shepherd it around when needed. It was great at the "follow me" command. Or mostly great. It could get distracted by dust bunnies and dirt particles, but tended to follow *and* sweep when given the command.

"Fabulous. I have you down here. I'll get you when it's time." He said and snapped the book shut.

"Thank you, Kang," Atmir finally spoke.

Kang had them wait briefly in the sitting area. Oracle re-read the plaque.

"Do you want to check out some of the jewelry before we leave?" Atmir asked her, after they began to look around the room for something to occupy the wait time.

"It couldn't hurt to look. There might be *something*."

"Ok. Let's look."

"Anything else I can help with?" Kang said, making Atmir and Oracle jump again. He appeared as if from the shadows. "Are you going to check out the armor or the enchanted jewelry? There is a little unenchanted jewelry too, if you're looking."

Oracle looked to Atmir, a little unsettled from the man's reappearance. Atmir looked unfazed and even a little brighter at Kang's suggestions.

"I don't think we need to look at the armor or weapons, do you?" He asked Oracle.

"No, but I would like to check out the jewelry. There could be something interesting there."

"Oh yes, very interesting things!" Kang said enthusiastically.

"Well, let's go then," Oracle said, rising from her seat. She led the way leaving Kang behind. Atmir followed, carrying the books they had gotten earlier. He wouldn't let Oracle walk around with them, but didn't fuss about the potion she had.

The jewelry room was about as big as the library room. It was a little more well-lit than the book area. Plain lanterns cast warm light over the room, making it feel cozy. There were display cases of all sizes and types here. They were filled with rings, necklaces, brooches, belt buckles, earrings, and bracelets. Much of the ware sparkled, even in the warm light. There were some items that looked well worn, and a few that looked worse for the wear. It smelled distinctly of metal. Oracle and Atmir perused the cases, reading the little labels for each item.

"Hey look!" Oracle said to Atmir and pointed at a ring. "This is a ring of fire starting. You could use that to light your stove instead of doing it by hand."

Atmir came over to look. It was a silver ring with a slash of red through it. The red was very shiny and had little tinges of orange at the edges.

"That's pretty, but I don't think I want to take shortcuts I'm not familiar with. Also, I'm afraid I'll burn the shop down."

"I'm sure you wouldn't." Oracle smiled up at him. Atmir kindly returned the smile.

They both continued to look. Oracle found several rings of warding, a ring of luck, and a ring of water bearing. She found necklaces to give the wearer the illusion of being prettier, necklaces to make you a little smarter, and a necklace that hummed a small tune when touched. There were lockets of sending that would be able to transmit a message to the person wearing the paired locket once a day. She thought of her mother, but decided that even a once a day reminder to come home to the city was too many guilt trips to bear.

Oracle looked over the brooches. Ivory ones, metal ones, stones embedded in intricately designed ones. They were very pretty. She then found a wooden one that was labeled 'Brooch of Druidcraft' and took it from the case. She pinned it on and waited to feel any augment to her magic. She felt nothing and put it back. She should have felt something.

At that moment, the flutter of beads from the doorway sounded and Kang entered with all the grace and regality of a nobleman addressing an audience there just for him.

"Wonderful selection, isn't it?" He said with another big smile. Oracle was again, taken aback at Kang's appearance. Why was he following them around?

"It's very nice, yes. Lady Lady has great options for jewelry. You said some of it was not enhanced?" Oracle asked, touching another brooch in the case.

"Yes, most are labeled 'normal' and most can be found on that wall Mr. Atmir is standing by." Atmir turned a little pink when being addressed and shuffled away from the wall nervously.

"I hadn't looked there yet. I was more interested in your magical jewelry." Oracle said.

"Oh, yes those are fantastic. Our jewlry used to have more variety, but we had to pull some out from storage given that last market a large group of adventurers came in and made quite a lot of purchases. Lady Lady took the opportunity to offer them a contract while they were here. We're looking forward to the results."

"Sounds…interesting," Oracle replied.

"Yes, very interesting," Kang said, looking expectantly at Oracle.

"I'm going to continue to look, if that's ok?" She said, waiting for approval.

"Yes, please be my guest. And if you have any questions or need any help, please let me know," Kang bowed and then retreated to a corner with his hands behind his back.

"Kang, how do we make our purchases?" Atmir asked.

"With me or another associate, whenever you're ready," He replied, smiling.

"Oracle, I'm going to buy your books and I won't hear you say anything otherwise," Atmir said as he marched over to Kang. He looked like he was trying to beat her there, though Oracle hadn't moved from the brooch case.

"You don't have to do that Atmir! I can buy my own books!"

"Let me buy them! I insist. You keep browsing and if you like something, you can buy that, ok?" He was holding the books in front of him toward Kang. Oracle couldn't even see them.

Oracle laughed, "Okay, I'll finish soon."

Atmir handed Kang the items he was holding and Kang made a mental note of what they were then wrote down a receipt for Atmir after he had paid. Oracle turned her focus back to the enchanted jewelry. She paused her gaze on some of the more rare items: a ring of wyrm summoning, a ring of wind, a necklace of animal speaking, a necklace of plant speaking, and a brooch of increase magic were all in a case by themselves. Oracle considered the necklace of plant speaking.

Her plants were healthy, but it would be helpful to be able to ask them what they needed. She wondered how long the effect lasted and how long it could be used. As if reading her mind, Kang piped up from where he stood in the corner.

"Once a day for one hour, Miss Oracle, you can talk to plants and some of them will talk back."

"What do you mean 'some' of them?" She asked, looking to Kang.

"Some plants are, ahem, too unintelligent to speak. Do not try to use this on mushrooms. They are not a plant, as such, and the necklace will not work on them."

Oracle opened the case and took out the necklace and put it on. It was a simple silver chain with a fern leaf in a circle and a small green gem for the pendant. She felt her magic augment. It was a feeling you had to be in tune with to feel. It took several years of practice and her mentor had insisted she learn. She was glad he did.

A brief buzzing sensation followed by an acclimation where she could feel her magic had changed. Her mentor explained that magic items were not inherently magical, and they instead altered the way the body processed ambient magic. The feeling, he said, was the ambient magic mages called on for casting spells interacting with the item and their own bodies.

It took but a moment for a body to readjust, and if mages were not paying close attention they would miss the telltale signs all together. Her mentor had been so good at this attunement he could tell when other people were wearing magical items. Oracle had never gotten that good, but she could reliably tell magical items from fakes when trying the item on. The necklace of plant speaking was indeed the real thing.

"I think I'm ready," Oracle said. Kang once again smiled his best smile and helped her make her purchases. One necklace, and one potion.

"Thank you for your purchases. If you're ready, Lady Lady will see you now," he said and bowed deeply to them. He didn't wait for a response and instead pulled aside the beads in the doorway and led them through the tent. In the far back was a large room, brighter still than the other rooms, with a couch and armchairs, a low table, lamps that glowed, a desk with several books and papers on it, and an old woman looking at them.

11. The Conversation

Sat in one of the armchairs was an old woman, lean and wiry, with jewelry that glittered in her ears, around her neck, and on her fingers. She practically shined in the lamplight. She stood as the trio entered. Oracle noticed a tea set and three cups on the low table.

"May I introduce Lady Lady," Kang said with flourish. He seemed to disappear as the woman approached. Obviously a practiced and perfected movement.

"Welcome, Atmir and Oracle," Lady Lady said warmly, coming in for a light hug and air kisses on each cheek to the both of them. "Please, sit down. May I pour you a cup of tea?"

"Yes, that would be lovely," Atmir replied sincerely. He never passed up an opportunity to try new teas. He and Oracle both sat on the couch across from Lady Lady's seat. She carefully poured from a teapot into the cups.

"Do you take an accompaniment with your tea?" She offered.

"No, thank you," they both replied.

They all took a sip of their tea. Atmir's eyebrows shot up and his eyes widened.

"Too hot, dear?" Lady Lady asked with concern.

"No. It's delicious. I brew tea here in Greenspring, and this is excellent. How do you get such a fine tea if you travel all the time?"

"Prying into my secrets already?" Lady Lady asked with a roguish smile.

"Oh, no, I'm sorry," Atmir said, shifting uncomfortably on the couch.

"I'm kidding, dear. I have one of my staff get the tea from Silverwood Supply in Atan. He goes regularly to keep my supply fresh," Lady Lady said, then sipped her own tea. Oracle had also tasted the tea and was surprised at both its flavor and its freshness. It was bold and flavorful, unlike any other tea she had previously. It tasted faintly floral.

"Atmir knows tea. His ingredient selection has very interesting properties," Oracle said, leaning forward as if sharing a secret.

"Is that so?" Lady Lady asked, looking back to Atmir. "What kind of properties?"

"*Magic* properties," Oracle said conspiratorially. Atmir, looking embarrassed, elbowed Oracle causing her tea to jostle in her grip.

"That's quite interesting. I would like to try some of your teas, Atmir. Would you brew me something?" Lady Lady inquired.

"I – uh- yes. I'd be delighted to. I can make you a blend to take with you, if you'd like?"

"I look forward to it. Now, while I enjoy visiting with all sorts of people, I understand you're here about an artifact?" Lady Lady took another sip of her tea. She sat straight upright in her chair, properly noble.

"Yes," Oracle said, "And one more thing if we have time."

"We might. To your first business. What is the artifact in question?"

"A semi-sentient broom."

"Semi-sentient you say?"

"Yes," Oracle continued, sitting back on the couch. "It sweeps all the time. Day or night. If it gets outside it will sweep for eternity, I think. It somehow senses the floor or ground is dirty and sets to work. It does rest, and it can answer yes or no questions."

"Where did you find an enchanted broom?" Lady Lady looked interested, and Oracle wondered if it was a mistake to tell someone outside of Greenspring about Broom.

"In the woods."

"In the woods," Lady Lady repeated, seeming to think.

"It followed Oracle home," Atmir added. He repositioned a pillow to rest his elbow on to support the tea in his hand.

"Yes. It can follow simple commands. So, I had it follow me home. It said it doesn't have a home, other than mine now. It answers to 'Broom.'"

"Quite curious," Lady Lady said, and she sat back in her chair taking a sip of tea. It was silent for a long time. Atmir and Oracle didn't know if she was waiting for either of them to add more to the story, or if she was thinking. They stayed silent. Lady Lady sipped her tea again, her many rings sparkled in the light as she raised the cup to her lips.

Finally, Oracle spoke. "I want to know, mostly, what the broom is about. Should I be worried about it missing from an estate somewhere? Should I trust it? Are there more out there? Or will trouble come to me by keeping it? It is handy to have in my shop."

"Shop?"

"I grow plants. Inside ones." It was Oracle's turn to shift uncomfortably in her seat. She took a nervous sip of tea.

"That's quite the achievement in Greenspring," Lady Lady said with interest.

"It is," Atmir said proudly, looking at Oracle. Oracle could feel heat in her ears as they looked at her.

"I would like one of your plants. I could use some green around here. It will go lovely with the purple," Lady Lady indicated the tent walls with one hand.

"Of course. I would be happy to supply you with a plant." Oracle said.

"*Plants* I dare say. What good is just one?" Lady Lady replied and laughed. It was a cozy sound that warmed you up to hear it. Oracle and Atmir smiled, and Oracle relaxed a little.

"Plants, then," Oracle said. They all sat in silence, sipping their teas.

"Well then. This broom," Lady Lady said, breaking the long silence. "To answer your questions, you might need to worry if an estate servant or the lord themselves comes looking for the broom, finds you, and you wish not to return it, or worse, are accused of stealing it. But that would be petty."

"I'd return it to its rightful owner, as much as I like it."

"That's good of you. It sounds a little like the broom had wandered off, but perhaps its enchanter or its home or its owner is no longer. It was simply seeking a new place, while doing what it was intended to do: sweep."

"That would be a relief," Oracle stated.

"I don't think any trouble will befall you if you keep the broom," Lady Lady said reassuringly. "It sounds like quite the boon, actually. As for others, there are indeed other brooms and tools like the one you describe. It takes a tricky bit of magic to produce such an item, making your broom very rare to be certain. I would protect it if I were you, lest it be stolen by someone looking to sell. That may be the only trouble you find."

"I'm a mage with a fire specialty, so I should be able to manage that."

Lady Lady sat straight in her chair again.

"A fire mage?" She asked with her full attention on Oracle. She brought her hand to her necklaces as if in shock. "You don't come across many young ladies who take that path. Let alone grow plants in their free time."

"Yes. I used to adventure," Oracle said with subdued tones.

"Used to? Pity. I am always seeking talented, skilled, and willing adventurers."

"I might get back to it," Oracle said with an awkward smile. Atmir looked straight forward, solemnly sipping his tea. Lady Lady smiled politely at her.

"The question of trusting the broom," Lady Lady said, returning to the subject and once again she relaxed into her seat, "is an easy one. Enchanted tools are very loyal. That's part of the tricky bit of magic. You can enchant something to do a job, and that magic eventually wears off, but to have sentience or semi-sentience is the tricky bit. Most enchanters make sure the tools are loyal so that their hard work doesn't wander off into the woods, or start doing their tasks for the neighbors. Have you noticed the broom trying to leave your shop?"

"No. Well, not on purpose besides trying to escape to sweep outside. It doesn't dart out the door any time it's open."

"There you have it," Lady Lady smiled. "It sounds like it's bound to you and will do its task for you and you alone now."

"Can someone steal it and bind it to them?"

"Yes. That's why I suggested you protect it."

Oracle considered this for a moment. She wasn't sure how to protect it exactly, but since nobody seemed more than curious about it, she figured she shouldn't be concerned.

"Do you have time to address a problem we have?" Atmir asked. He leaned forward and set his cup and saucer on the low table between them.

"I do," Lady Lady said, without checking a watch or clock. Oracle found that curious but figured she might not have other appointments to get to today. Atmir looked to Oracle to continue.

"I have read a book on sigils, but it wasn't very helpful. I was wondering if you knew or had heard much about them, or about them in Greenspring. I have a drawing," Oracle said while she produced the sketches from her clothes pocket. She passed it to Lady Lady, who set down her cup to unfold the paper. She looked at the sigils, studying it closely.

"Hmmm," She said thoughtfully. She looked a long time before returning the sketch to Oracle. "That's a very curious sigil indeed. I don't know that I have seen one like it, but surely someone has."

Disappointed, Oracle returned the sketches to her pocket. Lady Lady stood from her chair and glided to her desk. Interested, Oracle and Atmir watched her, turning in their seats to do so. She reached into a drawer and without a word, produced a key. She then glided across the room and slid a purple curtain away which revealed a cabinet with a lock. She put the key in, turned it, and then opened the cabinet door. It swung open silently. From their vantage point, Atmir and Oracle couldn't see into the cabinet very well. From what Oracle could glance it appeared to be books.

Lady Lady swept her finger down the spine of several until one gave a shudder when she did so, and the lettering on it began to glow faintly. She pulled this one from the cabinet and floated back toward the armchair, still silent as she walked. Oracle wondered if Lady Lady knew some magic and was actually gliding. It wasn't impossible. Lady Lady sat gracefully down. She opened the book with a little flourish and flipped through a few pages. Oracle and Atmir looked at each other, unsure if they should leave or say something. Lady Lady continued to flip through the book.

"Ah!" She cried. "This! I was looking for this. Here, see for yourselves."

Lady Lady turned the book toward Atmir and Oracle and they both craned their necks to lean in and see what Lady Lady wanted to show them. It was a very similar sigil to the one Oracle had sketched. Oracle became visibly excited, her eyes opened wide as she rose slightly from her seat.

"What else does the book have? Anything to say about it?" Atmir asked as Oracle stared at the sigil in it.

"Let's see, shall we?" Lady Lady turned the book around and Oracle sat back down. She grinned at Atmir, who humored her with a smile back. Lady Lady read through a few pages, nodded to herself here and there, and muttered a bit as she went. Oracle was almost bursting with anticipation, and Atmir placed a warm hand on her knee. This did nothing for Oracle's excitement but momentarily distracted her.

"Well," Lady Lady said, definitively, "the book isn't going to be a lot of help, but it does indicate that these types of sigils, specifically ones with the cross slash like you showed me, almost always come as a set – as cornerstones for each other – and can often be numerous. Something to do with the way the cross slash engages the sigil and interacts with the other sigils."

"Wow," Oracle said, then followed with, "Does it mention what the sigils are used for?"

Lady Lady looked down at the book again, the jewelry on her fingers gleamed in the lamplight when she adjusted it. She turned a few pages, read some, and then set the book down in her lap.

"This reference says these types of sigils with both a cross slash and that little swoop just here," she held up the book and pointed, "are indicative of a ward. It doesn't say if the ward was directed inside or outside the sigils, but it does say that depending on the swoop you can determine what it wards against. Judging by your sketches, Miss, I believe you have some sigils warding against the garden."

"What does that mean? Does that mean I need to look for more sigils? Is that why Greenspring can't grow anything? The garden?" Oracle asked.

"I imagine it does mean you'll be searching for more sigils," Lady Lady said, closing the book and resting it in her lap. "You might also be looking at the root cause of Greenspring's problem. At least, according to this book."

"What is that book?" Atmir asked.

"Ah, some secrets cannot be shared, love," Lady Lady replied, her eyes sparkling, and her hands neatly folded across the cover.

"I understand," Atmir said with a knowing smile, "I have recipes I don't share."

"Did it mention what formation the sigils could take? I know you said 'cornerstone' but does that mean a square?" Oracle asked. She was leaning in toward Lady Lady, her excitement mingling with frustration.

"It did not say, unfortunately," Lady Lady said.

"So, I have to look for a bunch more sigils in some unknown pattern. That sounds… difficult." Oracle frowned and looked away.

"Indeed it does," Lady Lady replied with a serene, unconcerned air.

"I agree," Atmir said, trying to sound dissuading, "It sounds very difficult."

"Maybe take a look through my wares and see if there's something that might help?" Lady Lady offered. Atmir and Oracle got the hint.

"Thank you so much for seeing us today. Your help and insight has been invaluable," Atmir said.

"The pleasure has all been mine," Lady Lady said, and they all stood up. She shook their hands, and Oracle found they were pleasantly warm, if a bit boney. "If you're ever interested in getting back into the adventuring life, do let me know. Your grief will not serve you any longer, dear. I can always use a good adventurer…or two."

Lady Lady winked at Atmir, who gave an awkward smile and glanced at Oracle. Oracle was looking at Lady Lady, frozen in place.

"Well I'll be sure to let you know if I ever take up that mantle again," Oracle replied in a slow, low voice. Atmir gently moved her shoulders to direct her out of the room.

"Delightful. Take care," Lady Lady said, and returned to her armchair, the jewels decorating her shined back a merry goodbye to them.

Atmir and Oracle exited out heavy purple curtains into the hallway. They walked in silence to the front of the tent. Oracle shielded her eyes as she exited the dark tent. The sun was bright and the day was warm. The market smells resumed bombardment of Oracle's senses, and she realized the whole of Lady Lady's tent smelled faintly like flowers and fresh laundered clothes, and none of the many market smells had permeated her space.

"Well, where to next?" Atmir asked.

"I don't want to make you carry those books for too long. I'm a bit anxious to open them up. Should we head straight to the hunters? It's almost time for them to close up, so I hope we haven't missed them. Is it Imanotep or Lestle today?"

"I will be glad to carry your books for you, Oracle. All the way home if you like," Atmir smiled down at her, also shielding his eyes, "Makes me feel a little chivalrous. So let me."

"Chivalrous, huh? Alright, carry the books," Oracle started walking to the right, Atmir at her side. "Let's head to the hunters' stall and then head home?"

"To the hunters and to home."

As Oracle walked home with Atmir, her mind began to wander. First to the sigils and what they could mean for Greenspring's barrenness, then to what Lady Lady had said about her grief, then to the plants, and then eventually, to Atmir himself.

12. Noodle Is the First Defense

Oracle woke up as Aquarius tugged at her scalp by walking on her hair and she begrudgingly rose from her slumber. She took the little dragon creature downstairs and fed him some fruit and dried meat. She herself wanted a cup of tea to help wake her up, but if she went to Atmir's she would be there most of the morning. She found it harder and harder to leave when she was there.

Instead, she went to wash her face and get dressed. She returned to the shop and flipped the sign to 'Open' and set to work with a propagation. She had a popular little plant that she wanted to grow more to sell. It was a thick plant with little round leaves reminiscent of curly hair. Her mother had sent her the starter seeds and had been in regular contact with Oracle via letters. She had been glad to hear of Oracle's success and told her she was proud of her no matter what she did.

Oracle's mom never wanted her to be a mage or adventurer and while she disapproved of Oracle's choice to become both, she never harped on her about it. She would gently mention it sometimes, but that was it. What her mom did harp on about was that Oracle didn't live nearby and she should come back to the city. Oracle had been back since becoming an adventurer, but things had changed so much when she was gone she couldn't see herself moving back there. She imagined what it would be like sometimes but generally came to the conclusion that she missed the city as she knew it but probably wouldn't like it now. It was too different from the one she grew up with.

Oracle was happy to get the correspondence from her mother, however, and kept the writing going. She wrote or received a letter almost every week. It was a lot easier to write and receive letters when she stayed in one place.

After all the regulars had left that day, Aquarius and Oracle set to work. Aquarius watered the plants. He was more efficient than Oracle, not needing to refill a watering can. He also had a knack for watering them the right amount, without having to ask. Oracle used her necklace of plant speaking, but mostly when she was not sure about a plant's condition. Then she would take advantage of the hour or so it gave her to talk to as many plants as she could.

She had also experimented with making her own plant food recipes. She had borrowed some brewing equipment from Atmir – the same travel set he had packed for her – and made a plant serum she'd found a recipe for. She had minor success with it. It didn't seem to have any effect on healthy plants, of which hers mostly were. It did seem to help the struggling ones. She thought maybe she would try tweaking the recipe herself but hadn't gotten around to it yet. She had tried to give the tea brewing set back to Atmir, but he insisted she keep it for her experiments. He occasionally gave her little packets of tea blends to make at home. Oracle was very careful to make sure there was no residual plant serum before making tea. She didn't want her hair to turn green, or worse.

The rest of the day had a steady stream of customers come in to Oracle's surprise. And nobody commented on the self-sweeping broom keeping itself busy. For as much trouble as she'd had in her first few weeks trying to grow plants, she never thought the shop would take off like it did. She had denied it was a bad idea. She had told herself that people would come around. She felt defeated previously, but now her resolve was renewed. Her magic had helped the plants grow and thrive and soon all Greenspring would have something green in their house or business. She was sure of it.

Oracle rearranged some pots and plants and took stock of her items. She thought it was about time to close the shop, and she was eager to head to Atmir's and share her day. She wondered how his day had been. She had put away her ledger and intended to change the sign to 'Closed' when the doorbells chimed again. *One more customer,* she thought.

"Oracle Moss. This is quite the shop you have. Blooms and Moss? Not so original, but it suffices," the reedy voice said. Oracle looked up at the person in her doorway. He was short - shorter than her - and wide. He wore long robes of black with blue accents. He also wore several rings and necklaces. The hood on his robe was up, but it didn't obscure his face. Oracle couldn't help herself and made a face. The man let the door shut behind him and took his hood down.

"Not happy to see your old friend? I thought you would be pleased to see someone civilized since you moved into this backwater. What are you doing here? I had heard you'd opened a plant store like your mother, but I hadn't realized how bad it was. Not in the game any-more?"

"What are you doing here Zevan? Or whatever name you're using," Oracle said.

"You can always call me Zevan, Oracle. You know I like it when you say my name," the man gave a grin akin to a snake that's found an egg. He stepped a little further into the shop.

"More reason for me not to use it. What do you want? Why are you here?" Oracle asked impatiently. Noodle started inching its way toward Zevan, perceptible only if you knew where to look. A lone tendril creeped silently down from the rafters.

"I just thought you'd need some comfort. I heard what happened to your last team." The words stung Oracle, but she fortified herself with the distaste she felt. Zevan continued after letting the words sink in. "I didn't think it was your fault. But there are some rumors about you.

Thought you might like to know what's being said. It's all untrue, of course."

"Zevan, we know this is a song and dance, but for what purpose? Get to the point," Oracle growled. Zevan stopped looking at her and reached up to touch the vines snaking around the room. Snaking toward him without his notice.

"A shuddering vine plant? These are fun. They almost never stop moving like the wind has them. A bit annoying when you mistake the movements for ghosts from the past though, isn't it?" He sneered at her.

"That's not a - never mind. What do you want, Zevan? I'm asking for the last time."

"A threat? That's unlike you," Zevan raised his hands, palms out to face her. "Ok, I give in. I need you. My team and I need you for a contract we took. It took a little bit to track you down, but when I found out you were planted in a small village, pun intended, I figured I'd come offer you the help you need. After your last team's demise, I thought you'd be happy to be in a team again. We're probably the only ones that will have you, you see. Word's gotten around. You know how people talk. Anyway, we wanted to give you the opportunity to work with us. In exchange, you help us on this contract. After that you can decide if you want to stay or go."

Oracle couldn't help herself, and let out a laugh. Zevan, surprised, raised his hands a little to prepare himself, unsure of what to expect from Oracle.

"Wait a minute. You came all this way to ask me to help you and your friends on a contract? You think I need saving from plants? And you thought I'd help *you* of all people? The backstabbing, sniveling rat who spent more energy on sabotaging his peers than actually studying magic? Does *your team* know what a piece of work you are?"

"Listen, water under the bridge, right? I'm just here to help you get out of this place. After losing your team I thought you'd be grateful to join any team that offered, let alone one of our caliber."

"Grateful? I'll be grateful when you get out of here. I don't need your help and I don't care if you genuinely need mine. You and your team can kick rocks for all I care!" Noodle had snaked very close to Zevan. Oracle noticed, but kind of wondered what would happen if Noodle got closer. Zevan didn't notice anything amiss. Noodle was mostly behind him.

"You know what? I was right about you. You're nothing without your mentor. That's why you're hiding here, *gardening*, instead of doing actual work. This town is going to pay for your mistakes just like your team did."

Oracle's hands lifted. Zevan's eyes widened. Broom skittered toward a corner as if it knew something was about to happen. She was about to do something drastic. Zevan raised his hands to counter her but instead he shrieked. Noodle had grabbed him and forced him backward toward its pot. In a matter of seconds most of Zevan was entangled in vines. He started to fight back but was bound tightly. A good mage could do some spells without saying the words to it, but anything with actual power needed the words. Zevan's mouth was clamped shut and most of his head had vines already wrapped around it. His eyes bugged out. Then Oracle smelled it - the acrid odor of burning flesh. Noodle was somehow *burning* Zevan. The little soft spikes that grew out of each vine were now glowing like embers. Zevan couldn't scream, but his frantic eyes said he was trying.

"Aquarius!" Oracle yelled and rushed over to Noodle and Zevan. She began to pry at the vines. Aquarius rushed over as fast as his little legs would carry him. He began to douse Zevan and the plant as best as he could from the floor. It didn't look as if the plant could consume him, but anything was possible at the moment. When prying at the vines didn't work, Oracle started to panic, trying harder to pull them off and failing.

"Don't start panicking!" Aquarius yelled at her, "Oracle! Focus!"

Oracle stopped and took a deep breath. She tried to steady her mind and focused on the plant. Zevan passed out, from the shock or the pain, Oracle wasn't sure. She closed her eyes and focused on the plant. She felt enraged and did what she could to tamp that down. She thought about things that made her happy, including her plants and her friends. She breathed deep. She counted and counted again. She thought of tranquil things and did her best to let the rage flow out and die down. She finally felt the rage subside and opened her eyes when she heard a soft thump.

Noodle had released Zevan, who crumpled in a heap on the floor in front of the door. The vines lethargically moved themselves back across the entryway ceiling rafters, as if it had been there the whole time. It settled down, not even a quiver. Oracle looked at Zevan.

Zevan had lots of little burn holes through his clothes and circular marks across his face where Noodle had scorched him. His clothes drooped soggily where Aquarius had hit him with water. Oracle nudged him with a foot. He didn't stir. Tentatively she leaned over him. She studied him and saw he was breathing. She released a big breath herself. She looked at Aquarius, who was staring up warily at the vines above him.

"I never thought that would happen," Oracle said.

"I warned you something bad would happen with that plant," Aquarius stated plainly.

"It reacted to my anger. I lost my temper, and it reacted. It moved *so fast*. Did you see that?" Oracle was looking at the vine plant now with curiosity and caution. She reached out a hand to feel the vine. It felt fleshy and ambient temperature, but not hot. It felt just like any other vine plant would.

"I did see that, and I'm terrified of it now. I was just scared before. It burned him, Oracle. Do you think that has anything to do with your powers? The plant is supposed to be unique to each person that plants it." Aquarius moved halfway across the room, out of reach of Zevan and Noodle.

"It must be. I don't have any explanation for why it would do that. Or how," Oracle said in amazement.

"Flip the sign to 'Closed'. We don't want to explain what happened
here."

Oracle flipped the sign to 'Closed' and then looked down at Zevan
again. Again, she prodded him with a foot. He made no sound or
movement.

"Aquarius, I know I shouldn't do this, but would you get the burn
salve from my pack? He won't have any. This rock-for-brains studied
air magic. He probably has a kite in his pack."

Aquarius didn't say a word and returned with a tin the size of
Oracle's palm. She took it and put it inside one of Zevan's pockets.
Then she cast a drying spell that made his clothes dry again. She didn't
bother to try to repair the burn holes. Instead, she walked up toward his head and scooped him up under the arms. She dragged him
across the shop to the back door, carefully but not altogether success-
fully avoiding her plants. She opened the door and pulled Zevan into
the back alley where she unceremoniously let him plop back to the
ground. He stirred.

"Get up Zevan," Oracle commanded. He didn't move at first and
she nudged him with her foot. "Get *UP* Zevan!"

His eyes opened and he laid in the alley staring. He took stock of
his appendages and then sat up.

"Ow."

"You have some ointment in your pocket. Consider it an act of
goodwill. Get out of Greenspring and leave me alone," Oracle said
fiercely.

Zevan gently touched his face, wincing and groaning each time he
hit a burn mark that now blistered, which was often. Oracle moved
back to the door and opened it.

"You can't even control your plants. No wonder you failed at adventuring. You're a liability," Zevan muttered. He stood up and felt in
his pocket the salve Oracle had put there.

"If I hear one more thing from you, I'm going to send *something else*
after you. Leave!"

Oracle slammed the door and locked it, leaving Zevan in the dark alley to tend his wounds.

13. I Want to Leave

The books Oracle had gotten at Lady Lady's turned out to be help-ful, but it didn't solve the sigil problem. Rosewater's Guide to Curses: Symbols and Sigils Edition had given Oracle a good idea that the sigil was *not* a curse. That was a relief. It still didn't tell her exactly what it was, but what she could gather from Rosewater's Guide was that it might be some kind of ward, or possibly a containment sigil. Two opposites the guide was not helpful in distinguishing. Oracle had written her mentor, but he would take some time to get back to her, not including the time it would take for him to find what she needed, if he could.

The book on identifying plants, on the other hand, had been really helpful. Atmir and Oracle had taken an afternoon to forage and they used the book to find some new things to try in teas. Atmir had a variety of new ingredients to try and would be quite busy with that. Oracle had promised to come by and help when she could.

The necklace of plant speaking had been a boon ten times over. Every day Oracle activated the necklace and spent an hour talking to as many of her plants as possible. She used their simple feedback to give them exactly what they needed. Most of the plants replied with simple one word answers, or simple two word phrases. "I'm dry", "Too Wet", "Roots hurt", "Happy", "Pain", "Tired", were some of the plants phrases and words she heard often. The exception, like so many times, was Noodle.

Green tendrils had crept across the ceiling crawling in all directions. They used the rafters for support. The long vines had short, stubby protrusions on them that had a slight brownish red color on the tips. Most of the time they hung inert, dangling like any other vine would. Except when Oracle was feeling a particularly strong emotion, like now. Oracle was frustrated, which made Noodle quiver and Aquarius uneasy. Aquarius tried to avoid Noodle but its massive volume and number of vines made it almost impossible.

When Oracle spoke with Noodle, it replied back with short phrases as well, but also would *ask* questions. It would ask how Oracle was. If it could have a treat – sugar water. If she would move the pot a little bit. "Move to sun" or "You well?" it would say. Of course, nobody else could hear what the plants were saying because they didn't have the necklace. It was very creepy at first, but Oracle got used to communicating with Noodle and the other plants. When she told Aquarius he had something snarky to say about it, of course. Noodle had asked "Why scared?" and "Aquarius friends" but it didn't persuade the little blue not-dragon of its magnanimous nature.

The shop itself had its ups and downs, like Oracle. Some days the shop was really busy with plant buyers. Other days it was quiet. The worst day yet was when someone came in to yell at Oracle, curse the plants, and generally be mad about a mage in town. Oracle didn't recognize the man, and didn't know why it had taken him so long to make his displeasure known. Her friends had defended her, which made her insides warm despite her own anger toward the man for his outburst. Noodle was precariously close to snatching the man up, but Oracle had gotten a hold of her anger before that happened.

She recognized that Noodle had very slowly crept near the man, winding a tendril of vine around his shoulder, and since she was worried about what it would do, she did her best to stay calm and shuffled the man out the door as best as she could. The vine snapped back easily, and the confused man brushed it off him with vigor. Oracle had shown the man the door and since his tirade hadn't so much as visibly

ruffled a feather, he left. Noodle the vine plant was probably dangerous she finally admitted to herself, but not dangerous to her. Oracle
decided it was probably worth keeping around just in case.

Oracle was feeling particularly low since the shop had a string of
things go wrong recently. Someone painted 'Go Away Mage' on the
window. It had taken the better part of the day to get rid of it, even
with help. An anonymous letter detailing the crimes of mages around
the world was slipped under the door one night. And business had
been very slow to basically dead for the last couple of days, except
for her regulars. Oracle wondered if there wasn't some kind of threat
against her clients for shopping here. She wasn't sure how to investigate that, or if she had the mental and emotional capacity to take
something else on. A few of her plants had withered overnight and
died, the other plants couldn't tell her why, and the few ones that were
looking sickly could only say "drain" or nothing at all. She felt very
much like an outsider despite the friends she had made. A failing outsider.

After closing Rosewater's Guide and reviewing her notes at her little desk, she sighed and rested her head in her hands. The sigil was
gnawing at her, but it wasn't the most important thing to be dealt
with. Her customer base, her failed attempts to grow anything outside, the dying and sick plants all needed her attention more. The sigil
just had a hold of her brain, but she wasn't getting very far with it.

Oracle stood up and announced to the room at large, which was
empty save Aquarius, that she was going to the Guiding Light and
would be back later. Aquarius was lounging in the dirt of a potted
plant in the sunspot from the skylight. He barely acknowledged the
announcement and continued warming himself.

Oracle walked down to the tea shop considering her day. She had
spilled an entire bag of fertilizer while trying to transfer it to smaller
bags. She had sheared a plant wrong and made it so ugly she wanted to
throw it out. She had even broken a stack of empty pots by knocking

them over. Today had been a rough day and she was looking forward to an uplifting tea.

It was evening, after the late afternoon rush. She would get to talk to Atmir for a while before the last customers came in for a bedtime tea. She would stay today to help make teas and get her mind off her own worries. She arrived and went in, the doorbells sang, and her nostrils filled with a sweet scent with something spicy in it. She inhaled deeply and let it settle in her lungs.

"A new brew?" she asked, walking to the counter.

"Newish," Atmir said from behind the counter. He had his notebook out and several ingredient bowls in front of him. On the stove there were two kettles of water, and on the counter two more containers with tea components in them. Atmir measured and noted carefully. He didn't look up at her, which meant he was focused.

"What is it?" Oracle asked as she went around the corner to read his notes.

"It's a new take on an old recipe. I'm subbing the Emspice for these peppercorns, and using a green leaf variant we found that's dried. The variant is a replacement for the ones I have to order in. If it works, that will save me some money."

"And what's this called? What's it supposed to do?"

"It's called Emberright Tea. And if I told you what it does, that would take some fun out of it."

"I have to be the taste tester?" She asked dourly.

"Well, I'm not going to be the first to try it," he joked.

"I like how you have confidence in your abilities. It's really inspiring," Oracle said with a straight face. They looked at each other for a moment and then burst with laughter.

"I'll try it. I'm sure it's totally safe, right?" She leaned against the countertop and let her arm brush against Atmir's. He didn't move it away.

"Totally," Atmir agreed. Atmir took another note down and prepared one more tea with what he had measured. Then he took out a mug and poured his brew for Oracle into it. Oracle smelled the tea first and gave her critique to Atmir. Atmir leaned on the counter and watched Oracle without hardly blinking. He leaned on his elbows which made him almost eye to eye with her standing there.

"Ok, so it smells spicy and sweet, but I'm not sure about that peppery scent. I hope it doesn't taste peppery. That would be off-putting, I think. Is there fruit in here? Why does it smell so sweet?" Oracle held the mug just under her nose and gave the tea a swirl.

"A little honey and a small amount of berries."

"Ok. Here goes," Oracle said and took a loud sip. "It's freaking hot!"

"I did just pour it not that long ago," an amused Atmir replied.

"I know, I know."

"I thought you couldn't be burnt. What did you think of this one?" Atmir was staring dreamily at Oracle, standing beside the forgotten tea notes and measuring spoons.

She took another sip, this time holding the tea in her mouth for a bit.

"It's not as sweet as it smells. And I was wrong. The peppery flavor is good. It kind of balances out the sweetness without being a complete opposite. It's subtly orange and berry and honeyed, with a peppery and cinnamon? – " Atmir nodded, " – taste. I like it. Now, to figure out what it does."

"Just wait a moment. Keep drinking."

Oracle complied and sipped the tea until it was gone. She set the mug down and waited, and waited.

"I don't think anything is happening? I don't feel anything."

Atmir frowned. He checked his notes.

"I'll have to work that out later. The latecomers are about to arrive, and I've got to get this cleaned up," he stood up straighter, indicating the tea ingredients and measuring spoons and containers on the counter.

"I'll help!" Oracle said cheerily, reaching for a container. When she moved she stumbled and spilled a container of water trying to catch herself. The water had splashed out on Atmir's shirt, his apron, the counter, and the floor soaking them all.

"I'm sorry! I didn't mean to do that!" Oracle said as she regained her balance. Another frustrating notch in Oracle's day had her feeling even more down. Her shoulders slumped and she sighed heavily.

"It's ok. I have another shirt. I'll just change and it'll be fine. Don't worry," Atmir said calmly.

"Ok. I'll clean up. Do you mind if I use a spell to help? It'll be faster."

"I don't mind. I'm going to change and then I'll help," Atmir took off his apron and hung it on a hook and reached behind the curtain into the small room Oracle had stayed that first night. He pulled out a shirt and set it behind him on the counter.

Oracle began the water cleaning spell. It would simply gather the water up and make a blob she could direct back into a container. She raised her hands and began the chant. Water from the floor rose up, water from the counter congealed and floated over to join the blob. Unexpectedly, Atmir's wet shirt began to float toward the blob. It was sitting on the counter and a shirtless Atmir was holding his dry shirt in his hands, about to put it on.

Oracle looked up at Atmir, then did a double take, losing her concentration. The water blob and wet shirt faltered in the air. The doorbell chimed and a few patrons walked in. Oracle, trying to regain her composure, turned back to the water blob and poured more magic into the spell to try to separate the water from the shirt. Which she did, but dropped the shirt onto the stove which caught it on fire. Oracle yelped and directed the blob of water at the flaming shirt, but it mostly evaporated in the hot flames.

Trying to think fast, she grabbed the end of the shirt off the stove, but she whipped it upward and her hands went into the shelves of Atmir's ingredients, knocking it upward off the supports and spilling jars of his tea components. Atmir dropped his shirt and went to catch the ingredients. Oracle dropped the flaming shirt and stamped it out, the crunch of glass and dried herbs could be heard beneath. It all happened in a matter of seconds.

Oracle looked at the smoking shirt and the mess of glass and ingredients. The patrons had gone quiet looking at the spectacle. Atmir had his arms full of the jars he had caught. It smelled like smoke.

"Are you ok?" He asked.

"Atmir. I'm-I'm so sorry," she stuttered. Tears filled in her eyes.

"It's fine. It'll be fine," he said. Oracle didn't believe him. A lot of supplies that were common to many of his teas were on the ground, ruined.

"No, it's not!" She burst out and let out a sob. She ran out the door and up the street not hearing his response. He tried to go after her, but only made it halfway out the door. He watched her run up the road and into the plant shop. He had patrons and a mess to clean. Not to mention he needed to put on his shirt still. He went back inside.

Oracle slammed through the door of the plants shop, alarming Aquarius. She went to run up the stairs but tripped and caught her foot on the ledge of the second stair and tore it off, pried upward. She fell down and let out a sob.

"Oracle what's wrong?" Aquarius shouted. Noodle the plant began to sway, agitated. Aquarius eyed it for a second and then turned back to Oracle who was picking herself up off the stairs, crying. "Oracle?"

"I've made a mess of things, Aquarius! I don't know if we should stay any more. I don't want to be here anymore." She cried harder. Aquarius climbed down from the plant he had been lazing in to approach Oracle.

"What's wrong? What happened?" He asked as he walked across the room.

"It's just...EVERYTHING!" She wailed and let out a new batch of tears. She sniffed and turned to sit on the fourth stair. Aquarius skittered over and went to climb up the stairs. He managed the first one fine, but the second one with the step torn up left a gap. A gap, Aquarius saw, that went *somewhere.* The step was hinged.

"Oracle," he said.

"Don't try to console me. I don't want to hear it, Aquarius. I want to get out of here –" Oracle wiped her eyes and blabbered on.

"Oracle."

"– We'll go back to the city and take small contracts, and we'll live with my mom until we get our footing again. We'll leave as soon as we can. I've done nothing right today. I'm an embarrassment. I can't even –"

"Oracle!" He said, finally raising his little voice.

"What?" She said sullenly.

"This goes somewhere."

"What? What does?" She sat up and looked over the peeled up step at him.

"Under the stair. Look. It's hinged."

Oracle tapped the step with her foot and it swung down with a clack, back into place. Back into looking like ordinary stairs. Oracle sniffed and stood up. She walked back down the stairs and flipped open the second stair again. It definitely was an open space that went somewhere.

"Maybe it has a basement?" Oracle offered.

"It looks as if it does. Should I climb in?" Aquarius asked.

"See if there's a handle or knob. Maybe it opens wider from the inside," Oracle said with a sniff.

Aquarius climbed inside and felt around the opening. Just a little beyond, about a forearm's length, was a lever. He reported that to Oracle, who reached in and pulled it. The staircase popped open on one side in a cloud of dust revealing that the first three steps swung to the right toward the front counter, like a door. Oracle and Aquarius coughed loudly as they choked on the dust. Below the stairs the floor had a handle and Oracle pulled it. It folded over flat two times revealing a staircase down.

"Just what I need to finish the day, a creepy staircase to a dark basement. Alchemist secrets, you think?" Oracle asked Aquarius. She wiped her puffy eyes and looked down the dark passage.

"It could be. Are you going to go down?" Aquarius asked, with just a hint of hesitation.

"What do you mean 'you?' *We* are going to go down," Oracle lit her palm and shone it down the stairwell. The passage twisted to the left and was full of dust and cobwebs. She didn't miss Aquarius' face. He would much rather go back to napping or watering plants than down the dark staircase. Nevertheless, she helped him climb onto her shoulder to ride down. He obediently took his perch.

The steps were stone here, and Oracle's footsteps made a soft click as she hit each one. When she made the left turn there were another eight or so steps into a room about half the size of the upstairs. It was a mess. There were old papers scattered on the floor, an extinguished candle in its holder on the floor, and an overturned chair. Oracle saw a desk, also covered in papers and a few books. She blew off the dust and looked at the title of one: 'A Primer to Alchemy.'

"It is Alchemist's secrets!" She said, her mood improving. "How did we not know this was here? How did nobody know this was here?"

"The Alchemist knew," Aquarius supplied.

"Very funny. I wonder if there's anything useful here?"

"Should we light a candle or lantern? Then you can have your hand back."

Oracle righted the overturned candle and lit it. She saw a few more candles in the room and took her time to light those as well. The space had gone unused for quite some time. She noticed an alembic on the table with dried substances in it. Some vials that also had dried substances stuck to the glass were spread on the desk. There was a chest and a storage cabinet also in the room as well as a long workbench scratched and worn that was mostly empty, save a few empty vials. A barrel stood in one corner.

Oracle let Aquarius down on to the desk. Then she inspected it a little closer. She gathered the dusty papers into a stack and put all the books in another stack. Under the papers and books was a well-used map, marked with inked notations. She recognized some of the places marked. She had been to some of those same places in her time adventuring.

"Aquarius, do you think the Alchemist went to all these places? There's quite a lot of them marked." She indicated a far mark on the map after locating Greenspring.

"Hard to say," Aquarius walked on the map, looking closely at the markings. "Maybe these places are where his components came from?"

"That's probably it. They were diligent in keeping track of where components came from so they wouldn't have to find new sources all the time. Must have gotten expensive to send adventuring parties out to some of these places. Look how far this one is," she said, pointing to another spot on the map.

She shuffled through the papers next, the stale smell invading her nostrils. A receipt, an invoice, another invoice – she couldn't tell if they had been paid or not – a recipe for sweet buns, a recipe for some kind of potion – it wasn't labeled – and a bunch of notes that looked like to-do lists. Toward the back of the stack there was a piece of paper folded in half. When she opened it, Oracle's eyes widened.

"It's a letter! Looks like it's to the Alchemist!" Oracle said excitedly.

"Well, what does it say?" Aquarius inspected the empty storage at the back of the desk, then walked back onto the map.

"Hold on, I'm reading it!"

Aquarius paced the map, looking at the places marked, softly he stomped his feet like a rampaging monster across a city. Oracle read the letter.

"Ok, the Alchemist's name was Carris. He was meant to go to the seaside town of Port Citrous in the south, but was delayed I guess. The letter writer, a person named Elandra – I'm assuming a woman – is basically wondering where the Alchemist is at and scolding him for not being at Port Citrous yet. It sounds joking, though, so I don't think the Alchemist was needed for anything serious. This letter sounds casual. Social even. Carris and Elandra must be friends."

"That's interesting. Do you suppose the Alchemist ever made it to Port Citrous?"

"We could write a letter and find out," Oracle said, then added quietly, "Or we could just go and find out."

"What else is in the papers?" Aquarius asked, attempting to distract her. He peered at the paper on top. Oracle looked at the last few of them. One was a recipe for a basic sleep potion, and one was a recipe for a basic medicine for an ache or pain. The last paper made Oracle jump.

"This is a letter from Carris to Elandra. It's unfinished though. Looks like a draft. There's a lot of scratch outs on it. It says…" Oracle trailed off as she read the letter. "It says they had something come up here and they were going to be to Port Citrous later than they had planned, but they were still coming. They had work to do here, but it sounds like something interrupted the work because that first part was scratched out and the next part says they're leaving as soon as they can pack. They indicate that it takes a long time to pack an alchemy workshop. Of course it does. And he would be to Port Citrous soon. The Alchemist addresses Elandra as 'my darling' so I guess they are more than friends."

"I wonder what business interrupted the Alchemist," Aquarius said. He had stopped stomping on the map and was looking for spiders to eat in the crevices and corners nearest him.

"The letter doesn't say. It looks like they packed up in a hurry, judging by the state of this place. I wonder if he took all the shop's ready potions with him. Can you imagine traveling so far with all that glass? No thank you," Oracle said. She set the papers back down on the desk and set her attention on the book stack.

"Let's see what we have here," She looked at the cover of each book. They were all basic alchemy books except for the last one. It didn't have a title and when Oracle opened it to look at the cover page she almost screamed. "It's a journal Aquarius! The Alchemist left a *journal* here. This is amazing!"

"Should we be touching that? What if it's been cursed?" Aquarius said and cautiously backed away from it.

"You think an Alchemist would curse their own journal?"

"You think an Alchemist doesn't have any secrets worth putting protection on?"

"I think if it was left here, it probably wasn't that important to the Alchemist and therefore, we don't have to worry about curses or traps."

"Suit yourself. I'm not helping you find a reversal though."

"Oh yes you would."

"Ok, but I won't do it without saying 'I told you so' many times during the time it takes to find a reversal." Aquarius went back to hunting spiders.

"I can live with that," Oracle said and opened the journal again to begin reading. The first entries were from the Alchemist's arrival in Greenspring.

I am enjoying this town already. Everywhere you look there is something green and blossoming. Maybe it's the time of year, but the flowers and blooms of fresh growth are giving me life. I am still mourning the loss of my friends, but Greenspring has me feeling renewed like I haven't felt since the accident. I am going to stay here and give up the adventurer's life. It's such a lovely little town. Big enough that I won't know everybody and I'll be able to find shop space, but small enough to be cozy and make some friends.

I've taken space next to a cobbler. He's a lively young man who inherited the business from his father. He's taken to come over and talk to me about my time in the world. He finds it strange I've travelled so much. I explained that is why I don't have much equipment with me. An alchemical adventurer is a tough profession. It was rewarding and I do miss it already. I plan to stay here for some time though. It's such a beautiful place. It sounds like I've come at the right time, too. There is a festival of healing taking place in the next month.

I've been told many people come to gather in the square and get a small blessing from – well, nobody actually knows what from. Or so the cobbler tells me. Anyone can go to the square at any time and get a blessing from this entity. It heals minor injuries – think a broken finger or a laceration, not anything life-threatening – and makes you feel uplifted for some time after. The townspeople make an offering of a special soup-like concoction. That whole thing is acutely disgusting. It's essentially a mix of fertilizers and compost fermented into a foul soup. They send the soup into special sections of the square and it disappears, and the blessing happens shortly after. A wild thing indeed. I intend to discover the secret behind this ritual. But not now. I am still settling in.

Today I was visited by an old friend, Cormander Bark. He wants me to join his party and continue to adventure, but I told him no. I am now settled here in Greenspring and have set up a workshop. I have stocked the shop above it with the most common of items people want. I do have a little section of more esoteric blends and useful potions for the traveling adventurers that sometimes wander into Greenspring, always on their way someplace else, thankfully. It's been peaceful here.

I'm working on a plant serum now. Greenspring is beautiful, but not all the plants thrive. I'm making a feeding serum that will help plants that are struggling to be resistant to whatever disease is striking them. I'm told the usual methods of saving the plants hasn't been working. A druid came in to look at some of them and offered advice. I think the serum will help, but not prevent the illness. There are a few local mages working on the problem as well. Nothing like a community effort! In truth, Greenspring is plenty green and growing. I think it just irks the locals when a plant turns brown and withers because they value and take such pride in their little town. Corman-

der was not happy with me, but he said he understood my reluctance to join him.

The feeding serum seems to work! It took about 4 iterations of the recipe to make sure it did, but it does. I now stock it in the shop. The recipe and my trial and error working on it are cataloged at the back of this book. I started it there, so I finished it there. It's a fairly easy thing to make, you just need a few supplies and brewing equipment. I don't even need the alembic for this. I'm starting to think there's something else afoot with the plants though. From my experiments, putting plants out and cataloguing their demise, I have determined they are dying in waves. Certain plants are dying all at once overnight. It's not the slow browning death of a mistreated plant, but an overnight withering. Very curious and disturbing. There is another odd happening. Some plants experience the opposite effect. They bloom and grow and fill up a space without regard to feeding or sunlight. I've had several plants nearly take over my main floor. Residents who experience this phenomenon chalk it up to Greenspring being a great place to grow things, but I'm not sold. This is odd behavior for plants. The two never occur at the same time either.

I received a letter from Elandra. She's moved to Port Citrous, south of Morkanth. She's told me how lovely it is and encouraged me to relocate there. It sounds like a quiet place as well. I'm not ready to leave Greenspring yet. The healing festival was great fun. I received a blessing as did many others. A cut I received down the length of my finger was restored, good as new. The effect was enduring. As with all festivals, there was a plethora of food and other vendors, dancing, music, and games. It was very lively. I enjoyed it. It's nice not having to worry about all that comes with adventuring. I think of my friends often, especially Tara, but I am quite satisfied with my life in Greenspring.

"Oracle, I've had my fill of spiders and I'm going upstairs," Aquarius hopped onto her lap. "Read the rest tomorrow. Or take it up with you. We still have a shop to run."

"You're right. I don't think we can hear the door from down here and I didn't flip the sign to 'Closed' when we came down." Oracle set the journal down after marking her place with a piece of paper. She stood up and stretched, putting Aquarius on her shoulder so he didn't plop onto the floor when she stood.

"Oracle?"

"Yes, Aquarius?"

"Why were you crying earlier?"

"I've embarrassed myself completely," She moaned.

"Do you still want to leave?"

"I don't think so. I don't want to show my face for a while, but I don't think I want to leave. I overreacted."

"I'm sorry. We can stay in the shop."

Oracle blew out the candles and hiked back up the stairs to the main shop. She closed up the secret entrance in the stairs. She thought about changing the sign and having a quiet evening alone in the shop, working with the plants. She flipped the sign from open to closed and continued to putter around after repotting all the plants that needed it. She had done almost all the regular work, and there wasn't much left to actually work on. The shop had been slow during the week and there wasn't much prep to do. The door opened and the bells chimed. She'd forgotten to lock the door.

"We're closed," Oracle said in an unwelcome tone.

"I can come back later," Atmir said softly.

Oracle stared at him and held her breath. Atmir looked right back at her. The silence was tangible.

"Are you ok?" Atmir asked, still standing by the door.

"Yes. I'm ok." Oracle said. She finally blinked and exhaled. "I'm really sorry about your shirt and your ingredients. And their containers." She looked away, pretending to check on Broom, who was sweeping as usual. Oracle admired the broom's ability to not care about a single thing except the dirt on the floor.

"It's just *stuff*, Oracle. I can replace it all." Atmir said. He stepped further inside the shop, away from the door.

"But I ruined so much. It's like everyone says, magic never goes well in Greenspring." Oracle threw her hands up.

"Beatran is an old gossip. She's never met a mage before you and is just telling you things she heard in old stories to have something to say and seem like a wise old lady. Trust me. Beatran isn't right about a lot of things. Especially that. And Harrad is just a grump."

"I – "Oracle fell silent.

"I promise it's fine, Oracle. There's no real damage. The Guiding Light is intact, all the furniture is fine. What's a few ingredients? I can order them in. We can get more on seventh day or another day. The glass I can replace tomorrow in town. It's fine. Really." Atmir crossed the rest of the way over to her and wrapped her in a hug. She started to cry again. "It's really fine. I promise it's not a big deal."

She cried into his shirt for a little while. His hug was solid and she let herself be engulfed by his strong body. She didn't know why she was crying so hard. She leaned back with her arms still around him and sniffed but didn't wipe her eyes.

"Now I owe you two shirts," she said with a stuffy laugh, her eyes puffy and red again.

"I can wash this one," Atmir said with a smile. "Are you sure you're ok? You're not going to disappear in the night or anything?"

"I promise not to disappear in the night."

"Can you promise not to disappear during the day either?"

She laughed, still sullen. "Ok, I promise not to disappear."

He let go of her and she wiped her eyes.

"Want to know a secret?" She asked.

"You know that I would love to hear one."

"This place has a basement."

"Where? There's no stairs down." Atmir looked around the room.

"Yes, there are. They're *hidden* stairs." Oracle said with a mischievous grin.

"No!"

"Yes! And below the shop, in the hidden basement, I found some of the Alchemist's things. Notes, and letters, and books, and even a journal."

"You didn't touch the journal, did you?" He said seriously. Atmir looked concerned.

"I tried to warn her!" Aquarius shouted from across the room.

"I did touch it. I read some of it. And there is some very interesting content."

"Like what?"

Oracle sniffed again.

"Can I tell you over tea?"

"Of course you can," Atmir embraced Oracle again, looking deep into her eyes. She looked up at him a little too long. At that moment, he leaned down and kissed her. She kissed him back. When they broke apart, he grinned and she looked a little flustered.

"I just wanted to make sure that we're on the same page," he said.

"That's – ah – you're – I think – we are, yes."

He leaned in and kissed her again slowly.

"Yes. That's probably the same page," Oracle said, now grinning at him.

"Should I try again to make sure?"

"Maybe," Oracle said coyly. "Ok. Yes. You have to lean again down because I can't levitate up to you."

Atmir laughed and leaned in.

14. Attican Braun

This morning was overcast and dreary, unlike the consistent sunshine they'd been having. Aquarius and Oracle had slept a little late today, but felt refreshed when they awoke. They plodded down the stairs together, Aquarius chose to scale the walls instead of the stairs, and Oracle set out his breakfast. She walked over to flip her sign to "Open" and unlock the door. She took in the clouds for a moment through the door's window and wondered if it might rain.

She peered down the street for potential customers or regulars heading her way. She saw only a lone man, older, with a wispy white beard and beautiful deep blue robes lined with gold and gold stitching. Oracle recognized the man. The man recognized Oracle peering out the window and waved when he saw her. She smiled and held the door for him as he approached. Even though he was old, he was still nimble. Age hadn't gotten to his bones and joints yet.

"Oracle Moss. It seems you have performed a miracle here in Greenspring," the man said by way of greeting.

"Professor Braun. What are you doing here?" Oracle asked, not able to hide her excitement. She backed up and let the man inside.

"I had heard about the loss of your team. My condolences. I had also heard strange rumors of my very promising student giving up the adventurer's life for gardening," he said and looked around the shop, still smiling pleasantly.

"It isn't exactly gardening, Professor," Oracle replied shyly.

"Please, Oracle. Call me Attican. I'm not your professor anymore."

The man took a few more steps into the shop and looked around at the plants. He touched a few leaves on some of them. When he heard the scratching of Broom he looked up and grinned.

"A self-sweeping broom! Did you make it?" He asked, stepping closer to Broom.

"I found it. Do you know anything about them?" Oracle walked over and stood next to him. Broom continued to sweep across the room.

"Found it! What a find. I've seen them before. I know they take some clever magic to make, but I have never done it. I've never tried too hard, however. Usually, they are bound to a house or manor of sorts and can't pass the threshold. No good to sweep the grounds outside." He said, amused.

"Actually, I found it outside. In the forest. It was sweeping leaves. Did you know they communicate?"

"Do they now?" Attican curiously watched Broom sweep.

"Broom, stop. Stop!" Oracle commanded. The broom stopped. Oracle approached. "This is my mentor, Attican Braun. Do you know him?"

Sweep sweep.

"That's a no. Do you like it here?"

Little bow.

"That's a yes. I can't ask it anything more advanced than yes or no questions, but it's reliable in its answers. It can follow too. That's how it got back here. Followed me out of the forest. It seems content to sweep all day. Sometimes all night, too."

"That's quite curious. May I ask it questions?"

"Of course."

"What is its name?"

"I just call it Broom."

"I know where to start then," He said walking up to Broom. "Do you have a name?"

Little bow.

"Is it 'Broom?'"

Little bow.

"Would you like a different name?"

Sweep sweep.

"Do you get tired of sweeping?"

Little bow.

"Very interesting," Attican mused. "Does it ever stop sweeping on its own?"

"Sometimes, yes. It puts itself in the corner, but not for long," Oracle said. "I can't make it stop sweeping or it gets upset."

"Have you always been a broom?" Attican continued.

Sweep sweep.

Oracle's mouth dropped open, and Attican smiled sympathetically.

"Is this a curse?"

Sweep sweep.

"A mistake of some kind?"

Little bow.

"Do you need help?"

Little bow.

"Well then, Oracle. I think you have another problem to solve," Attican looked at Oracle over his shoulder. "If it wasn't always a broom, and this is not a curse but a mistake, what could that mean?"

"Do you suppose it was a mage that's had an accident? But wouldn't it have a name then? It indicated it didn't have one. One besides Broom."

"Unfortunately, I am not here to solve mysteries, my dear," Attican stopped looking at the broom, which started back sweeping, and instead turned to Oracle.

"What are you here for?" she asked.

"You."

"Me?"

"Yes."

"What do you want with me? To have traveled so far means it must be important."

"I need to engage in your services," Attican said, folding his hands in front of him.

"My...services? You want me to grow something for you?" Oracle asked, nonplused. He laughed heartily, and Oracle was a little embarrassed.

"No, my dear. I need your fire expertise. I need a relic, and I am hand picking a team of adventurers to descend into a fiery pit, so to speak, to retrieve it. The relic is guarded by a special contraption that requires a bit of wit and a lot of fire. I immediately thought of you. I have already sent people to investigate; I just need someone capable to retrieve it for me."

"Is that why Zevan was here?" Oracle crossed her arms.

"Zevan?"

"Yes. He came to see me to get me to work with him. I refused." She uncrossed her arms.

"Wise choice," Attican said. "No, not Zevan. I haven't seen him since before you left. He went off to study somewhere else. Last I heard of him he was still a mediocre mage, but had gathered some favor with a party that needed one. My knowledge of him ends there."

"Well, he probably won't be coming back after our chat."

"I don't want to know," Attican said, examining a leaf on a nearby plant.

"And I won't bore you with the details," Oracle said wryly. "So, what is this relic?"

"It's an ancient scroll that an incredibly old fire dragon produced once. That's why the contraption requires fire to open. It's also meant to be a little bit of a puzzle. If I recall, you were very sharp when it came to thinking on your feet and working out puzzles. So, when the team I hired returned to me with the details, I immediately thought of you. There was just one problem."

"What?"

"I had no idea where you were. The letter you wrote to me failed to mention it. I apologize for not finding the related book you needed. There are a lot of books at my disposal. You understand." Attican started to wander the shop. He examined and touched plants as he went. He even smelled one.

"I do. Maybe if you do find something you can send it to me. Sorry for not mentioning where I relocated. Someone must have figured it out and spread it around though. How else would Zevan find me?" Oracle followed Attican a few steps behind.

"Indeed, someone did. The wizard you last worked for had come to the city looking for another team to harvest the wyrm you destroyed," he said, then added gently, "and recover the bodies." Oracle blinked a few times and balled her fists. Attican continued. "He described the affair and how you were the sole survivor. He wasn't clear on the details, but had assumed you'd had an accident. He said you had walked off into the night afterwards, and he hadn't seen you since. I took it upon myself to ask your mother – "

"My mother! Zevan had to have visited her. Oh, ick," Oracle said, "I don't want to imagine him anywhere near my family."

"I'm sure he did, but your mother can handle herself. He must have seen the correspondence you wrote, as did I. Your mother chased me out, much the same she must have done to Zevan. She didn't hide your letters though. They were plain on her desk and it was easy enough to see that it was you. And that you were in a place called Greenspring. She needs to work on her security measures." Attican smiled warmly.

"My mother left my letters out and you read them?" Oracle said with a hint of embarrassment.

"Not quite. I browsed through them when she was distracted and gleaned the name Greenspring and various tidbits about plants and growing them. I pieced together where Greenspring was exactly and came looking for you. To my amazement, here you are, healthy and growing plants. An unusual trade in a place that can't grow anything," he said knowingly.

"You have done some research," Oracle replied.

"I have."

"So, you want me to go with an adventuring party to retrieve an ancient dragon's magic scroll?"

"That's the sum of it, yes." Attican stopped again to sniff a plant. Oracle watched him, amused.

"Who are these adventurers?" She asked. Attican looked at Oracle.

"Very seasoned professionals. They have been together an exceedingly long time and are much older than you. Their experience is very valuable, and I trust their judgement and their talents." He looked her directly in the eyes.

"Child minders, then?" Oracle crossed her arms.

"No. Guardians, maybe. You're not a child, Oracle." Attican turned and felt the waxy leaf of a nearby plant between his finger and thumb.

"It must cost a lot to hire these people."

"It does indeed," he said, feeling another leaf and examining underneath it.

"And what is the reward? I can't just up and leave. I have a shop to run," Oracle said with a smile. Her brain flitted briefly to Atmir and then away again.

"Lots of coin, of course. A spot in the history books, maybe. A parade perhaps? Honestly, Oracle, you could probably name your price." Attican had turned again to look Oracle in the eye.

"It's that important?"

"It is that important."

Oracle considered for a moment. Then she decided she couldn't decide.

"I need time to think about this. When do you need to know?"

"There's little urgency, so take your time. I am staying the night in town and then starting the return journey tomorrow. You may post a letter with your response if necessary. Or you can show up at my door. You're always welcome." He patted Oracle on the shoulder and headed for the door. As he walked out, Atmir walked in.

"A customer this early? You never thought you'd be this busy, did you? What's wrong?" Atmir saw Oracle's face and became concerned.

"That was my mentor. Former mentor, I guess. I studied under his guidance for a long time."

"Was it not a welcome visit?" Atmir came in and stood right in front of Oracle.

"It was...unexpected. That's all." She thought about Attican smelling the plant. "He offered me a job."

"A job?" Atmir asked.

"Yeah. Kind of an important one. It would require my fire abilities and travel. I'd be gone a long time."

"Are you considering this?"

"I am."

"Oh."

"I need to think about it some more, it sounds like it could be very dangerous. I'm not sure if I am ready for that kind of danger again," Oracles said after a long pause.

"Would tea help? I brought you something special. I have been working on using those iridescent mushrooms you brought me and I think I have something worked out with them. Since I have so few I've been sparse with them. I have the result and I think you'll really like it."

Atmir brought out a sachet of tea and held it so Oracle could see. It had little iridescent bits in the mix, making it seem like the sachet was sparkling.

"Will it turn me into a vampire?" Oracle asked in a low voice.

"Do you want to be a vampire?"

"No."

Atmir put his arm around her shoulders, leading her toward the counter. She didn't mind and let him guide her.

"Good. And no, it won't turn you into a vampire."

Oracle took a long look at the handsome man with his arm wrapped around her shoulders. Adventure was what she wanted to do for so long, but the loss she had suffered made her scared to commit to that life again. She thought she had the right amount of adventure here, with little quests and a mystery that could satisfy the itch that gnawed at her. Was that enough of a tether? Was that enough excitement to keep her planted? Oracle admitted to herself that even though she didn't really want to leave adventuring behind, she also didn't want to leave Atmir behind either. She enjoyed her little shop and her little group of friends, too. What did that mean?

She wanted to say something to him, about how important he was to her, about how much she liked their time together, what a solid person both figuratively and literally he was, and about how she really would like to spend all her time with him because her heart beat a little faster any time he was around, and she really liked the feeling. She couldn't do it though. Instead, she stared for a bit too long.

"Are you ok?" Atmir asked, concerned again.

"I'm fine. Yes, let's do the not-a-vampire tea."

15. Festival Talk

The cloud covered sky didn't offer much light today. Oracle lit a few candles to brighten the space a little bit. The plant shop regulars had brought her a cup of Atmir's tea with theirs this morning. She hadn't seen Atmir much lately, mostly because she had been too embarrassed to go to the tea shop but partially because the regulars regularly brought her tea. She had felt a simple sort of *want* when given her mug. Maybe she would save it and make him come get it back. Or maybe she could leave on the pretense of returning it. Normally one of the regulars brought it back with theirs on departure, but she could hide hers with enough ease.

Oracle rearranged a display with small plants on it, while the group chatted happily behind her. Her group had become her friends. Adam often watched the shop so Oracle could run errands midday. Indy would come in and help repot or propagate sometimes when she wasn't working. Jenna and Edalyn would often come to the seventh day market with Oracle to help her carry items while they shopped for themselves. Tullus was a fixture in the shop, offering sage advice you could only get from an elder. She appreciated them more than they could know.

Their chats had become a sort of soundtrack to her mornings. The rhythmic sweeping of Broom and the chatter of her friends was a pleasant melody. Oracle carefully rearranged the plants on the display and listened to her friends talk. When she was done, she took her tea mug and sat down with them. It had become its own ritual, only disturbed by customers coming in, and Oracle found she missed it on days nobody made it in. It was unusual to have an empty shop now because of her friends almost always being there.

"What do you guys think of the healing festival?" She asked at a pause in the conversation.

"What healing festival?" Tullus asked. He gave Aquarius a piece of dried fruit.

"The one that used to take place here. Have you never heard about it? I figured if you all knew of the Alchemist, maybe the festival was also remembered."

"We've never heard of such things," Tullus said, "I'd remember."

Oracle looked at the others.

"I've never heard of a healing festival," Jenna said and everyone agreed, except Adam.

"I have, actually," he said. Indy sat forward to give him her full attention. Her full attention always made him talk faster and stumble with his words. "I c-copied a m-manuscript once. It h-had something in it about a festival of healing."

"What did it say?" Oracle asked.

"Not a lot," Adam shrugged, "I-it only mentioned the f-festival. There w-weren't any details."

"So, what is this festival? And how did you find out about it?" Jenna asked.

"A long time ago when Greenspring was still green, there was a healing festival once a year. There was an offering made. You know those weird spout-looking things in the square? They'd pour a peculiar mixture down those as an offering and soon after everyone was sort of blessed with minor healing. The type that fixes broken fingers and minor cuts and bruises. I don't think it healed diseases or anything severe," Oracle responded then sipped her tea.

"So, no regrowing legs or arms or replacing eyeballs," Indy said. Everyone gave a little laugh, and Adam looked at Indy as he did.

"I don't have a lot of information, but to my knowledge, no. No re-growing eyeballs," Oracle said.

"Makes you wonder what's under the square. Where did the offer-ings go?" Edalyn asked.

"Into the dirt. The square has to be built on solid ground to take the weight of all the townspeople," Tullus said in his deep voice.

"The spouts could be connected to a pipe of some kind, leading it away somewhere," offered Jenna.

"Nonsense," Tullus replied, which made Oracle smile. Tullus had a stubborn mind and it was hard to change it, but she had seen him change with the right information before.

"Maybe the spouts hold the mixture until it can evaporate?" Adam said.

"That is a good idea," Indy said. She reached out and patted his arm. Adam's cheeks only pinked this time.

"Thanks," he said quietly.

"I don't know if it would evaporate. It sounds like the concoction was pretty gross – rotted food and other decaying things," Oracle said.

"Sounds disgusting," Tullus said.

"I'm sure it was. It sounds a little bit like the fertilizer I make. I don't put rotting food in mine though. That sounds like too much to me. I do think it's related to something I discovered earlier though, about a plant that lived under the square." Oracle took a sip of her tea, letting the savory flavor settle in her mouth. While many of Atmir's teas had minor magical properties, some of them didn't. Atmir was generally careful not to provide Oracle with tea that would interfere with her work. She waited.

"A plant?" Edalyn asked.

"Yes. I read some folklore in Harrad's about a plant, gifted by a god, that lived under the square. Well, it lived in the square before ours was built. I *think* the spouts must be connected."

"Why do you think the plant stopped giving blessings?" Indy asked. "Could it have died?"

"I'm not sure, yet. I've been looking into it. I think it's related to a symbol I found while out with Atmir foraging, but I can't be sure yet. I've been researching the symbol and what it does, but nothing conclusive came up. Or hasn't yet," Oracle took another sip of tea, looking around at the group.

"That's fascinating," Indy said.

"Did you also learn about the festival that way?" Adam asked.

"I found a different book that mentioned the festival, but didn't have a lot of information about it," Oracle replied.

"What else happened at the festival? Do you know?" Jenna asked, completely ignoring Oracle's explanation. Oracle didn't bring it up again.

"I imagine regular festival activities. There would probably be food, dancing, music, and maybe other entertainment?" Oracle suggested.

"We don't have any festivals. Have you been to many?" Indy asked Oracle.

"I've been to a few. There's a large one in my hometown and a few smaller ones throughout the year. Sometimes they aren't that fun. Too crowded and easy picking for pick pockets and the like. The city is dangerous that way." Oracle replied.

"I don't think any of us have been to one," Edalyn commented.

"I have," Tullus said. They turned to look at him, but he didn't elaborate.

"Do you want to tell us about it, Tullus?" asked Adam after they all waited a moment for Tullus to continue.

"It was in a city a long time ago," Tullus started in his usual way. "I was on a leave. I think the name of the city was Chapel Peak. It used to be called Dragon Peak, until the dragon was defeated. It took a large army to defeat that dragon. I wasn't there when it happened. Too young. But the dragon would take people from the city and destroy things. I think it was only a town then. It didn't get to be a city until the dragon was defeated and the population could grow some."

"Tullus," Edalyn said gently, "What of the festival?"

"What festival?"

"The one in the city. Chapel Peak?"

"Oh right," Tullus cleared his throat and continued. "They had a festival to mark the dragon's defeat. I was on leave of sorts. I was sent with a message to the local authorities about a possible conscription. I was supposed to wait until the festival was over, but since I arrived early I got to spend time there. The authorities wouldn't be pleased with the news, so I was instructed to wait until after the festival. There was a duke in charge of the whole city. He had a palace, which didn't really sit right with me. Rulers should be of the people. This whole idea of – "

"Tullus?" Indy interrupted.

"What?"

"The festival. What was it like?"

"They had a festival to mark the dragon's defeat. The town was called Dragon Peak until the dragon was defeated. Then it grew into a city and they renamed it Chapel Peak."

"Yes, you've said," Edalyn took a turn now. "What was the *festival* like? Was there music? Dancing?"

"Sure there was. The crowd of people was very large, and the general feeling was happy. No. Joy. Joy is a better word for it. Everywhere you went people were singing, dancing, eating, and laughing. I remember one fella who had too much to drink. He fell over trying to–"

"Oracle?" Jenna interrupted, "What was your festival like?"

"Oh, um…it was good. Like Tullus said, there were always a lot of food vendors, and it's a bit like seventh day market except there's way more people and more dancing and singing. There's always a lot of bards. There used to be a big parade that went through town. People would perform tricks like acrobatic feats. There were stage plays and street plays. Puppet shows. All of them telling the story of the reason for the festival. In the city I grew up in, it was a celebration of defending against invaders from – I don't know – several hundred years ago.

We were told it's so we wouldn't forget. Nobody has, to my knowledge, forgotten we defeated them. It happens every year and we learn about it growing up from whoever is in charge of our education."

"So, it wasn't dangerous or anything?" Adam asked.

"I like a little bit of danger," Indy said suggestively to Adam, who missed her motive entirely. Everyone else pretended not to hear.

"It wasn't dangerous like meeting a beast in the dark is dangerous. You could get drunk and end up without your belongings. Or a cut purse could come by your coins without your consent. Sometimes fights would break out, but generally everyone is there to have a good time. Festivals are fun."

"Drinking, dancing, and food," Indy said wistfully.

"That sounds lovely," Edalyn said agreeably. The door chimed and an older man walked in. Oracle got up and greeted him.

"Welcome!"

"Thanks. I'm looking for something, but I'm not sure what. Can I just look around a bit?"

"Of course. If you have questions or need help please tell me and I will sort you out," Oracle said with a smile. She'd been practicing toning herself down for customers.

"Ok, I'll do that," the man replied, then walked a little further in to look at a display of medium sized flowering plants. Oracle went back to her tea and the table.

"A festival would be nice. Something to celebrate is always nice. I can't imagine the whole town celebrating though," Adam said.

"That would be a sight to see!" Jenna said. The group fell silent for a bit. The only noise was Broom's scratching.

"I wonder if we could get people on board with another one. Not necessarily the old one, but maybe a new one?" Indy asked after a while. "There's plenty of deities to appease. We could hold a celebration for one of them."

"I-I like that i-idea," Adam replied directly to Indy. She beamed at him and he turned red. She rested her hand on his arm and he shifted in his seat. Oracle thought she saw a bead of sweat emerge from his forehead and silently chuckled. Poor guy.

"I don't know. We don't have any temples in town, or nearby. Everyone travels for their god. Could we celebrate the market? Or maybe the number of years Greenspring has existed?" Jenna suggested.

Jenna and Edalyn looked at each other. Jenna said, "This is hard. I don't know that people will want to celebrate Greenspring. It's barren here and we don't have a lot of –"

"– culture?" Edalyn finished.

"Yes. I don't think Greenspring has enough culture to support a festival." Jenna finished.

"Pardon my interruption," the man who had entered the store had turned to the group and they all faced him to see what he had to say, "I was listening. Sorry. I have to agree with the lady though. Greenspring is barren and all we're known for is having to import everything because ground crops don't even grow. We have no temples, no famous heroes, and nothing positive we're known for. Maybe the mine, but it isn't that special. We don't have festivals because there simply isn't anything to celebrate on that scale. It's why there are so many vacant buildings; people leave and they don't come back to the place that doesn't grow anything."

The irony was not lost on Oracle, that the man was standing in a shop full of green growing plants.

"Well, I'm going to change that," Oracle said defiantly.

"Good luck," The man said and turned back to the plants he was looking at.

Oracle stared at the man's back for a minute before returning her gaze to the group.

"Are you really? I mean, are you going to change the ground?" Edalyn asked with hopeful eyes.

"I have a plan that should restore some fertility to the ground here, so plants can grow outside. I haven't worked it all out yet, but I have been working and testing solutions," Oracle said. This was only a small fib. Oracle had been working and testing soil, magic, and fertilizer combinations, but on soil she had brought from outside into the shop. She hadn't tried planting anything outside yet. She wasn't quite sure how to do it best so the plants would grow.

The group looked at her, amazed. Even Tullus, who normally dozed off when he wasn't the one talking, looked at her with his eyebrows raised.

"That would be something," he said decisively.

"Are you serious?" Adam asked.

"That would be incredible," Indy said.

"Completely," Adam added.

Jenna and Edalyn just nodded with wide eyes.

"It's not possible," the man said over his shoulder. "Nothing grows in Greenspring."

"You're looking at things growing in Greenspring right now. How can you say that?" Jenna asked, indignant.

The man paused for a second and then pointed to a plant. "These aren't imported?"

"No. I grow them here," Oracle said slowly.

"Oh," the man said. He scratched his head and looked around. "You grow all of them here?"

Noodle started to twitch like there was a breeze in the room. Aquarius opened an eye from Tullus' lap. Broom scooted across the floor, sweep-sweeping out of reach of the vine plant.

"Yes," Oracle stated with some obvious agitation.

"I apologize," the man said. "I didn't know. I didn't think anything could grow here. I thought you imported them, like everything here. Do you really grow them?"

Noodle stopped trembling.

"Yes. I use a combination of plant knowledge and minor magic to ensure they grow."

"So not naturally grown then. You use magic."

"The plants are naturally grown. The magic just helps protect them from *the elements*," the undertone being 'whatever kills everything here.'

"I see," said the man. "Maybe if you do get plants to grow in the ground it would be worth celebrating. I don't think this is going to be it."

And before anyone could retort, the man walked himself out of the shop. The group just looked at each other. Some were appalled; some were disheartened. Oracle was a little perturbed, but it quickly turned into determination.

"We'll have something to celebrate. I promise you that," she said to the empty entry.

"I think we can make a new festival eventually, when Oracle gets things growing outside again. That *would* be something to celebrate," Jenna said.

"I think you're right," Edalyn said, "Everyone in town would celebrate that."

"Should we start to plan it?" Jenna asked.

"Oh. Uh, probably not yet. I haven't really been successful outside," Oracle said.

"I think it could be fun to plan it, just for ideas for the future," Indy offered.

"I agree," Jenna and Edalyn said together.

"Well, let me know what you guys drum up. I think it would be good for Greenspring to have a festival again. It's not exactly a hub of activity," Oracle said.

"Well, I think I'd better get on with my day," Indy said. The others followed her lead and began to gather their things to leave. Oracle was not quick enough to hide her mug and Jenna took it up with hers, while Edalyn took Tullus' mug. Tullus even got up, gently set Aquarius down on the floor, and grabbed his walking stick.

There was a shuffle of people, "so-long" and "see you tomorrow," and the group filtered out. Adam was last, making sure Tullus got out ok. Oracle held the door as everyone streamed out.

"Adam?"

"Yes, Oracle?"

"Have you thought about asking Indy to do something with you?"

"W-what? Why w-would I do that? Like what-what would I ask?"

"Listen, buddy. It's very obvious she's into you, and you're into her. Everyone knows it and watching her flirt and you blush is getting to be too much. Just ask her to do something with you. Go to the market, or for a walk, or get a cup of tea. It doesn't have to be anything fancy or extravagant. Just pick something and ask. She's gonna say yes." Oracle put a reassuring hand on Adam's shoulder.

"How do you know?" He asked.

"Just trust me on this, ok? Ask her. I don't know why she hasn't asked you yet, but –"

"She has."

"What?" Oracle was taken aback.

"She's asked me to go to the market with her. I was busy practicing scribing with my opposite hand and didn't need anything at the market. She asked me to walk with her to the baker's once too, but I didn't need anything there either. Actually, she's asked me every week to do something, but it's never something I need to do."

"Oh wow. Ok. Ok, listen, Adam. Go do the next thing she asks. It doesn't matter if you don't need anything from wherever she's going." Oracle patted his shoulder.

"It doesn't?" He shifted awkwardly where he stood half in the shop half out of it.

"No. Not at all. Just go with her. Whenever she asks, if you have time, go with her. Go for the walk. Go to the baker's or the market, even if you don't need anything. I promise that you'll find something anyway."

"What if I don't have anything to say while we're walking? I get a little panicky." Adam drug his hand down his face.

"Just try to talk about her family, her goals, her work, or her dreams and ambitions. Ask questions and listen to her answers. You're already a good listener, so just listen."

"Ok. The next thing she asks me to do. Family. Goals. Dreams. I got it," he said. He smiled at Oracle then. "Thanks, Oracle."

He walked out the door and when he was partially down the street she called out to him, "Also, do something dangerous."

"What?"

She just smiled and waved. Confused, Adam continued down the street. When she closed the door her face dropped and she began to consider how exactly she was going to get something to grow outside when she was still experiencing some waves of death for her inside plants. She set to work that day with a pain in her head and a lump in her heart.

16. Sigils

"And that makes 13," Oracle said to Aquarius, who was riding in her pocket. She noted the number in her notebook next to a sketch she had made earlier. This sigil was carved into another rock as most of them had been. Unlike the pulsing sigil, all the others appeared to be intact and glowing brightly. She had noted that she was almost all the way around the town. The sigils made a big circle around the town when they were connected.

"How many more could there be?" Aquarius asked.

His head was poking out of the top of her pocket along with his front legs. He was happily munching a piece of fruit and looking out at the surroundings. He could also curl up and be fully inside the pocket, which Oracle thought he'd do after his snack. He was not fast enough to walk with her, and he didn't have wings to fly.

"One or two or none. We've made it almost around the whole town now."

"It only took forever."

"Not forever. A long time, though, I'll give you that."

"Can we go back or are you going to trudge along and look for another? I'm ready to go back and eat something more than fruit," Aquarius said.

Oracle looked at the sky and then her notebook.

"If my sketch is close, I think there are actually no more sigils to find. We have time to make the loop back to the first sigil. Then we'll know for sure. They're all almost equidistant from the town and each other. It shouldn't be too hard or take too long to find the last one. Or find out there isn't a last one."

"So, we must trudge on and starve." Aquarius sighed and sunk into her pocket a little deeper. Oracle took out a piece of meat from her pack and slid it in.

"There. Now improve your attitude a little. You're not starving."

"Not anymore!" Aquarius said happily.

Oracle walked onward. She was in the section of land that was the most obvious transfer of growth. On one side there were trees and the black rocks that jut up from the ground were not as frequent. On the other side the black rocks were tall towers scattered among sandy brown grassland. There were a few trees where Oracle walked, but they were sparse. There were no trees on the town side of the invisible divide.

She had been thinking as she walked that maybe she had made a mistake telling Attican no. She had written shortly after he had left town, telling him that the opportunity to get the relic for him was enticing, but she had problems to solve here. Hunting sigils to a puzzle she didn't understand was not the glorious adventure she had in mind all those years ago when she decided to learn magic. But she had committed to Greenspring. This was her home now. When she wrote she reminded him to send her a book on sigils, but hadn't heard back from him yet.

Oracle toed the imaginary line checking the backs of rocks and trees for any of the sigils. Over the weeks, she discovered there were three distinct kinds of sigils. They all glowed white, except the first one she found. She concluded the sigils were likely the culprit behind keeping Greenspring in a state of barrenness. It appeared to be a large ritual circle where Greenspring was at the center. What she didn't know was how the ritual was actually affecting the town, and whether or not the broken sigil was a good thing or a bad thing. She had yet to determine what the sigils were doing, or what to do about them.

If the broken sigil caused the ritual to fail, or partially fail, is that why her plants could grow? If the ritual was something else, is that why her plants were growing erratically? It had gotten worse in the last few weeks. Every day she woke up she wasn't sure what she would find below. Dead or dying plants, overgrown ones, ones blooming too early. Not all the plants were affected, but Oracle couldn't find rhyme or reason for the ones that were. It just didn't make sense. Not even magic, nor the plant serum she had made according to the Alchemist's recipe, nor her own brews made a lick of difference to which plants were affected.

Add to that, the sigil ritual could be the only thing that kept Greenspring green once upon a time. If the broken sigil interrupted the ritual of making Greenspring artificially green, that would make sense why everything else was so sparse. Oracle didn't like this last theory. It didn't explain the magical divide she was walking along.

She and Atmir had discussed at length the different possibilities. She had some good ideas, but no answers yet. She was still determined to find out what was happening. She was busier than ever at the shop though, and a lot of her free time was either spent trying to research or with Atmir.

"Ah. Here it is," Oracle said out loud. Aquarius had finished his snack and was asleep in her pocket. The late afternoon sun warmed her, and she knew Aquarius couldn't help it. She took out her notebook to compare. "As I thought. This is the same one I already have down. The circle is complete. 13 sigils, one not working, and no closer to answers."

Oracle leaned back against a rock and closed her eyes. She let the sun beam on her face for a moment. A breeze whipped through the rocks. Oracle tried to clear her mind. It was nice to be outside. She opened her eyes, checked on Aquarius in her pocket who had fallen asleep after his snack, and then put her notebook away.

Town was not too far off. The weather was still nice, but the days were getting shorter. Cold weather would roll in before she knew it.

Oracle walked in silence, slowly through the sandy soil. The rocky outcroppings became fewer and fewer before disappearing into the ground, leaving just a trace of loose rock behind. The brown grass became more prominent and soon Oracle found one of the main roads into town. She followed it to her shop.

Aquarius woke up as she entered and the bells chimed. He yawned and stretched in her pocket and she took him out and put him on the counter. Oracle took a moment to look at her plants. Some of them were still wilting, and some were overgrown. She had patrons come in over the last short while with similar problems.

"Did you solve it while I was asleep?" Aquarius asked, interrupting her thoughts.

"Of course. It was simple."

"What? You did?" Aquarius looked at her with wide eyes.

"Of course I didn't, Aquarius. Don't be silly," she said, putting her pack down behind the counter. "I think I'm going to go for a cup of tea. Do you want to come down with me?"

"No. I had my nap. I'm going to patrol," Aquarius said. That meant he was going to eradicate flies and spiders and other insects from the shop. The little beast seemed to always be hungry, or napping. Was he growing? Oracle had only had him for a little over a year. Now that she thought about it, how big would Aquarius grow? She looked at him for a long while.

"What?" He asked when he noticed.

"I was just wondering if you would grow larger. And how large you might get."

"That's a good question. I have never met another one of me. I don't even know what I'm called. Maybe I will turn into a true dragon!"

"Let's hope not."

"You're right. Maybe I'll get wings though. That would be helpful."

"Mmhmm. I'm going to get my tea. You keep dreaming," Oracle said. Aquarius sniffed and continued his hunt.

Oracle walked down to The Guiding Light. The lantern was lit, as usual. She peered in the doorway and there was nobody inside. It was late, so that made sense. Atmir would be cleaning up for the day and getting ready for bed. He kept the lantern lit and had a bell system that would ring in his bedroom if anyone entered. Oracle thought it a pain to always be interrupted like that, but it rarely happened. When it did, it was usually of some importance, so Atmir didn't mind.

She pushed the door open, and the bells chimed happily. Atmir was in the back and came out. His smile reached his eyes almost immediately upon seeing her.

"Good evening, Oracle. I have been expecting you." He came from around the counter and wrapped her in a hug.

"You have?"

"I have," he leaned back, but didn't let go. "I have a guest this evening, but we can wait until morning for introductions. I also have a book for you, and I have already blended a tea. Just give me a moment to brew it."

"A guest? And a book? *And* a tea? I'm feeling very special right now." She sat down at a table. She looked over at the plant Atmir had bought from her. It sat happily near the window. It looked as if it had grown a lot since leaving the shop. This took a little weight off of Oracle. One hadn't died.

"One of my cousins is here," Atmir began, "Though he's sleeping right now. He's back from what sounds like a very difficult journey. He promised not to leave too early tomorrow, so that I could introduce you."

"I feel weird meeting your family."

"Why?" Atmir took the water container off the stove and poured it over the tea he had blended.

"It feels too….official? Too…I'm not sure. Fast? No. It just feels a little weird."

"Well, I promise that Orbak will not come off as weird. Boisterous maybe, but not weird. Do you not want to meet?" Atmir took the steaming mug from the counter over to Oracle. He set it down in front of her, gave her a kiss on top of the head, and sat down across from her.

"I am happy to meet your family," Oracle replied genuinely.

"Good. Because once Orbak meets you, everyone will know about you and we can probably expect more of my cousins to come through."

Oracle didn't say anything. She took a sip of her tea, and Atmir watched her. The tea was a bit chalky in her mouth, but tasted like roasted apples and clove. Altogether it was not bad. Until she noticed the green tinge to her skin.

"What does this tea do?" Oracle demanded, half in a panic.

"It's called Orbak's Blend. My cousin. The green is temporary," Atmir said reassuringly. "It gives you extra strength for about 10 minutes. Physical strength. You have to drink another blend for mental strength."

Oracle examined her hands and arms and gently touched her face. She did feel a little stronger, but the green hue to her skin made her look almost sickly.

"Why did you give me this?"

"I thought you'd relate to Orbak a little better when you meet tomorrow. Sorry it's not more relaxing." Atmir had a mischievous grin on his face.

"Can I try out the extra strength?"

"On what? Don't go breaking tables or chairs in here. I happen to like them a lot."

"I'm going to hug you." Oracle said.

"Oh, please don't. You're liable to squeeze me to death." Atmir replied.

"You can't stop me. Not for about 8 more minutes."

"It gives you extra strength, not super strength."

"Want to wager on it?" Oracle said with a devilish grin.

"I do not," Atmir said and stood up from his chair. Oracle got out of her chair and gave him a bear trap hug.

"Ok, pry me off," she said.

Atmir gave a feeble attempt at Oracle's arms.

"C'mon you can do better," she said.

"I kind of don't want to," Atmir said, smiling down at her.

"Well, I can't hold on to you forever."

"Can't you though?" He didn't stop smiling.

"Oh stop," she said. She let him go as she felt her face flush. She sat back down to sip on the tea some more. Atmir returned to his seat and then stood up suddenly.

"The book! I almost forgot. Guess who brought it in?" He walked back to the storeroom and got out a book. He sat down again with Oracle and turned the book to face her. The title read *Wards and Containment Magic.* Oracle read the title out loud.

"I don't know. My mentor?"

"*Harrad.*" He said, just above a whisper.

"No," Oracle said in a hushed tone. "Why would he do that? He hates magic and avoids me at all costs."

"I think deep down he wants you to be successful and wants magic to really work. I think he would really like magic to not be a bad thing. He's probably read enough books to know that in other parts of the world magic is wonderful. For some reason, it's not as great here. I think he just wants to witness it being great. He's too old to travel. This is his little token of hope," Atmir finished. He took his eye off the book cover and looked at Oracle.

"Have you looked inside?" Oracle asked. She ran her fingers over the cover, feeling the woven texture. She flipped it open and looked at the first page.

"I was afraid to open it. You warned me about magical books."

Oracle laughed.

"I'm glad you listen to me. This one is fine though. No magic," She fanned through the pages to demonstrate that nothing would happen.

She then flipped back to the contents page. She ran her finger down the list and stopped.

"There's a chapter on sigils! This is great. Put, like, 5 teas on my tab for Harrad."

"He won't accept. He 'accidentally' left this book, and he never accepts your tea purchases."

"Tell him they are from someone else. I don't care," Oracle said. She flipped to the chapter on sigils and started reading.

"Do you want Reader's Delight tea next? I have some in sachets I can send home with you. You're going to be up all night with that. And speaking of sigils, is that where you were all day?"

"Yes," Oracle said, looking up from the book. "I found 13 of them in a circle. They aren't all the same design. Greenspring is at the center of the circle. How did Harrad know I needed a book on sigils?"

"I think Adam told him."

"Gods bless Adam for doing so."

"Which gods? Should be more specific," Atmir said.

"All the ones that offer boons and benefits."

"That's better. Don't need Adam with a blessing from the gods of wars, famine, deceit and the like."

"Funny man tonight," Oracle said and took another drink of her tea. She started to pore over the book.

"So, no Reader's Delight, then?" Atmir asked.

"What does that one do again? The fingers?"

"Yes. It makes your fingertips glow. It's great for reading at night without worrying about falling asleep with a lit candle near you."

"I think one tea is enough for tonight. I am feeling energized. And a lot less green," Oracle said, holding out her hands and looking at them.

"Green is a nice color on you."

"Maybe on my clothes."

"So, what is your next step?"

"I'm going to read this book on sigils. After that I will have to decide what's next. If I didn't have this book I was going to spend the night reading the Alchemist's journal. I might still, depending on if this book is helpful or not."

Oracle turned back to the book. Atmir stared at her a long while, watching her read. She eventually looked up at him.

"Oh! Sorry! I should get going. I'm keeping you," Oracle said. She stood and closed the book.

"You don't have to go."

"No, I should get back and read in bed. I'm going to fall asleep reading this anyway, so I might as well be in bed instead of at a table."

Atmir resisted a quip about falling asleep in his bed and instead stood up. He went up a lot higher than Oracle did when standing.

"Can you levitate yet?" He asked.

"What? No, I can't levitate," Oracle said confused. Atmir chuckled and then leaned way over to kiss her.

"Oh. Yeah. That," She said after, "Maybe I'll work on levitation after this sigil business."

Atmir just smiled at her and walked her to the door. He opened it for her and said goodnight and Oracle walked out into the night, back to her shop and home. It was a clear night, and all the stars were out. Oracle walked with a little pep in her step, holding the book snugly to her chest.

Aquarius was playing with a ball when she got there. Chewing it and bouncing it around. Broom was sweeping behind the counter. What Broom was sweeping, Oracle didn't know. The shop floor was almost always spotless because of Broom. She bid them goodnight and took the book straight upstairs and to bed where she read the chapter on sigils. She found what she had been missing. The sigils had to be a ward. Actually, three wards. She flipped to the back of the book. There was a reference guide to various sigils and what they were most commonly used for. She found all three in the book. All three were containment wards meant to seal something away. But what? What in Greenspring needed to be contained in a way that made plants die?

She looked at the sigil in the back of the book that looked like the broken one. It was most often used to contain *mint or other invasive plants*. This was not making any sense. There was a ward again mint surrounding the town? Nothing grew because of these wards, but why invasive plants? Did something try to take over the town at one point and this was the solution? Did a mage have a grudge and placed these wards to hurt Greenspring? And were things growing now because the wards had been partially broken?

Oracle had so many questions she didn't know how to answer. She was confused after her initial elation. She re-read the chapter on sigils. She looked again and again at the reference drawings at the back of the book. It didn't add up. Then she had a thought. The journal might have more information on the wards. It was so long ago that maybe the Alchemist had seen the change in Greenspring and that's why they left. Oracle set the book down and picked up the journal from her bedside table.

She flicked through pages, scanning for anything that jumped out at her. She was so tired from the day but determined to find something. And she did find something. The blessings stopped at one point, and the Alchemist determined it was because there was some kind of damage to the offering spouts. Soon after, weird things happened to the plants and crops. Some grew abundantly, and some withered unexpectedly. The town had earthquakes. She kept reading.

The town had hired an adventuring party to find out what was wrong with the town. They didn't come back and nobody knows if they just took the town's money and left, or if they died on their adventure. The Alchemist surmised they died after going underground to trace the path of the offering pipes. They thought that the offerings were not getting to where they needed to go, and that angered whatever was down there. Desperate, the town hired a mage from a distant city to help, after their local mages were unsuccessful.

Apparently, this mage offered a solution that was not ideal – warding against whatever was down there. The Alchemist thought it was a plant after an earthquake revealed the green tendrils of something growing under the square. After some inspection, some research, and some testing with various plants, the Alchemist surmised it was a very large semi-sentient plant that had some connection to a god. After interviewing some townspeople for folklore they might know, the Alchemist was convinced it was a plant and the relation to the god is how it offered blessings.

The mage and the Alchemist had discussed this, and the mage decided to ward against invasive plants. It took several weeks to do so. The town suffered earthquakes, which they thought was the plant coming up through the ground. Buildings and streets were ruined. When the mage was done, however, the plant wreaking havoc on the town retreated and went quiet. The mage left and town was peaceful again, though without the magic blessings they previously received.

The peacefulness didn't last very long. Plants across town started to die. The crops died. Everything withered. The plants that had been growing wildly stopped. Greenspring turned into the sandy, dusty place it was today. Nobody could find the mage that had placed the wards, and nobody was quite sure where the wards were. The Alchemist decided it was time to retire to a more pleasant place and headed off to the coast to meet his friend.

There was no more account of Greenspring or the strange happenings. This was the only account. Nobody in town could remember what happened after a few generations it seemed. The town persevered by importing things, but the population dwindled some. A lot of buildings were left empty and life went on, the knowledge of the plant's existence fading to nothing over time.

Oracle wondered if the plant was still below the town, if it had survived somehow. From the book she found at Harrad's it sounds like the seed planted by a god theory was true. Oracle wondered why nobody had hired another adventuring party to track down the wards the mage had put in place. She silently thanked the Alchemist for leaving the journal. They must have done so on purpose.

She blew out the candle as Aquarius snuggled into bed with her. Her mind was racing over all that she had just learned. She wondered if she could alter the sigils and break them. Then she thought that it would be a bad idea if the plant below the town was still alive. She decided her next course of action would be to venture underground and determine the state of the invasive blessing plant, if that's really what it was. She slept in fits and starts.

17. Cousins

Oracle awoke a little groggy. The sun was up and shining on her through the bedroom window. She had slept late. She suddenly sprung from bed, remembering she was to meet Atmir's cousin. She dressed and hurriedly gave Aquarius some food, explaining where she was going as she did so. She rushed out the door grabbing her cloak as she went, only slowing when she approached the windows and could be seen from the outside of the tea shop. She gave herself a little pep talk, smoothed her cloak, and went inside.

A few of Atmir's usual customers were seated at their favorite tables enjoying their usual brews and baked goods. What was unusual was the very large, very green man with lower teeth protruding like tusks. Oracle had seen orcs before but there weren't any in Greenspring. She tried not to let her surprise show as much as patrons tried not to let their stares be noticed. The big orc was sitting with Atmir. Atmir was tall, but not as tall as this guy. Oracle belatedly realized this was Atmir's cousin, Orbak.

"Oracle! We've been waiting for you," Atmir said, beaming. Oracle walked over.

"Sorry, I had a late night," She replied, a new set of thoughts racing through her head. Atmir greeted her by way of a hug and gestured for her to sit.

"Oracle, this is my cousin, Orbak. Orbak, this is Oracle," Atmir said as he released Oracle. He made his way behind the counter to brew tea for Oracle as she approached the table. Orbak also stood up and held out his hand. Oracle took it, or rather, was swallowed by it. He was firm but gentle in his shake.

"The famous Oracle! Atmir wrote to me about you, so I am pleased to finally make your acquaintance. He's told me a lot about you!" The big man boomed. It almost rattled the mugs on the tables.

"Pleasure to meet you," Oracle said, meeker than she'd meant to.

"The pleasure is all mine!" Orbak said. "Atmir says you're an adventurer. I am too. My party is having a break right now. We've just returned from a five month long stint in the Ryodai Desert. Have you been? Lovely people there, but the sand wyrms are the worst. We went to eradicate an outpost and that turned into several more outposts, a town, and a small fishing village on the opposite side of the desert. We trekked all over that place, let me tell you!"

Oracle got the impression that Orbak would be telling her, whether she wanted him to or not. Atmir returned with a mug of tea and pulled a chair out for Oracle to sit. The three of them sat down at the table. Atmir had put a pastry in front of Oracle as well. She bit into it and looked at Atmir.

"Oracle is growing plants now. She is quite exceptional at it," Atmir said proudly.

"So you've said! I would like to see this plant shop. It is a miracle, truly. Nothing has grown here for many years. Nobody knows why. The town won't hire any adventurers to find out. Say they don't have the coin and don't want to raise taxes. That seems a bit ridiculous. The townsfolk probably would like things to grow again, right Atmir?"

"I think everyone has just grown accustomed to the way of life here and many can't relocate for one reason or another. It probably doesn't have anything to do with coin, really." Atmir replied.

"So, Oracle," Orbak turned to her as she swallowed her food and took a sip of tea. "What are your intentions with my cousin, here."

Oracle choked and spit tea out all over the table. Orbak laughed mightily and Atmir pulled a rag from his apron to start wiping the mess.

"Sorry Atmir," she said when she recovered.

"Not your fault," he said and sent a stern look to Orbak.

"I'm sorry, I couldn't resist trying," Orbak said. "Anyway, Oracle. What do you think of Greenspring so far?"

"I haven't been here too long, but the spring and summer have been pleasant. The people here are good and I've found a niche I like with growing the plants. It's a nice change of pace from adventuring, but I do get out now and again for something other than tending green things."

"I have a joke about tending green things that I will keep to myself," Orbak said and chuckled. He took a drink of tea and Atmir put his palm to his face and looked at Oracle. Orbak continued, "I'm glad you like it here. It's not for everyone. I don't know why my cousin stays."

"Here we go," Atmir mumbled.

"He had so much potential and he's just letting it go to brew tea. Tea!"

"Potential?" Oracle asked.

"He hasn't said anything? It's worth bragging about!"

"Orbak, don't –" Atmir started but was cut off.

"Atmir was the best bare-knuckle boxer this side of the Sword River for many years when he was younger! A fighter through and through. He was unbeatable. Big opponents, small opponents, fast opponents, it didn't matter. Atmir tore through them all. And the man is handy with a battle axe. You couldn't pay me enough to challenge him. He might be out of practice now, but I bet he'd pick it up again no problem and be almost as fierce as he was back then." Orbak finished, with Atmir looking a little dour.

"Is that true, Atmir?" Oracle asked incredulously. The gentle tea-brewing man of The Guiding Light was a fierce and maybe decorated warrior.

"It was another life," he sighed, then faced Orbak. "Orbak, you know I don't talk about that for a reason. I've given up all of that, and

I am perfectly happy here working on my tea and bringing a little joy with it. You don't have to remind me of my past. I was there. I lived it. And I've given that side of me up for good."

"Sure, sure. It's just bubbling beneath the surface though. I know how it is. Your talent is wasted on tea, but that's your choice. If tea brings you joy, I am happy for you, cousin."

"Thank you," Atmir said sincerely.

"I never would have guessed," Oracle said plainly.

"I would never have wanted you to," Atmir said back.

"And if this lady brings you joy, then I am happy for that too. Promise me you will come visit and bring her with? Della and Kablin would be excited to meet her and to see you. Even Eli would probably be glad to see you."

Atmir sighed and said, "Even if Eli was glad to see me, I'm not sure I would be as glad to see what became of the house and garden when visiting to see him."

"Oh, it's not so bad as all that. He's done a nice job, and he kept the garden," Orbak said and then stood up. "Speaking of, let's go look at your garden, Miss Oracle. I need to be on my way, but I'm not going until you show it to me."

"I guess I could keep you hostage for a while then, if I refused to let you in?" Oracle said, her eyebrows raised. Orbak guffawed.

"I like this one, Atmir. Spirited!" He said, still laughing. "Miss, if you want to try keeping me from where I want to go, by all means go ahead and try!" He stood up straight and puffed his chest out a little before relaxing and laughing more.

"Don't go tempting fate, Orbak," Atmir warned. He scooped up their empty mugs and set them behind the counter to be washed.

"Are you coming, Atmir?" Orbak asked.

"Sure, just a second." Atmir hung his apron up and met them at the front door. He didn't meet Oracle's eyes when she looked at him, and she knew something was bothering him. The three of them set off to the plant shop.

"What is the shop's name?" Orbak asked.

"Blooms and Moss," Atmir said warmly. "It fits nicely, I think."

"I like it!" Orbak said exuberantly. "You have a gift for naming things, Oracle."

"I like it," Oracle said, "but Atmir helped me name it. Actually, he did name it."

"Well then cousin, you have the gift! Sorry, Oracle," Orbak laughed.

They passed the large window with the plants in it, and Oracle led the way through the front door. Orbak proceeded to comment on the plants, touching them, asking questions about them. He was surprised and amused by Broom. He jovially inspected the workbench, the propagation station, the shears and bags of fertilizer, commenting the whole time on what a nice thing this or that was. Oracle hung near Atmir and whispered to him.

"Are you ok?"

"Yeah," he whispered back, still not looking at her.

"What's wrong?"

"I just wish Orbak hadn't mentioned battle axes and boxing. I'm not that person anymore."

"I don't think less of you for having a past, Atmir," she whispered and took his hand. She gave it a gentle squeeze. Atmir squeezed her hand back. He released her hand and took a couple steps toward Orbak.

"Orbak, I don't mean to rush you, but you do need to leave sometime and let Oracle get to her work."

"That is true. I need to get on the road. I'm still a few days from home. But first," He stood up from examining a small plant on the floor. "Oracle, I want one of these to take home to Della. My sister is a druid and would love more plants. She loves plants. All the plants."

"All the plants," Atmir agreed.

"Does Della have indoor accommodations? These plants need to be inside for the most part."

Orbak laughed and said, "Yes, she has a house. Well, a cottage. She doesn't travel like I do. I wouldn't be home enough to care for a plant, but she would love another to add to her collection."

"Any particular size or price range you want to get into?" Oracle asked as she stepped over to the display Orbak had been examining.

"I think a small one that has the potential to grow large. She would love to be able to take a baby plant and grow it huge. I imagine she knows a few spells to make even a regular plant grow larger than it should, though."

"She probably does," Atmir said, amused. "Della is a little eccentric. She would probably like an unusual plant if you have any."

"Eccentric is putting it nicely," Orbak looked at Oracle and in a stage whisper said, "She's weird."

Oracle laughed and said, "I think she will probably like this little guy right here. It will get fairly large and it can be brought outside for sun. It will survive a few day's travel outside as long as you water it appropriately and don't let it get too cold at night. The weather is still good enough for that. This plant is unusual in that it will flower one big, black or grey bloom. It needs to grow a bit more before blooming though. So, probably next year it will bloom."

"Perfect!" Orbak cried out. Aquarius, who had been peeking around the stairs at the noise, jumped backward and went upstairs again.

"I think Della will like that one," Atmir supplied.

"How much for it then?"

"I would like to give it as a gift."

"No! I can't do that!" Orbak put his hand up at Oracle and shook his head.

"I can. I want to give it as a gift of future friendship. If I come to visit, or if she's ever in the area, I hope she remembers the gift and it starts us on the right foot."

"She's not the one handy with the axe, but I see where you're going with this. And you mean 'when' you visit, right?"

"Right," Oracle said, smiling. She plucked up the plant and put it gingerly in Orbak's big hands.

"Thank you, Oracle. I'm sure she will love it. Atmir, cousin, thank you again for your hospitality. I'm going to collect my things and head out."

"I'll go with you," Atmir said.

"We have things to talk about later, Mr. Battleaxe," Oracle said sweetly, hardly containing a smile. Orbak roared with laughter.

"Please don't call me that." Atmir gave Oracle a flat look and then shared it with Orbak.

"Ok, Mr. Bare-Knuckle Boxer." She sing-songed at back at him.

Orbak roared again. Atmir shook his head and walked out, Orbak nodded at Oracle and walked out right behind him. Oracle could hear Orbak say, "I like that one" as the door closed behind him. He clapped Atmir on the back in front of the window and they disappeared from sight.

Oracle finished the day caring for the plants, taking care of customers who arrived, and chatting with the regulars who stopped in. They hadn't been able to stay the morning since she hadn't been open for most of it, but she promised tomorrow she would be open earlier and they could all chat then.

Oracle had gone to bed that night thinking about what she'd learned so far. The sigils were a ward. There was a giant plant – possibly - under the city. The Alchemist left the journal on purpose. Atmir was a half-orc barbaric fighter and his much bigger orc cousin was afraid of what he could do.

That last bit rotated around in her brain a lot. Atmir, a fighter? It seemed hardly possible, though his strong physique didn't suggest he made teas his whole life. The gentle man who was kind and sweet and thoughtful didn't equate with a bloody fighter, battle axe or not. She felt a little bad for Atmir and wondered if he was running from something in his past, despite what he had told her. She didn't think Atmir a liar, though, and quashed that line of thinking.

She woke up in the morning feeling refreshed, but the thoughts from last night lingered in her brain. She tried to push them out, but they doubled down, so she just let them roll around while she tried to focus on her routine. When she went downstairs to open the shop she stopped dead in her tracks not even all the way down the stairs.

18. A Wave of Decay

All the plants were dead, except Noodle, who wasn't dead, but was definitely worse for wear. She stood in shock on the stairs unable to move at first. Her eyes lingered over each pot of brown. She took a hesitant step down. Then another. The whole shop was dead. Another wave of decay had swept through the shop overnight decimating her little green prizes.

"What happened?" Aquarius asked. Oracle couldn't answer. She stepped the final step down and reached out to touch the first plant she could. Its leaves cracked and crumbled, disintegrating into her hand.

"All my work," She murmured, staring at the dead plant before her. "What are we going to do, Aquarius?"

"What happened?" Aquarius repeated in disbelief. He was going plant to plant, looking at each closely. There were no obvious clues or evidence present. He was baffled. There was a knock at the door. Aquarius looked up to see Adam knocking. She hurried over and opened the door.

"Oracle, my plant died! But overnight. It was –" he trailed off as he saw the room behind her. "What happened?"

Before Oracle could say anything Indy and Jenna had shown up with Edalyn and Evan in tow. Each of them held a dead plant.

"We rushed right over to see if you could tell us what was wrong," Jenna started, but stopped when she saw the shop. "Oh gods, Oracle! What's gone wrong?"

"Come in," Oracle said and moved out of the way of the door. Everyone entered, carrying their sad, dead plant. Noodle dangled limply around the entryway, still green, but pale and unmoving. They all looked around sadly at the brown.

"I thought it was something I did," Edalyn said.

"Obviously that's not the case," Jenna said. "Oracle, is it something…is it somehow the way you prep or grow the plants? Could this be some kind of backlash?"

Oracle thought back to the rituals and magic she performed. There should have been a short time limit of effectiveness on each, but no backlash. She had a thought then, and got out a small dropper of the plant serum she had made from the Alchemist's recipe. She put a couple of drops at Noodle's base, while the others watched. Miraculously, Noodle perked up and looked a little greener. Oracle sighed.

"I don't know what happened, honestly," Oracle said. "What I do to the plants shouldn't affect them beyond maybe a week. If there was backlash, it would happen when the effects wear off, not weeks or months later. Even so, it wouldn't have killed everything all at once. It would have happened in stages, since that is how things grew here. I didn't grow everything all at once. This has happened a few times now, but I thought it was ok because it hasn't happened in a while."

"What are you going to do, Miss Oracle?" Evan asked timidly.

"I'm going to stop what caused this," she replied quietly. The others looked around at each other.

"What do you mean?" Indy asked. "What did this?"

"I think the wards around the town – the sigils are three wards. I think it caused the plants to die. It's not quite right. One of them is broken, but the sigils make it so nothing grows. I think this was a burst of protection from the remaining sigils, but it's killing the wrong things. The sigils are supposed to be a containment and a ward. I think the containment sigil is malfunctioning because I ruined a sigil and the ward is maybe malfunctioning too. That's why plants can grow, but they die sometimes when the sigils sort of work. I'm going to go break them all."

"How do you do that?" Indy asked.

"You just vandalize the mark," Oracle said. "I'll make Greenspring green again."

"Do you need help? Can we help you?" Adam asked.

"Yes, let us help you," Indy said.

"Let me get some things first. Meet me at the southern entrance."

The group left, leaving their dead plants on the table they normally sat at with their teas. Oracle went upstairs and got her pack, her notebook, and then went to the workbench downstairs where she did the plant ritual. She grabbed chalk and a hammer, put them in her bag and headed to the front door. Atmir rushed in.

"Oracle! What happened?" He asked, worried. I came because –"

"- your plant died? I don't know what happened but I'm going to fix it. I think the wards are acting weird because of the broken sigil."

"Wards?"

"Right. We haven't had time to talk about the rest of that. The sigils are three wards. They are preventing anything from growing here. I'm going to break them. They were in place to protect the town from an evil plant that's probably dead by now."

"Slow down. Evil plant?" He asked, his brow furrowed and his mouth frowning.

"I said evil, but it's a plant, so it probably was just doing whatever plants are wired to do. It was being destructive and the town resorted to putting up the sigils, but it's been so long nobody remembers them going up, or how Greenspring used to be green. I'm going to destroy the sigils."

"What if something bad happens?" Atmir asked, warily.

"Like what? Plants growing again? Look at this place, Atmir! All my hard work was decimated for nothing because some mage couldn't figure out how to contain a plant!"

"Well, if the plant was like that one," Atmir pointed at Noodle, "then I can understand how that might be a challenge!"

Oracle looked at him. He had never raised his voice before at her or anyone.

"Sorry," he added and looked apologetic. "Oracle, you don't really know what the sigils are doing. You have a pretty good idea, but what if undoing that mage's work results in something worse than plants not growing?"

"I can think of a lot of worse things to happen to a town, but destroying the things keeping it from really prospering isn't one of them."

Atmir scoffed and Oracle felt anger rise.

"You don't have to help me."

"You don't have to do this."

"And what am I supposed to do?" She yelled. Fire burned in her eyes. Atmir stared at them wordlessly.

"I don't know," he said finally.

"I have to do something. I'm not going to regrow all my plants to have this happen again and again. I'm going to destroy the sigils and then I'll figure out what to do next. I still have an offer from my mentor. Maybe I won't even stay here. There's not much here for me now." She said fiercely.

Atmir recoiled a little and flinched. Oracle was immediately sorry.

"I didn't mean that. I didn't mean it to come out like that," she said quickly.

"Maybe you should just stick to adventuring." His aggression made his filed down tusks stand out.

"What?" Oracle snapped.

"Adventuring. You should leave and just stick to it. You want to, don't you? That's why you're always looking for danger –"

"I'm not looking for it!" Oracle exclaimed, her temper rising. Noodle was too weak to do much more than quiver at its tips.

"Well, you didn't say no right away when your mentor came back. Are you holding that in your pocket so you have an excuse to leave?"

"What is this about, Atmir?"

"Nothing. Go do what you have to do," Atmir growled as he looked her in the eye. Oracle glimpsed the warrior he once was. His voice was intense but the fire went out in his eyes. He left. Oracle wanted to say something as he was going, wanted to stop him, but she didn't know what to say. She watched the door, hoping he'd turn around. When he didn't, she walked out of it and met her friends at the edge of town.

She had told everyone how to find the sigils and what to do when they saw one. They were to carefully draw with chalk a random pattern that intersected with the sigil. Oracle would march around to each one, cast a fire spell which would melt the chalk, score or hammer a piece off the tree or rock the sigil was carved into, and let the magic out of the sigil rendering the ward inert. It was going to take all day and into the night to get all 13, but she was determined. When the last sigil had been drained of its energy, the sun had already set and they were all holding lanterns, except Oracle, who lit up her palm.

"Is that all of them?" Edalyn asked.

"That's thirteen," Oracle said. "All of them that I found around town."

"Now what? What happens next?" Indy asked. They all looked at Oracle expectantly.

"It's a bit anticlimactic, but we go home. With the sigils broken, things should start growing again. It's going to take some time for me to replant and restart, but everything that grows should be fine now."

"What about outside? This ground?" Adam asked toeing the sand.

"I think it probably needs some amendments to put nutrients back in, but without the ward hampering the growth, it should be fine."

"Should be?" Edalyn asked.

"I don't actually know what will happen outside. I just know that the ward is broken and that should free up plants to grow. Crops too," Oracle replied, rubbing her head.

They stood around in the lantern light, not saying anything.

"Should we go back now?" Jenna asked softly.

"Yes. The sigils are broken. Let's go back. Thank you all for your help. It would have taken a lot longer for me to do it by myself," Oracle said to them. They replied by nodding and saying variations of "of course, we're friends."

They walked back together until they entered the town, then they went their separate ways. Oracle noted that Adam and Indy walked off together even though they lived at opposite ends of town. Oracle approached The Guiding Light and saw the lantern was extinguished. Her heart broke. She went up to the door and tried the handle. It was locked. It was never locked and the lantern was never unlit.

Oracle peered inside. There was nobody in, and no candles glowing. She thought about knocking but didn't. She backed up and looked upstairs, but the lights were out there as well. She suddenly felt very heavy. Oracle continued up the street, a bit slower than she'd walked all day, even through the rockiest sections of her trip. When she arrived at her own darkened shop, she walked inside and leaned against the door after she shut it. Tears formed in her eyes and she felt a pressure rise up in her chest and throat and face. She slid down to the floor, her back still against the door.

"Oracle?" Aquarius called softly. He was somewhere downstairs on the main floor with her.

"Yes, Aquarius?" She choked out, her voice thick. He didn't say anything else. He found her in the dark and climbed into her lap. She stroked his scaly back gently. She began to cry then. The tears poured out, and then snot. She put her face in her hands and sobbed in the dark. Noodle quavered above her, still sickly.

When the tears ran out, Oracle sat in the silence of her shop among the dead plants. She made no effort to move to bed or anywhere else. She leaned her head back against the door and closed her eyes. That's when she felt it. At first, she thought she imagined it. It didn't register as being real. Then it intensified. The earth was shaking below her. The floor rippled in impossible waves and the whole building swayed.

Oracle did her best to stand. She put Aquarius in her pocket and braced herself as best as she could. When the shaking stopped, she heard people outside wondering what had happened. She went out too. Some of the buildings nearby had partially collapsed. Her side of the street appeared to be mostly fine. She looked around at her neighbors. They were all frightened. Oracle had a terrible thought. *The plant.*

"Aquarius. I think I've made a mistake," She said to her pocket, trying to keep the fear at bay. The echo of Zevan's words ran through her brain. *"This town will pay for your mistakes."* She shivered.

"What are we going to do, Oracle?" Aquarius asked, slightly muffled from his spot.

"I have to find the plant and get rid of it. That's the only thing that makes sense. The Alchemist said there was a plant under the square causing earthquakes before the sigils went up, and it's tied to a god. If the sigils were really warding and containing the plant that has to be what's causing all this. We have to get rid of it!"

"How do we do that?"

"We'll have to go underground. It's under the square."

"How do we get underground? And how do you know that?"

"There has to be an entrance somewhere to get under the square. The blessing funnels all lead under the square. It makes sense that the plant would be there."

"It's in the cemetery," a voice said behind her on the sidewalk. Oracle whipped around to see Atmir. He was carrying the lantern and the light cast across his face made him look downright scary. He was standing tall in a tunic of dark material, and light leather armor. He had an axe at his side. "I'm going with you."

"Atmir? What? Is that an axe?" she asked. She did nothing to hide her shock.

"Yes, I kept it. I'm sort of a sucker for keepsakes," he said matter of fact.

"How do you know how to get underground?" she asked.

"You weren't the only one doing research. I thought we'd discuss it next, but things sort of forced our hands here, didn't they?" he said and crossed his arms. This Atmir was not one Oracle recognized.

"Yes, they did. Listen, I'm sorry about what I –"

"Don't." He said flatly, not looking at her.

"I'm sorry for what I said. It was thoughtless and not at all how I feel about Greenspring. Or about you. Mostly about you."

"Apology accepted," he said coolly. His tone cut Oracle. *Who was this man?*

"Let me go inside for a few things and then we'll go?" She asked.

"Sure," he replied, still distant.

When she went inside, Aquarius said, "I don't like this Oracle. It doesn't feel right."

"What do you want me to do? Run away?" She hissed.

"That's an option!"

"That is not an option," she growled back through gritted teeth.

She hurried inside and put a few things in her pack she thought she might need. She wasn't sure exactly how to fight a plant, but she thought fire was probably one of the more effective methods. She was good to go there. She packed a knife as back up. Her pack already had most supplies an adventurer would need, so she wasn't worried about it. She had even put the potion from Lady Lady's in there right after she had purchased it, and she always had the necklace of plant speaking on.

"What else? Think!"

"You have everything, Oracle. Except maybe the good sense to flee," Aquarius said, still in her pocket.

"We can't run away. I can't make a mistake and not fix it. I have to fix this." She was adamant.

Aquarius didn't say anything more. The ground rumbled again. Oracle dashed down the stairs when a strange wave of energy shot through the shop, through her, and out the other side. She noticed Noodle recoiling. The energy had hurt Noodle, but nothing else. She felt fine.

"Aquarius did you feel that? Are you ok?" She asked frantically.

"I'm fine. What was that?"

"I don't know. It hurt Noodle though."

"Oh no," Aquarius said facetiously.

"Shut it. That's a clue. Why would that hurt the plant and not us?"

"It's a plant attacking other plants? That's new for, ah, plants." Aquarius responded.

"Let's go."

Oracle rushed outside to find Atmir helping people across the street get outside of their building. The top floors, where most shopkeepers lived, had started to collapse further. Frantic people were trying to get out before it crumbled completely. The rubble piled up with each wave of quaking.

"You can shelter in the plant shop if you want," Oracle told them. "Atmir, let's go before another wave hits!"

He nodded, Aquarius climbed into Oracle's pocket, and they took off at a steady run. Oracle had to take almost two steps to Atmir's one. His long legs drove him forward powerfully and Oracle was losing the pace. Fortunately, Atmir slowed a little when he realized she couldn't quite keep up.

"Oracle," Atmir stopped suddenly. Oracle did the same.

"Before we go after this plant. I think I should apologize too. I was hurt. I am hurt – thinking that you're going to leave here. I shouldn't have said it like I did. I should have explained to you how I was feeling. It feels like you're going to leave, and I don't want that."

"I'm not leaving, Atmir."

"Not even for treasure and glory?"

"I told Attican 'no,' Atmir."

"You did?"

"I wrote to him and declined his offer. I might not be done adventuring all together, but I think there's enough adventure around here to be getting on with," she gestured with her arms wide to indicate the town. "I kind of like what I have here. I don't want to lose anything more."

Atmir looked at her until the ground quaked again, causing them to stumble in keeping their balance. They continued to run. They entered the cemetery through a wrought iron gate, and he headed toward a marble statue.

"How did you know this was the right place?" Oracle asked.

"I told you. I did some research too. I kind of figured you would want to go underground eventually. I was hoping to impress you -," he grunted while he pulled down a lever hidden behind the statue and a grinding like stone on stone could be heard. "- with this information."

Oracle watched the stone in front of the statue slide away leaving a dark abyss. She lit up her palm and held it out. She couldn't see anything besides a passage down.

"Who put this here?"

"I don't know. I didn't uncover that. Uh…ladies first?" Atmir said. Oracle rolled her eyes and went down the passage. Atmir followed with his hand on her shoulder. "I only said that because I can't see in the dark, and you have the light."

"Uh huh. Sure," Oracle replied.

She knew he couldn't see her smile in the dark, but she imagined he was smiling too. The passage had a stone floor that sloped steeply down into more darkness. It was only wide enough for one person, and Atmir had to hunch a little to avoid scraping his head on the ceiling. They traveled down and down. The stale air became significantly cooler as they trekked.

"How would a plant live down here?" Atmir asked.

"Magic," Aquarius and Oracle replied.

"I guess that's reasonable," Atmir said.

They continued down the passage even further. Finally, it ended in a door with a torch holder on the wall. Oracle reached out to try the door. It was unlocked. It creaked open and in the darkness Oracle still couldn't see anything of interest, or danger. They walked forward. This passage was taller than the entry. Atmir could stand at his full height with several more feet of space above him. Ahead, Oracle could see a chamber open up. She paused to listen. A wave of energy pulsed out and hit them, but it had no effect.

"It's there," she whispered. Atmir nodded in the dark, forgetting he couldn't really be seen. "Aquarius, scout."

Aquarius took the command and hopped out of Oracle's pocket. He skittered to the wall and climbed up it. Staying in the dark, he disappeared around the corner and into the big chamber. Oracle held her breath and listened. Atmir held his too. A moment later Aquarius came back.

"It's huge, but mostly dead it looks like. Lots of brown, tangled, brambly limbs. It's looking very unwell," he reported. "The room is large, but mostly filled with the plant. You were right, Oracle. It is a plant. Or it looks that way from here. My dark vision isn't great at a distance."

"Ok, hop back in," She said and crouched down. Aquarius did so, disappearing into Oracle's pocket. Oracle cast a spell and several motes of lights flew up to illuminate the space.

"Plants can't really see, so those should help us," she explained.

"What's the plan?" Atmir asked.

"I thought you had the plan?" Oracle retorted. Atmir opened his mouth and then closed it again. "You just stay there and look cute. I'll go out and figure out what's wrong."

"Not a chance," He replied and pulled her backward a step. "We'll go out together."

"Fine but follow my lead." Oracle didn't have a plan. She had some ideas that a spell might work on the plant, but she had nothing concrete to go on, and in the spirit of adventure thought she would rely on her skills to get her through.

"Ok."

Atmir drew his axe from its holster. A beautifully carved weapon that flashed in the light showing off its intricate design. Oracle couldn't help but stare at it for a moment.

"You like it?" Atmir asked, tilting it a little left and right to catch the light.

"Can we talk about that later?"

"Oh. Right. Yeah." He steadied it.

Oracle drew a breath and released it. She ran around the corner, arms outstretched and ready to cast a spell. She saw the dead limbs first. Tangled, brown, and brambly as Aquarius had described it. Following the limbs up, you could see where some of them turned green again, but were a sickly hue. It looked as if the green was climbing up to the center of the plant. In the center was a large bulbous body of green and red. It looked sickly as well, sagging to one side.

Another pulse ran out from its body, and it heaved its great limbs upward clawing through the ceiling. Oracle thought of Noodle dying as the room shook and dirt fell on her. Noodle being tied to her might have given it extra strength to withhold the waves of death her other plants experienced, but it couldn't last forever.

She readied her hands. In them, a growing orb of fire appeared and she pointed her palms at the plant. A large particle of fire shot from her hands and flew across the room. It hit the plant's limbs and erupted in a sizzling bang. The dried brown limbs caught fire instantly and the room began to fill with smoke. Oracle shot another fireball out toward the dried limbs. Atmir, taking the clue, took his axe and charged in. He hacked at the dead limbs and cleared them away.

"Oracle?" He yelled.

"What?" She yelled back, casting another fire ball.

"WHY"

HACK

"ARE"

HACK

"WE"

HACK

"PRUNING IT?" He said, driving his axe through a bramble again.

"We're just clearing a path to the body!" She yelled, a little exasperated.

When the dead limbs were cleared away the main plant started to move wildly. Its sickly green tendrils began to reach out in all directions, searching for them. Oracle had to jump and then quickly duck to avoid them. Atmir was doing a dance of his own to avoid them.

"Now what?" He shouted.

"Attack the main body!"

Atmir roared and charged forward, hacking at the green limbs as he went. Oracle cast fire spell after fire spell. The plant whipped its branches out. One of them caught Atmir before he could reach the main body. The red and green body pulsated a little bit and more appendages whipped out and wrapped around him. He swung his axe with precision, but couldn't cut as fast as the vines were encompassing him. Oracle, beginning to panic, cast more spells at the base of the limbs holding Atmir.

"Don't panic!" Aquarius reminded her. She took a deep breath and stopped casting spells for a moment.

"Oracle! I still need your help!" Atmir yelled. He squirmed in the plant's grip, but it was tightening around him. The plant had picked him up off the ground. It sent another pulse out and began rooting above itself into the dirt causing the earth to shake again.

"I have it! Don't worry. I know what to do!" She shouted. She wasn't sure what to do and her mind and heart raced. She felt like she was going to explode.

"Could you do it quickly please?" Atmir tried to keep his panic from his voice. The plant began to squeeze him, cutting into parts of his body.

Oracle's mind sprinted through ideas for what to do next. Fire spells were not working. She tried a wither spell. Nothing happened. A shrinking spell next. Again, nothing happened. A vine shot out and sliced Oracle's face.

"The necklace!" Oracle said, realizing late that she could talk to the plant. She activated her necklace of plant speaking and cried out, "Stop! Stop!"

The plant didn't stop. The plant continued to dig above them, holding Atmir aloft, and green vines raced and grabbed for Oracle. She backed up out of their reach and looked at the helpless Atmir. She was about to lose another important person and the dread rose into her throat and lodged like a stone.

"What's wrong with you? What do you need? Stop!" She yelled, desperate.

"Pain. Hungry. Sick."

"What?" Oracle said, breathless. It took a moment for the words to sink in.

"It's sick. It's sick. It's sick," She repeated. "I know!"

She dumped her pack off her back and started to rummage through it. Aquarius hopped out of her pocket. Frustrated, Oracle turned her pack upside down and poured everything across the floor. All her items scattered. Half of them rolled or fluttered out of reach.

"What are you looking for?" Aquarius asked urgently. He was standing among the scattered items at the ready.

"The potion!" Oracle cried.

Aquarius dashed through the items looking at each one. He found the bottle Oracle had purchased at Lady Lady's and picked it up. He brought it to Oracle in his mouth and dropped it into her hand.

"Oracle!" Atmir cried out again, panic evident now.

"I'm coming!" She yelled back.

She thought for a second on how to get the healing potion to the plant. Frantic, she threw the small bottle as hard as she could toward the plant body. It bounced off and Oracle thought she heard breaking glass. She hoped she heard breaking glass. She ran to Atmir and began to pry vines from him.

"What are you doing?" He yelled down at her.

"I'm freeing you!" She screamed back.

Oracle worked as fast as she could but as soon as she pried a vine off, another took its place. She was getting frustrated when she noticed the plant vines turning from a sickly green to a vibrant green. Atmir noticed too.

"What's happening? Oracle, what's it doing?" Atmir called down to her.

"I – I don't know. I think I healed it."

"Healed it? Are you out of your mind?" It was his turn to scream at her.

"No! It's sick and hurt! It needed healing. It didn't need fire. It needed healing!"

"And now that it's healed, what is it going to do?" He yelled, strained.

Oracle turned to the plant body. It was glowing slightly and pulsating. It wasn't digging into the ceiling anymore, but it wasn't putting Atmir down. As if the thought had willed it to do so, the plant vines dropped to the ground, with Atmir still in them. He began to peel away the limbs and Oracle helped. They both stopped when they saw something happen with the main body. It was *blooming.*

Atmir, temporarily stunned by the bloom, stopped peeling vines away. Once he snapped out of it he began to work faster at freeing himself. Still holding a vine, Oracle couldn't look away. The body went from red and green to solid, vibrant red. Layers started to peel away in petals. The flower was beautiful, huge, and blood red. It smelled strongly and Oracle heard the plant. It sighed. Oracle had a hard time reconciling this because plants don't have lungs. She stared at it, confused.

"How did you know that would work?" Atmir asked as he stepped away from the vines.

"I didn't. It was the only thing I could think of. Like a wounded or trapped animal, it was just acting out. It didn't get the offerings from the townspeople and that's why it started to become destructive. Why is it down here anyway?"

"Trapped. Spirit trapped. No release." The plant unexpectedly replied.

"You're trapped here?" she asked. Atmir looked at Oracle, confused, because he couldn't hear the plant. Oracle stared, wide eyed at it.

"Need healing. Need sustenance." The plant replied.

"I think the offerings were feeding it. It's just…hungry? When the spouts deteriorated the offerings weren't making it down to the plant and it turned destructive. The sigils didn't kill it. They just made it really weak. The sigils did contain it, but they also killed off everything that grew in Greenspring. The plant needs the offerings to survive, and it needs to be healthy to offer the blessings!" Oracle exclaimed. The puzzle was coming together. "I bet when I broke the first sigil, that's what allowed my plants to flourish, but it also allowed this plant to act out and kill mine. When I broke all the sigils, this plant was still weak but could resume its destructive phase. That's why everyone's plants died again."

"What do we do with it?" Atmir asked.

"I don't know. I wonder if it was giving the blessings before or if that was something else?"

"Spirit. Bless." The plant said.

And with a wave of gentle energy Atmir and Oracle had been healed of all their minor scrapes and cuts. Oracle looked at Atmir. Atmir looked at the plant. They didn't say anything for a long time.

"So now what?" he asked.

"I think we have repairs to make."

"The plant?"

"That's probably a start. There's quite a bit of town that probably needs some repair as well. We could help there. What do you think people are going to want to do with it?" Oracle asked.

"I don't know. It is a bit scary to have something like this down here."

"Not afraid." The plant said.

"I don't think we have to worry about the plant now. If only Lady Lady knew she had the answer the whole time."

"What was the answer?"

"The plant healing potion I got from Lady Lady's. I threw the bottle I had at it."

"That was quick thinking."

"Panic thinking."

"No, adventurer thinking." Atmir walked over to Oracle and put her in a firm embrace.

"I didn't know if it would work or not. It was a risk." She said quietly to him.

"Sometimes risks pay off," Aquarius interjected from the floor, still with Oracle's scattered items.

"I guess they do sometimes," Oracle said. She looked over at the plant.

Atmir didn't pick up his axe right away. Atmir reached to her face and gently pulled it to look up at him. He leaned over and kissed her deeply. She melted in his arms for a moment and let the feelings soak into her.

"I know it's maybe too soon for anything *official* official, but remember when we were at Lady Lady's? When we got the books and the potion? I bought something I want you to have, if you'll take it. I, uh, I mean it as a future thing, not like a right now thing. But kind of a right now thing? I guess it is sort of a both thing..." Atmir said.

Oracle was amused seeing the big man nervous. Atmir pulled out a beautiful black ring and held it up for Oracle to see it. It was hard to see in the low light, but Oracle could see it was inlaid with silver wavy lines and red stripes that looked like fire.

"I've been carrying it everywhere, trying to decide what the right time was to give it to you and I guess now is as good as any. I just wanted to…In case someone else thought they might like you more…I didn't want anyone to get there first," Atmir said.

"It wouldn't matter," Oracle said, looking up at him. "I wouldn't like *them* more than you."

And with a lot of focus and a little help from Atmir, Oracle levitated up to kiss him.

19. Epilogue

"Oracle, on behalf of Greenspring we would like to gift you these seeds," Beatran said loudly, so the crowd could hear. "They are a representation of our everlasting gratitude to you for saving our town, and giving us something to celebrate; the return of the blessings we didn't know could be possible, as well as turning Greenspring green again. None of us ever knew it was possible. Thank you."

Atmir stood beside Oracle and he positively radiated his smile at her. She smiled broadly at Beatran and accepted the seeds with a little gracious bow.

"They are perennials, I'm told. They will come back year after year, a permanent reminder of your service to us. We hope you'll sow your seeds here," Beatran said and winked at her. She turned around to face the crowd and said loudly, "Let the festival begin!"

The crowd erupted and music began to play. It had taken almost a whole year to repair the town, explain what the underground plant was about, and fix the offering spouts. During that time, Oracle cared for the underground plant. After some research, many letters to her mentor, and a trip back home to visit the library, Oracle had more information.

The plant, it turned out, had been a special seed planted by a god thousands of years ago. It had once been the focal point of a city, but for some reason was covered up by a square. It could thrive in the dark and would produce minor blessings on behalf of the god when it was pleased. What pleased a dark-dwelling plant? Food and fertilizer.

Oracle had crafted a special fertilizer for the plant using the Alchemist's serum formula with help from the townspeople. It was to be used today for the offering. She had also checked in on the plant in person, using her necklace of plant speaking to understand if it needed anything else to be contented.

It was thriving, somehow without sunlight. It grew bountiful in the dark with regular feedings of "offerings" from townspeople above. And with the wards broken, Greenspring was able to grow crops again. The sandy soil, as it turned out, was fine for corn, potatoes, wheat, blueberries, hops, pumpkins, peaches, watermelons, and more. Greenspring also exploded with houseplants and flowers. The dead planter boxes were almost always filled with beautiful, colorful flowers now. Grass had grown back full and thick in front of the buildings that had space for it. Oracle's shop was constantly busy with people in and out.

With some prodding and planning, Oracle and her friends had convinced Beatran to bring back the festival. She cited the Alchemist's notebook and their description to help convince her. As Greenspring blossomed in the springtime, Beatran relented and planning began. The festival took place during the middle of summer, hot as it was.

Atmir put his arm around Oracle's shoulders, and Oracle put her arm around him and leaned in.

"You've done another miracle," he said. "Did you ever think this is how you'd get your adventuring glory? A plant festival?"

"It's a *healing* festival and no. I never thought I'd open a plant shop or fight a giant plant by healing it. I always figured my adventuring career would look like the ones you hear about growing up. Heroes and dragons and enchanted swords. Those kinds of stories."

"Overrated," Aquarius piped up.

They looked at the crowd from where they stood. The music was loud and happy. People were talking animatedly and dancing wild and spirited. The square was full of vendors and every once in a while, someone would pour a little offering down one of the spouts to the plant and a vibrant burst of energy would pulse out over them all, causing people to dance, laugh, shout, and toast with their ales. Aquarius was busy eating treats the townspeople tossed up to him.

"Tell me," Atmir said over the crowd, "Since this is a healing festival and not a plant festival. Do you feel healed?"

Oracle thought about it, taking stock of her feelings. She squeezed Atmir and said, "I do."

"One more question."

"Go on."

"What are you going to do about Broom and Noodle?"

"I think that's another adventure calling me. Broom isn't just a broom, after all. Noodle, I am not sure yet. It's getting awfully large, isn't it? And I have another secret."

"Another secret?"

"Yes. When I discovered Broom it led me to a box under a tree but I have never been able to open it. I'm going to focus a little bit on that, too. I haven't had time for many other mysteries."

"Are you going to leave?"

"I don't think I'll have to, but if I do will you come with me?"

In answer, Atmir grasped her in both arms, lowered himself, and kissed her intensely among the hoots and hollers of bystanders.

Acknowledgements

Acknowledgments

I'd like to acknowledge and thank K.A. Smock and Laura Anderson for their invaluable editing skills and advice. I'd also like to acknowledge and thank my friends Jamie Eddy and Jessamyn Corpus for putting up with constant talk of my book, the process, and my victories and woes. All this support has made this dream come true and I am deeply grateful for them.

About the Author

About the Author

Megan lives in Eastern Oregon with her husband, two kids, and two dogs. She enjoys trips to the Oregon coast, spending time with friends, playing boardgames, and imagining little stories in her head.